GIANT SPECIAL EDITION!
Twice The Action And Adventure On America's Untamed Frontier—In One Big Volume!

TRAPPED!

"Maybe we've given them the slip," Nate said.

"No," Shakespeare said, pointing. "There."

"Damn!" Nate fumed. "They've found our trail."

"They're guessing," Shakespeare disagreed. "They've figured out that we're trappers and they know most trappers head east to one of the forts when hard pressed by Indians."

Vague shadows moved at the limits of the night, a compact group sticking to their trail like sap to a tree.

"They can't be doing that," Nate snapped. "It just can't be done, not at night."

"Someone forgot to tell them."

From the bench Shakespeare and Nate wound down into a canyon and through it to a steep incline that brought them to the top of a sparsely treed tableland. It wasn't until they came to the opposite rim that they realized their mistake; the tableland ended at a sheer bluff hundreds of feet high. They had inadvertently boxed themselves in!

Wheeling, the trappers went to retrace their steps to the slope but they were too late. Advancing toward them in a skirmish line were their pursuers.

T5-AQQ-379

WILDERNESS

ORDEAL

David Thompson

LEISURE BOOKS   NEW YORK CITY

To Judy, Joshua, and Shane.

A LEISURE BOOK®

April 1995

Published by

Dorchester Publishing Co., Inc.
276 Fifth Avenue
New York, NY 10001

Printed in the United States of America.

WILDERNESS
ORDEAL

Chapter One

It was an accident, plain and simple. Nate King certainly had no desire to tangle with a furious bobcat, no more than he'd care to confront a riled grizzly. Yet that was exactly what happened, all because he happened to be in the wrong place at the wrong time.

Nate had just gathered an armful of wood for the fire he was set to make. He strolled back to the clearing, admiring the blaze of pink and orange streaks that framed the jagged western horizon. Around him birds sang gaily. Somewhere higher up on the mountain a hungry hawk shrieked. Deer grazed in the verdant valley below, while off in the distance a small herd of shaggy buffalo drank at a meandering stream.

It was a tranquil scene. So Nate had no reason to expect trouble when he stepped from the

7

pines and made toward the middle of the clearing. Lying there was the buck he'd shot 20 minutes earlier, and as he strode into the open, he saw something move beside it.

With twilight shrouding the countryside, Nate was unable to see the creature clearly. Suddenly it rose on all fours to utter a savage growl, and Nate froze. He hoped the bobcat would wander elsewhere if he didn't provoke it.

Seldom were bobcats dangerous. Unlike their much larger cousins, bobcats were rarely seen and always fled when encountered. Almost always, anyhow. Occasionally trappers ran into contrary bobcats and wound up sporting nasty scars.

Nate King already had more than his share of scars and no hankering to add to them. He stood stock still as the cat took a slow step toward him. Burdened as he was with firewood, he couldn't resort to his flintlock quickly even if he'd wanted to. And his prized Hawken was propped against a fir tree across the way.

The animal crouched, ears flat, thin lips curled to expose razor-sharp tapered teeth. Over five feet long from nose tip to tail's end and packing upwards of seventy pounds onto its sinewy frame, the cat was capable of disemboweling a man.

Nate saw blood trickling from the bobcat's tufted chin and figured the scent had drawn it to the carcass. Normally, bobcats shunned carrion.

Again the creature advanced, body slung low to the ground, wide paws soundless on the grass.

A gut feeling told Nate the cat was going to attack. It was an instinctive feeling born of years spent in the raw wilderness, of honing that most basic of human drives, simple self-preservation, to the keenness of a finely tempered blade.

The bobcat's stubby tail twitched as it slunk forward. Nate cast a longing glance at his heavy-caliber rifle, knowing he couldn't reach it before the cat reached him.

There was one trick Nate could try. Hoping to spook the bobcat, he stamped a moccasin and vented a Shoshone war whoop. Instead of fleeing, the bobcat snarled and lunged at Nate.

So fast were the feline's reflexes, it was on Nate before he could so much as move. Without thinking, he let go of the firewood. The broken branches clattered at his feet, causing the bobcat to weave to one side. Nate stabbed at a pistol as the cat swung, its claws digging into his shin deep enough to draw blood.

Nate back-pedaled, drawing as he did, the bobcat pressing against him, its paw moving so fast the motion was a blur. He had no idea how many times he had been cut when the flintlock cleared his wide leather belt. Thankfully, the bobcat didn't leap at his chest or neck, giving him the opportunity needed to level the pistol and take a hasty bead.

As if the creature possessed an uncanny sixth sense that warned it of imminent death, it abruptly whirled and fled, streaking into the forest too swiftly for Nate to react and shoot. In the blink of an eye it was lost in dense undergrowth, its parting snarl carried by the stiff breeze.

Nate lowered the .55 and examined his leg. The legging had been shredded below the knee and there were a dozen or so stinging furrows, some deep, some not. Hardly life-threatening, but there was always the risk of infection.

Working briskly, Nate removed his fire steel, flint, and tinder box from his possibles bag and soon had a fire going. Pulling his butcher knife from its beaded sheath he proceeded to slice his legging higher so he could tend the wounds, but his task was interrupted by footsteps at the south side of the clearing.

Shakespeare McNair was an elder member of the trapping fraternity. Some claimed he had been the first white man to ever set foot in the central Rockies, a claim McNair never disputed. Sporting long hair and a bushy beard every bit as white as the snow-crowned peaks of the mountains he called home, McNair was widely regarded as the best trapper in the business.

Now, coming across the clearing, Shakespeare saw Nate's leg and grinned. "Lordy, this coon can't leave you alone for five minutes without you getting in a racket with the local wildlife."

"It was a bobcat," Nate said.

"No fooling. I heard it cuss you in cat talk." Shakespeare deposited the full water skin he had brought from the spring and sank to one knee beside the younger man. "Let me have a look, Horatio. You're liable to chop off your own foot by mistake."

"Keep badgering me and we'll be the ones getting in a racket."

"Go, go," Shakespeare began quoting from the book he knew as well as he did the palms of his hands. "You are a couterfeit cowardly knave. Will you mock at an ancient tradition, began upon an honourable respect, and worn as a memorable trophy of predeceased valour, and dare not avouch in your deeds any of your words? I have seen you gleeking and galling at this gentleman twice or thrice."

"Like hell," Nate grumbled. "I've never gleeked anybody, so far as I know." He paused. "And once, just once, I'd be happy if you spoke normal English like everyone else."

"Normal English?" Shakespeare repeated, then cackled as if demented. "Son, Americans don't know the meaning of the word. We take to mangling language the same as we mangle everything else."

"If you say so," Nate responded. His leg had begun throbbing, and he was in no frame of mind to spar words with his mentor. "Do you happen to be toting any poultice makings in that bag of yours? I'm plumb out."

"I've got me some woodie leaves," Shakespeare said, referring to a type of plant commonly used by the Shoshones to treat war wounds. "Not much, but it should be enough."

"Have at it." Nate leaned back, gritting his teeth against the pain, which grew worse with each passing minute. It was as if he'd been stung by a hundred bees.

The grizzled mountaineer removed a battered coffeepot from a worn parfleche. "I'll have to boil

11

water first." He chuckled. "Gives me a chance to tell a story."

"Oh, no," Nate groaned, but he secretly pricked his ears.

"Yep. This reminds me of the time old Bob Walker came up short in a tussle with a bobcat." McNair commenced pouring water into the pot. "It seems his Nez Percé wife wanted to fringe all her dresses with bobcat fur. Something to do with a dream she had. She believed the fur would be right powerful medicine. Turn Old Bob into a tiger under the robes at night."

"You're joshing me again."

"As I live and breathe, that was her reason," Shakespeare swore. "So Old Bob went traipsing all over Creation after bobcats. The hide had to be from kittens for the medicine to work, which meant he was poking his nose into every hollow log and under every fallen tree he came across. He found a few dens, too, and naturally the she-cats weren't none too thrilled about having him take their young, so he had to fight them off first."

"Hardly seems worth the bother," Nate commented.

Shakespeare arched an eyebrow. "This from a married man. When was the last time you told your wife to go take a walk off the nearest cliff when she gave you something to do?"

"Get on with your tale."

"Well, long about the fifth or sixth den, Old Bob met his match. He had to reach way down into a tree stump, and when he did that she-cat

12

boiled out of there like a hairy volcano. About tore one of his cheeks to ribbons and bit off the end of his nose. Left a big hole, she did. He had to put a ball in her brain or she would have rubbed him out for sure. Then, proud as could be, with enough kitten hides to hem a dozen dresses, he rode back to the village."

"Must have made his wife happy, I reckon."

"No. She left him and moved back in with her folks."

"Whatever for?"

"She couldn't stand the sight of him without his nose. That big hole about made her sick to her stomach every time she looked at him."

"The nerve! After all the poor man had been through."

"That wasn't the worst of it."

"What was?"

"She took those hides with her and used them to decorate the shield of her new lover."

"How did Old Bob take her treachery?"

"He got so drunk at the next rendezvous, he challenged the lover to a duel. Her new beau got to pick the weapons and he decided on lances, from horseback."

"Did Old Bob win?"

"Not hardly. I saw the fight with my own eyes. They were sitting on their cayuses, waiting for the signal, when Bob sort of oozed off his animal like all his bones had turned to mush. Out cold, he was, for a whole day. When he came around he didn't remember a blessed thing."

"So that was the end of the affair."

"Almost. The woman married the warrior. About a year later they were in their lodge one night when someone pushed on the flap and tossed a big sack inside. Before they quite knew what was what, a bobcat came barreling out of that sack primed for battle. A she-cat, it was. She scratched the warrior something awful, then tore into that woman and ripped off her lower lip."

"Old Bob."

"No one could ever prove it," Shakespeare said. "The Nez Percé grumbled for a spell about making war on all whites for the outrage, but they were just making chests for the benefit of their women."

"What did Old Bob do?"

"Married his woman when she came crawling back, begging his forgiveness."

"I've done lost your trail."

"Didn't I tell you? That warrior didn't want any part of her after the bobcat was through. Without her lip she couldn't kiss good enough to suit him, so he sent her packing. Since no one else wanted her either, she had to choose between Old Bob and spinsterhood." Shakespeare fed a few small limbs to the fire. "Goes to show there is justice in this world of ours, no matter what those with blinders on might say."

They lapsed into the amiable sort of silence only the best of friends can enjoy, Shakespeare pleased with himself for having taken Nate's mind from the cuts if only for a short while, Nate thinking about his wife, Winona, and wondering whether she would still love him if he were to be horribly

14

disfigured as Old Bob had been, which, given the violent sort of life he led, was a distinct possibility.

Not that Nate dwelled on such morbid matters. Since leaving the choking confines of New York City for the untamed frontier, he'd never sincerely regretted his decision or fretted over the future. "If it's meant to be, it's meant to be," he liked to say when looking ahead to specific events.

At this particular moment the young free trapper was quite content with his lot in life. He had a dependable wife, a strapping son and a lovely little girl. They lived in a remote cabin high in the Rockies with eagles and bighorn sheep for neighbors. Their water came from a spring as pure as any in the Garden. Food in abundance was theirs for the taking most months of the year. To Nate's way of thinking, he dwelled in paradise and wouldn't trade places with anyone for all the gold ever mined.

Shakespeare McNair was equally content but for different reasons. Like Nate, he had a devoted wife. Like Nate, he lived far back in the mountains where other men left him alone to do as he damn well pleased.

But Shakespeare had the added perspective of a man well on in years, of someone who had lived life to the fullest, who had wrung every precious drop of enjoyment there was to wring from existence and could count his cup as full.

Only one piddling fact marred Shakespeare's outlook, a trifling desire he had harbored for more years than he cared to recollect, a strange pulling on his heartstrings that had nothing to do with physical love. And for a mountain man it was all the more bewildering because it didn't concern the land he so passionately cherished.

Shakespeare had told no one. Not Blue Water Woman, not Nate or Winona. Yet he wanted to confide in someone. "There's something I've been meaning to bring up," he said casually while checking on the water.

"No, I won't lend you a hundred dollars until the rendezvous," Nate joked.

"What's here?" Shakespeare quoted. "The portrait of a blinking idiot, presenting me a schedule." He shook his head. "No, I wanted to talk about this hankering I have."

"For painter steak?"

"No, not panther meat."

"Fly-blowed buffler meat?"

"You're a funny gent."

"A prairie queen?"

"My wife would shoot me and you know it." Shakespeare laughed, then turned serious. "I want to see the ocean again."

Nate sat up, his brow puckered. McNair despised the civilized life as much as he did, and he couldn't see the old-timer making the long journey to the Atlantic just to stare at the sea. "It would take months," he remarked.

"Years."

"The Atlantic Ocean isn't that far."

"I was thinking of the Pacific."

Ordeal

Shakespeare might as well have announced he wanted to fly to the moon. It would have had the same effect on Nate. "You're touched in the head. No one has done that except Lewis and Clark, and they had a whole expedition to back them up."

"Wrong," Shakespeare said. "Jedediah Smith went to California in '24. Joe Walker went just a few years back. Kit Carson has been there, too. So has Ewell Young."

"There must be a regular highway," Nate said, only half in jest.

"You know all this," Shakespeare chided. "You're just trying to get a rise out of me." He gazed wistfully westward. "But this hos meant what he said. I'd like to see the Pacific again before I die."

"Getting there and back would take the better part of a year," Nate noted.

"I know."

"You couldn't leave Blue Water Woman for that long."

"I know."

"And there are all sorts of things that can go wrong. You'd have to contend with hostiles, grizzlies, rattlers, long spells without water and food, the fickle weather—"

"I know all the perils," Shakespeare said testily. "I'm the one who has been there, remember?"

"When, might I ask?"

"That's right. I've never told you, have I?" McNair propped himself on his hands. "It was in 1798. I got an itch to see the Oregon Country,

17

so I set off with a pair of Delawares. Ever met one of their tribe?"

"Can't say as I have," Nate said, distracted by the question. He was eager to hear the story.

"Upstanding tribe. Generous and reliable to a fault. The Lenni-Lenape, they call themselves. They greeted the white man with open arms and were forced from their homeland by their white brothers." Shakespeare gave a little snort to show his contempt and was about to go on when he glimpsed movement on a ridge to the southwest. The encroaching darkness kept him from distinguishing details, but the glimpse was enough to galvanize him into lunging, grabbing the water skin, and upending it over the fire.

Nate didn't bother seeking an explanation. They had ridden together so long they knew each other's thoughts. Despite the pain, Nate pushed himself erect and gathered their belongings, rushing to the horses with parfleches, packs, and bales of plews. It took ten minutes for the two of them to slap their gear on their pack animals and saddle up. They'd done a sloppy job but neither made an issue of it. Staying alive was more important.

Shakespeare led off into the pine forest, winding among the tightly spaced trunks with marvelous skill.

Nate twisted often to check their back trail. The stock of the Hawken rested on his right thigh. He had forgotten about the pain in his leg.

From a hill a quarter of a mile from their camp they surveyed the night, and Shakespeare said, "They were bound to have spotted our fire."

"But they can't track at night. Maybe we've given them the slip."

"No," Shakespeare said, pointing. "There."

They had the aspect of centaurs prancing under the dim starlight. A full dozen riders roved over the camp site, scouring for sign.

"Hostiles, you reckon?" Nate whispered even though they were well beyond earshot.

"Blood country is closest," Shakespeare answered, referring to one of the three tribes that constituted the dreaded Blackfoot Confederacy. Along with the Blackfeet and the Piegans, the Bloods waged relentless war against all invaders, white or otherwise.

"They don't like to fight at night," Nate remembered.

"Not ordinarily. But they will if they're hungry for coup."

The centaurs had fanned out, bearing eastward.

"Damn!" Nate fumed. "They've found our trail."

"They're guessing," Shakespeare disagreed. "They've figured out that we're trappers and they know most trappers head east to one of the forts when hard pressed by Indians."

"Then I say we go north."

The carpet of pine needles underfoot enabled them to travel quietly for the next hour. They shied from meadows and valleys, staying in the shelter of woodland where they could safely ride undetected. On a rocky slope they reined up to scour the land they had crossed, and Nate saw the dully glittering lances first. "I'll be dogged! How the devil are they doing that?"

"Your guess is as good as mine."

Onward into the night the two trappers galloped, taking risks now that their lives were at stake. Shakespeare had an uncanny knack for sniffing out the path of least resistance. Toward midnight they finally halted for the sake of their animals on an upland bench that afforded a sweeping view of the countryside.

"We've shaken them now. I can feel it in my bones," Nate said, wiping sweat from his brow with the sleeve of his buckskin shirt. He took off his beaver hat to let the crisp air cool his head.

Shakespeare had risen in the stirrups. "That's rheumatism, you dunderhead."

"Calling yourself a doctor now, are you?"

"Take a look and you tell me, Horatio."

Vague shadows moved at the limits of the night, a compact group sticking to their trail like sap to a tree.

"They can't be doing that," Nate snapped. "It just can't be done, not at night."

"Someone forgot to tell them."

Their tired mounts balked and had to be goaded into resuming the flight. Nate resisted a wave of fatigue that threatened to dull his mind and senses. He'd been on the go since before first light and had worked hard all day raising beaver. So had McNair, yet the older man was as spry as a bantam rooster. One thing Nate never tired of doing was marveling at his mentor's constitution. He hoped he'd be half as lively

Ordeal

when he was the same age, provided he lived that long.

From the bench they wound down into a canyon and through it to a steep incline that brought them to the top of a sparsely treed tableland. It wasn't until they came to the opposite rim that they realized their mistake; the tableland ended at a sheer bluff hundreds of feet high. They had boxed themselves in!

Wheeling, the trappers went to retrace their steps to the slope but they were too late. Advancing toward them in a skirmish line were their pursuers.

Chapter Two

Nate King and Shakespeare McNair were not about to let themselves be taken alive. They knew all too well the horrid tortures countless of their kind had endured at the hands of pitiless captors. Resolved to fight on for as long as breath remained, they started to swing around behind their pack animals to allow the beasts of burden to serve as a buffer between their attackers and them. Suddenly one of the oncoming figures hailed them in English, and to say the trappers were surprised would be an understatement.

"Hold on there, you two! We're Americans and we mean you no harm! We'd just like to talk."

Nate and Shakespeare exchanged puzzled looks as they drew rein. It was McNair who replied, bellowing, "Stop right where you are! Come no

22

further until we've jawed with the captain of your outfit."

"That would be me," the speaker said, his voice deep, and resonant. "I'll be unarmed, so for God's sake don't shoot."

The tall figure handed weapons to a companion. Nate watched the man knee his mount forward while holding his arms aloft to show he was defenseless. Nate had to admire the stranger's grit even though he suspected it was a trick of some kind. The only Americans in the mountains at that time of year were trappers, and this bunch lacked both traps and pack horses.

The stranger wore an expensive riding outfit and heavy coat, a flowing red scarf, and polished black boots. "My apologies for accosting you in this manner," he declared as he neared them. "But I'm hoping you've seen two men—" He broke off, gawking at them. "Can it be? After all this time?"

"What the dickens are you raving about?" Shakespeare prompted.

"Your white hair and beard. And the young Atlas with you," the man exclaimed. "Do I at long last have the distinct honor of addressing Thaddeus August McNair and Nathaniel King?"

Nate was so shocked by the disclosure that he swung toward his friend. "Thaddeus August?"

Shakespeare studiously ignored him. "You do," he told the stranger. "Who might you be?"

"Cyrus Porter, at your service," responded the other with a flourish. "And I have been searching for the two of you for months."

23

"With a small army?" Shakespeare asked, nodding at the 11 riders waiting patiently for their leader.

"Hirelings, all save one," Porter said, then leaned forward. "Oh! There is so much we must discuss. I don't really know where to begin."

The mountain man hefted his Hawken. "Mister, for the past six hours you've been dogging our trail like a hound dog after coons, and in the process you've about run our horses into the ground. Before I'll offer you a glad hand, I want to know why. Just the meat will do. I don't need chapter and verse."

Cyrus Porter stiffened, then sniffed as if afflicted with a cold. "Fair enough, Mr. McNair. I have traveled to this godforsaken country all the way from Connecticut to find my daughter, who went missing out here about a year ago. I've been asking around, and everyone tells me that you're the man best able to track her down, as they say in frontier parlance." He leaned forward, hands propped on his saddle horn. "I trust you'll be civil enough to hear me out. If not for my sake or that of my darling Hetty, then for the one thousand dollars which will be yours once you've accepted my proposal."

"A thousand dollars is more than most folks make in a whole year," Shakespeare remarked.

"To me, it's a paltry sum, a mere pittance," Porter said matter-of-factly. "I probably make that much interest on my money every day."

Nate's curiosity had been piqued and he had

to ask, "What exactly do you do for a living, Mr. Porter?"

"I count the interest on the money bequeathed to me by my parents," Porter said sarcastically. "Yes, gentlemen, I'm as rich as Midas and I make no bones about it."

"It's not a fact I'd advertise hereabouts, were I you," Nate cautioned.

"Why not, pray tell?" the New Englander inquired with perfect innocence.

"Some of the men living out here would slit a man's throat for a hundred dollars. Imagine what they'd do for wealth beyond measure."

"I'm not worried. I'm amply protected." Porter gestured at McNair. "What is your decision? Will you hear me out or not?"

"I will," Shakespeare announced. "You and your men can lead the way. The first suitable spot, we'll pitch camp and put a coffeepot on the fire."

"Wonderful. Simply wonderful." Porter nodded happily, then rejoined the members of his party. In a group they rode eastward.

"What do you make of all this?" Nate wondered as he guided his pack animals in their wake.

"I don't rightly know yet," Shakespeare replied. "He seems sincere but I'll reserve judgment until we've heard him out."

Below the tableland, in a clearing in a tract of fir trees, the rich man's party tethered their stock and built a roaring blaze. By the time Shakespeare and Nate finished with their own string, a coffeepot was boiling. Both noticed that Cyrus Porter was waited on hand and foot by an elderly man wearing a formal suit, of all things. Beside Porter sat a man of 25 or so who wore an expression of perpetual melancholy.

"This is Adam Clark," Porter introduced them. "His father and I are the best of friends, and Adam was very close to Hetty before she went off on her lark."

Clark shook hands with all the vigor of a limp rag. Nate masked his reaction as he took a seat on a log that had been strategically placed close to the fire for their benefit. "I'm pleased to meet you," he said to be polite. Clark simply nodded.

"Not half as glad as I am to meet the two of you," Porter avowed. "You're hard men to locate." He stretched his legs and sighed. "I swear, I've spent more time in the saddle in the past sixty days than in all the years before combined."

"You get used to it after a while," Nate said.

"Not at my age." Porter faced McNair. "Before I take up more of my valuable time and yours, of course, I must know a crucial fact." He paused as if half afraid to go on. "Have you ever been to the Oregon Country?"

Everyone stopped whatever he was doing to stare at Shakespeare. Adam Clark perked up, waiting expectantly.

"I have," the mountain man admitted, puzzled by all the fuss.

"Thank God!" Porter cried, leaping erect in his excitement and clapping Clark on the shoulders. "We've found our man!"

"I'm not the only one who has been there," Shakespeare commented. "There's—"

Ordeal

"I know. I know," Porter rudely cut him off. "Smith and Young and Fitzpatrick, to name just a few. But Smith is dead, Young is too busy to help, and Fitzpatrick is the last man on this planet I would hire."

"Tom is a good man. I know him well."

"That may be," Porter said, "but since he's partly to blame for my daughter's plight, I wouldn't demean myself by looking him up."

"The idiot!" Clark chimed in.

Again Shakespeare was perplexed. He'd trapped with Fitzpatrick back when the Rocky Mountain Fur Company was a going concern, and they'd shared many a tall tale around campfires just like this one. Fitzpatrick was intelligent, soft-spoken, and moderate in all his habits. Not an idiot, by a far sight, and Shakespeare declared as much.

"Please don't be offended," Porter soothed. "Adam is letting his feelings show, is all. You'll understand better once you hear the whole story."

"My ears are primed," Shakespeare said.

Nate was being largely ignored, which didn't bother him in the least. It gave him an opportunity to study the rest of the New Englander's party, and he didn't particularly like what he saw.

Of the ten men, eight wore the cocky insolence of St. Louis river rats on their grimy sleeves. Clad in city clothes and boots, they were as out of place in the mountains as the two from the East. Most favored short beards; all carried a brace of pistols and a pair of knives.

The ninth man was a rarity, a Mexican in flared

trousers, boots with spurs, and a broad-brimmed sombrero. Around his slender waist was a red sash into which he had slid two fancy pistols, both with inlaid silver butts.

The last man was difficult to pin down. He wore buckskins, but they were new and ill fitting. He mingled freely with the river rats, but his bearing and conduct were more on the order of an aristocrat than riffraff. In added contrast, his hair was sandy blond, his eyes strikingly blue; the others all had dark hair and eyes.

Cyrus Porter had begun pacing in front of them, hands clasped behind his stout back. "To fully appreciate why I've sought you out, Mr. McNair, I must tell you about my daughter, my pride and joy."

"Your only child?" Shakespeare guessed.

"Yes. Born twenty-two years ago in Hartford, where she lived all her life until intoxicated by the spirit of adventure and the charms of a serpent."

"Pardon?" Shakespeare said, thinking he had missed something.

"A rogue by the name of Oliver Davin. Swept my sweet girl off her feet with his rakish ways, then convinced her to journey to the frontier to seek out a new life together. They joined a group of twenty settlers heading for the Oregon Country and hired Tom Fitzpatrick to guide them."

"Ah," Shakespeare grunted, making the connection.

"I protested against the foolish enterprise, to no avail," Porter lamented. "To all my entreaties, dear Hetty would bat her eyes and say how it was her wifely duty to stand by her husband." Emotion choked him a moment. "I raised her well, Mr. McNair. Perhaps too well."

No one interrupted and the New Englander went on.

"Perhaps if my beloved Martha were still alive, we might have prevailed. Hestia always listened to her. But my wife was lost to the coughing sickness about five years ago."

"I'm sorry," Shakespeare said to be polite.

Porter bowed his head a moment. "But I digress. The main point is that Hetty and Oliver departed Independence in the company of those other misguided souls and headed westward in wagons." He shook his head in disbelief. "Wagons! In this awful country!"

Nate opted to mention, "They say it can be done."

"And they say men will travel everywhere in trains one day, but only an utter jackass would take it as gospel." Porter stamped his foot in anger. "I tried and tried to dissuade her. I talked until I was blue in the face. Yet off she went with that worthless vagabond. Only later did I learn they didn't make it all the way to the Oregon Country."

"They didn't?" Shakespeare asked. This was the first he'd heard of Fitzpatrick's expedition. Based on prior experience, he doubted the man had up and abandoned them in the middle of nowhere.

"No, sir. Apparently they camped in the Bear River region and decided they'd gone far enough.

That was where they'd settle down and plot their homesteads." Porter glanced at the mountain man. "Are you familiar with the region?"

"Been there a few times."

"Excellent." Porter held his palms out to the crackling flames. "That's where we'll have to start."

"Start?"

"Other parties have been through the area since. There was no sign of the settlers. Not a trace."

"You're sure?"

"Of course!" Porter exploded. "Did you think I would give up on my Hetty? I hired a man in Independence whose sole job was to contact anyone and everyone leaving for the Oregon Country and to request that they check on her welfare, if possible, and send him a note with returning guides or travelers."

"Where could they have gotten to?" Nate mused aloud.

"That's the most crucial question in my life," Cyrus Porter stated, "and the reason I've spent so much time and money outfitting an expedition to go find her. Which is where you come in," he addressed McNair.

Shakespeare stalled by giving a loose moccasin more attention than it deserved. The idea appealed to him, if only because he could push on beyond Bear River clear to the Pacific and fulfill his heart's desire, but he foresaw problems, serious problems, so he hedged by saying, "You want me to guide you to the Bear River Country, I take it."

"You take it correctly."

"Forgive me for saying this, but you do realize there's no guarantee we'll find your daughter?"

"I must try."

"The journey could prove more costly than you expect."

"I must try," Porter stressed.

Nate had listened intently to the exchange. His mentor's tone told him that McNair was inclined to accept, and suddenly he had a powerful hankering to go along. It might be the only chance he ever had to visit the Oregon Country, and he meant to take advantage.

Shakespeare was fiddling with a moccasin. "You mentioned organizing an expedition?"

"The men you see here, plus four others with our pack animals."

"Where are they?"

"Camped at your cabin."

McNair shot off the log as if it was scorching hot. "You've been to my place?"

Porter nodded, appearing disturbed by the frontiersman's gruff bearing. "How else did you think I knew where to find you? A trapper gave us directions to your cabin, and after I explained my dilemma to your wife, she graciously gave us a map showing where you were going to trap this season." He cocked his head. "Is something wrong? She assured me it would be all right."

"She would," Shakespeare said absently. "Blue Water Woman doesn't have a mean bone in her body."

Nate saw his friend glance at the river rats and

could imagine his thoughts: Four of their notorious ilk were alone with his wife. In confirmation, Shakespeare shifted toward him.

"Will you bring my pack animals?"

"Did you even have to ask?"

Moving rapidly, McNair grabbed his Hawken, jogged to his white horse, and began saddling up.

Adam Clark roused himself to speak. "I don't understand, Mr. King. Where is he off to in such a hurry?"

"Home," Nate said, conscious of the glares bestowed on the mountain man by several of the St. Louis crowd.

"But he should wait and travel with us," Porter said.

"He wants to ride fast and light," Nate elaborated. "We'll get there in a week and a half. It'll only take him three days."

"No man can cover that much ground in so short a span," Porter declared.

"You'd be surprised," Nate said. "Knowing the lay of the land makes all the difference in the world." Draping his own rifle across his legs, he frowned while watching McNair vault astride the horse, whip the reins, and speed off into the night without so much as a parting wave. Nate didn't blame him. Were the situation reversed, he'd be doing the same—after punching Porter square in the face for stupidly endangering his wife.

"How odd," the New Englander said as the clatter of hooves receded. "Is your friend always so impetuous?"

Ordeal

"Shakespeare McNair is the most level-headed man you'll meet this side of the grave," Nate said. He would have liked to explain but dared not with so many river rats right there, listening. It wouldn't do to antagonize them any more than they already were if they were to travel hundreds of miles together.

Porter abruptly cursed. "He never said whether he'd help me or not!"

"Ask him again when we reach his place," Nate suggested, inwardly adding, "And pray to high heaven his wife is all right or your missing girl will be the very least of your worries." Rummaging in a parfleche, he came across his tin cup. Steam rose from the coffee when he poured. The heady fragrance was unlike any he had ever smelled. "Delicious," he remarked after taking a sip.

"A special Colombian brand I'm fond of," Porter said, staring after the absent mountain man.

"You might as well sit and enjoy some," Nate said. "First light will be here before you know it, and we have a heap of riding to do today."

So did McNair. He drove his horse to limits that would have ruined most mounts, stopping for ten minutes every three hours and for half an hour every six. Sleep was banished, eclipsed by anxiety for his wife's welfare.

Shakespeare was no greenhorn. He'd been most everywhere, seen most everything. Including the tempestuous melting pot known as St. Louis, a bustling city that reveled in satisfying the baser human urges, especially along the waterfront district where there were more taverns and bawdy houses than a man could visit in a month of Sundays.

Men who worked the river frequented those dives regularly. Lusty men these were, ready to fight at the drop of a hat, ready to make love on the whim of the moment. They honored no masters save themselves, bowed to no one for no reason.

On occasion mountain men visited St. Louis. Being for the most part as carnal as the river rats, they often wound up in riotous battles with the river men. In Shakespeare's younger days he had been in a few brawls and learned the hard way that the boatmen were as wild and woolly as any Nature's son who ever donned buckskins.

He tried not to dwell on their lusty side as he galloped madly to the southeast. He tried assuring himself Blue Water Woman was a full-grown female and could handle herself as well as any man. Yet in the end his mental assurances counted for naught. Worry nagged at him like a red-hot poker.

By dawn Shakespeare was exhausted, but he shook off a bout of drowsiness and pushed on.

By noon he was hungry enough to eat the proverbial bear but paid no heed to his stomach's rumbling.

By evening both rider and mount were soaked with sweat and racing pell-mell without a conscious thought between them. Their minds had shut down. They were at the point where a weary

Ordeal

body resigns itself to the inevitable and performs the motions mechanically.

Three days of this they endured. On the afternoon of the third day Shakespeare crested a ridge and spied the familiar outline of his home in the verdant valley below. He saw no movement, no sign of anyone.

Shakespeare flew down the slope and nearly lost his horse when it misjudged and stumbled in a rut. Righting itself, the animal took to the trail as if wings adorned its ankles. In no time they pounded up to the front of the cabin and Shakespeare jumped down before his mount stopped moving.

The door stood ajar. Within, silence reigned.

Cocking the Hawken on the fly, Shakespeare barreled inside. His worst fears were realized when he discovered the furniture in scattered disarray and household items littering the floor. "Oh, God!" he cried, then dashed back out into the sunlight.

"Blue Water Woman!"

The whispering wind mocked him.

Shakespeare bent low to examine the soil. Too much time had passed, and the jumble of old tracks only added to the difficulty. He moved in steadily widening circles, ascertaining where the four river men had been camped and where the pack animals had been tethered. He counted 30, a surprising number. All loaded with goods for the trek, goods an enterprising river rat could sell in St. Louis or elsewhere for thousands of dollars.

"Porter, you're a jackass," Shakespeare said.

On the trail leading southward were the freshest prints. Shakespeare galloped after them, his heart heavy, his blood roaring for vengeance. He'd taken the trails so frequently, he knew every bend, every dip, from memory. No one else could have ridden as fast.

Shakespeare figured he would overtake the river rats in three or four days. So he was mystified when he beheld a column of smoke ahead and simultaneously electrified by the faint notes of a wavering scream. It could only be one person, he reasoned, and thundered on with bloodlust in his eyes.

Chapter Three

At the very moment that one mountain man bore madly down on those who had abducted his wife, another rode at the head of a column of men and horses listening to a smug New Englander justify his actions.

"Hetty and I were always close until that damned Oliver Davin came along," Cyrus Porter declared. "He turned her against me, made my own flesh and blood see me as some kind of ogre."

"The two of you didn't cotton to one another?" Nate said idly. He had no real interest in their squabbles, but it was all Porter wanted to talk about. The man was downright fanatical on the subject.

"You must be joking!" Porter responded with a bitter, dry laugh. "What could the two of us possibly have in common? Davin was a nobody, a clerk my daughter met at a dry goods store, of all places." Porter muttered under his breath. "She could have taken her pick from any eligible bachelor in Hartford, in the whole damned State, yet she picked someone who pushes pencils for a living!" He muttered some more. "I wouldn't have minded half so much if Davin possessed a smidgen of blue blood."

Nate decided then and there that he disliked the highborn Hartforder, immensely. The thought of spending months in Porter's company was enough to sour him on the proposed trip.

The aggrieved father continued. "What Hetty sees in him, I will never know. Davin is so ordinary, he's worthless. He'll never amount to much, in my opinion."

"In your opinion," Nate deliberately emphasized.

Porter glanced around. "I don't want you to misconstrue my attitude, Mr. King. I'm not one of those doting fathers who are unwilling to let go when it's time for their brood to leave the nest. I would love for my Hestia to marry the right man and bring a whole flock of grandchildren into the world."

Ordinarily Nate refrained from sticking his nose into others' affairs. Among those who made their living by trapping, there was an unwritten Eleventh Commandment: "Thou shalt mind thy own business." But in this instance Porter had brought the subject up and wouldn't let it drop, so Nate commented, "Your daughter must believe this Davin is the right man."

"Then she's mistaken."

"I see. Father knows best," Nate said, an edge to his tone. Porter reminded him a lot of his own father, sparking memories better left to gather cobwebs in the inner recesses of his mind.

"In this case, yes," the New Englander insisted. "I can look at the situation in a detached, logical manner, while dear Hestia is a victim of her immature heart. She let a handsome rascal sweep her off her feet when she would have been smart to wait for a man of more substance."

Adam Clark, who rode a horse as listlessly as he did everything else, interjected, "I'm a man of substance but she didn't want me." He sniffed in indignation. "I wasn't good enough for her."

Porter clucked like a mother hen. "You were doing just fine, son, until Davin came along. After the drudgery he's put her through, I'd wager my bottom dollar that she'll greet you gladly. And with a bit of persuasion, maybe we can convince her to forsake that cad for you."

Nate had to look away so they wouldn't see his resentment. It rankled him that Porter had the gall to think he was better qualified to pick Hetty's husband than she was. He dropped the subject, though, so as not to antagonize his new acquaintances.

Twenty-five yards in front of the main body rode the Mexican, a rifle slanted across his thighs. His horse was a superb bay, its coat as sleek as glass. Man and mount moved as one, the horse prancing as if putting on a show.

"That Chavez sure can ride," Nate said.

"What?" Porter replied absently, then gazed ahead. "Oh. The greaser. Yes, he can. Fine rider, fine tracker. I get my money's worth out of him."

"He's too much the loner for my tastes," Adam Clark said. "He hardly ever talks to anyone."

Nate could understand why, given their sentiments and those of the clannish rivermen. Since the horses under his charge were being handled by a pair of the latter, he was free to apply his heels to the flanks of his stallion and overtake Chavez. "Mind some company?"

The tracker betrayed surprise but regained his composure and answered, "Not at all, señor."

"The air back younder is getting a mite whiffy," Nate said, jerking a thumb at the column.

Chavez digested that awhile. "You do not like Señor Porter's company?"

"Let's just say I'd rather hug a polecat and let it go at that," Nate said, grinning.

The Mexican did the same. "I think I like you, hombre. We have much in common."

"Then why do you work for him?"

"Dinero, señor. Money. I need a lot of it before I can go home again, and he has agreed to pay me more than I could make in two or three years if I will go with him to this Oregon Country."

"Seems to me a man can go home any time he wants," Nate said. "Money ought not to be a factor."

"It depends on one's situation," Chavez responded cryptically.

Nate didn't press. He stared at the tracker's rifle, a brand new Hall's breechloader in .52 caliber. Indeed, all of Porter's men had been armed with similar rifles, a contingency against hostiles. From a distance, at night, the long guns could readily be mistaken for lances, as Nate and Shakespeare had done. "Do all of you get to keep your rifles, too?"

"Those who stay with Señor Porter until his hija, his daughter, is found, yes." Chavez pointed at Nate's Hawken. "I have heard much of the Hawken brothers and their guns. Excellente, it is said. I hope you will let me fire yours sometime, and I will let you shoot mine."

"You have a deal."

A series of steep switchbacks required their full attention. Once at the bottom they reined up to observe the progress of the rest.

Chavez pushed back his sombrero and pulled a leather pouch from under his short embroidered jacket. "Care for a cigarrillo, señor?"

"No thanks," Nate replied. He waited while the tracker's slim fingers adroitly handled the paper and tobacco. As Chavez took his first puff, Nate indicated the twin pistols. "Speaking of excellent guns, those pistols of yours are without a doubt the finest this coon has ever set eyes on."

"A gift from a very special person," Chavez said proudly, giving one an affectionate pat. "These are dueling pistols. English made, maple stocks with silver decoration, in .60 caliber."

"May I handle one?" Nate asked.

Chavez hesitated, only a moment. He neatly plucked out the left-hand pistol, gave it a little flip to reverse his grip, and handed it over butt first.

Nate was a far cry from an expert but he knew an outstanding sidearm when he saw one. It was exquisitely crafted, with superior balance. A smoothbore, like his pair, but five times as expensive. The trigger was thinner and shorter than his by half.

The tracker noticed Nate's puzzled features and stated, "It is called a hair trigger, señor. A tiny tap and the gun will fire." He grinned. "After it is cocked, of course."

"Of course," Nate said, returning the pistol. The idea struck him that Caesar Chavez was probably slicker than hot grease with those guns. He tried to judge the man's age but couldn't. Chavez had the smooth skin of a man in his twenties yet his eyes were old and haunted.

By this time the main party had descended and Cyrus Porter came up. "I don't pay you to smoke on my time," he told the tracker. "I want you on point. There's no telling when we might run into a pack of savages."

"Yes, señor," Chavez said, then trotted off.

"I wouldn't worry too much about chancing upon a war party," Nate said. "We're in Crow country and they're friendly. In a few more days we'll be in Shoshone territory, and they're even friendlier."

"I was led to believe that the Blackfeet roam all over these mountains as they damn well please."

"True, to a point—" Nate began.

"Then don't tell me not to worry. I have too much at stake. If anything happens to me, what will become of sweet Hetty?"

Nate saw no need to point out that as far as they knew Hetty was alive and well. Any number of reasons could account for her absence from the Bear River region, and the whole expedition might well turn out to be a monumental waste of energy and money.

Adam Clark cleared his throat. "I wouldn't mind meeting a few of these Blackfoot hooligans I've heard so much about." He wagged his rifle. "I'd teach them to pester their betters."

Sighing, Nate fell into step alongside them. More than ever he sorely missed his mentor's company and hoped McNair had found Blue Water Woman safe and sound. A glance at the somber rivermen hinted otherwise.

Many miles eastward, Shakespeare McNair burst from the forest into a lush meadow and spotted the 30 heavily laden pack horses clustered at the far end, with others. The scream was repeated as he let his mount have its head. This time he realized it was a man, not a woman.

A number of Indians were gathered in a circle near the pack horses. Shakespeare recognized them as Flatheads, his wife's people, some of whom turned as he pounded to a stop and leaped among them. Shouldering his way to the center, Shakespeare was vastly relieved to see his wife standing to one side. She uttered a joyful cry and sprang into his open arms, her warm breath fanning his neck.

"Husband," she said softly in her precise English.

"Wife," Shakespeare said huskily.

"I missed you."

"I missed you too."

The Flatheads had fallen silent and stopped what they were doing. Shakespeare stepped back from Blue Water Woman and saw four rivermen bound hand and foot, on their knees, in a row.

A tall warrior wearing fine buckskins, his braided hair flecked with gray, smiled and beckoned with the bloody knife clutched in his right hand. "You have come just in time, Wolverine," he said in the Flathead tongue, referring to McNair by the Flathead name McNair had earned. "We caught these whites mistreating Blue Water Woman and have decided to punish them."

Lying on the ground in front of the first captive was a severed tongue. The river rat slumped, drooling more blood and spittle.

"This one," the tall warrior said, tapping the man's head and causing him to jump, "would not stop calling us foul names and insulting our mothers. Anyone who cannot control his tongue has no use for it."

Shakespeare reverted to Flathead and asked his wife, "What happened? I know all about Porter paying you a visit and leaving these four to watch his horses. Take it from there."

Blue Water Woman bobbed her chin at the quartet. "There is not much to tell. They behaved themselves until yesterday. Then they took me against my will and were stealing the pack animals when Buffalo Horn happened by."

"We were out on the prairie, hunting buffalo," the tall warrior said when she paused. "A dream told me to stop, so I did."

"Thank you," Shakespeare said hoarsely.

"They did not hurt me, husband," Blue Water Woman said, "except for the one with no beard. He slapped me and tried to reach under my dress."

"Did he now?" Shakespeare said. Without warning he drew a flintlock, walked to the offender, and put a ball through the river rat's head. The man barely so much as flinched when the shot rang out.

Immediately the two scoundrels as yet untouched cowered and pleaded in pidgin English mixed with liberal French for their lives.

"Please, monsieur! *Je regrette!* We meant no real harm. *Comprenez-vous?*" one wailed.

The members of the hunting party said nothing. Because it had been Shakespeare's wife who had been abused, he had the right to seal the offenders' fate as he so wished. He stalked to the next boatman and slowly unlimbered his other flintlock.

"Have mercy, monsieur!" pleaded this one. "I did not lay a finger on your wife! I swear, as God is my witness!"

"You can lie to Him in person if you want," Shakespeare said coldly while lifting the pistol. He wasn't deceived for a minute. The river rats were going to spare his wife until they were safely away; then they would have used her and disposed of her. They didn't dare leave a single witness.

"What have I done?" the man protested.

"You broke the trust of the man who hired you. You stole. You kidnapped another man's wife. Need I go on?"

"But I don't deserve death! Please let us talk this over. Maybe we can be friends, *non?*"

"No," Shakespeare said, and shot him, too.

That left the man who had lost his tongue and one other. Shakespeare tucked both spent pistols under his belt and pulled his tomahawk. The object of his attention had marshaled some courage and squared his shoulders.

"Do your worst, pig of a trapper! I spit on you, your squaw, these filthy heathens, and the sow who gave birth to all of you!"

The man opened his mouth to add more insults, but Shakespeare's arm flicked out and the flat side of the tomahawk struck the river rat on the temple, felling him on the spot. "Such bad manners," Shakespeare said in the Flathead language, eliciting laughs from several of the warriors.

Blue Water Woman materialized at McNair's elbow. "Don't you think that you have done enough?"

"I'm just getting started."

"No real harm was done."

"By pure accident. If Buffalo Horn and his bunch hadn't wandered by when they did, you'd have been worm food before too long." Shakespeare started to bend over the unconscious

46

ruffian. "I've never scalped someone using a tomahawk before. Should be interesting."

"Please," Blue Water Woman persisted. "Let my people deal with the last two. Take me home."

Reluctantly Shakespeare replaced the tomahawk, took his wife's hand, and headed for his horse. "Do with them as you want," he announced to the warriors. "Then bring their horses to my cabin and we will smoke a pipe and share old times."

The screaming resumed when they were halfway across the meadow. Neither looked back. Blue Water Woman sagged against Shakespeare, her arms around his waist, her cheek on his shoulder.

Nor did either of them speak until they came to the cabin. Shakespeare simply let the reins fall when he wearily climbed down. The long hours of hard riding combined with lack of sleep at last took their inevitable toll as he entered and his legs buckled. Embarrassed, he caught himself and shuffled to a chair which he righted and plunked down in.

Blue Water Woman sat in his lap and studied his rugged face while running her fingers through his great beard. "I feared I might never see you again."

Shakespeare tenderly touched her lips, then quoted in a whisper, "If I profane with my unworthiest hand this holy shrine, the gentle fine is this. My lips, two blushing pilgrims, ready stand to smooth that rough touch with a tender kiss."

Blue Water Woman smiled. "Only you could think of that at a time like this."

"I was trying to wax romantic, woman," Shakespeare said, feigning anger. "After all I went through to get here, you could have the decency to play along."

The reminder made Blue Water Woman look through the window at his exhausted horse. "Where is Nate?"

"With stuffy Cyrus Porter and company."

"You came on ahead? Alone?"

"Had to."

"The risk you took," Blue Water Woman chided, but love radiated from her like light from a lantern. "How did you know I would need you?"

"I know river rats. The wonder of it is that they took as long as they did to get up the nerve to run off." Shakespeare embraced her and kissed her as he hadn't kissed her in a long time.

"You should quote *Romeo and Juliet* more often," Blue Water Woman teased. She rested her head on his chest and looped a whang around a finger. "What would you like to do? Sleep, eat, or just have coffee?"

"Talk."

"About Porter's expedition?"

"What else?"

"Would you like to go?"

"I'm ashamed to confess that I surely would."

"Why ashamed, husband?"

"A man my age having a hankering to see the ocean. It's plumb silly." Shakespeare chuckled. "Maybe my mind gave out on me and we just don't realize it. Maybe I'm thinking I'm twenty again."

"We will go."

Shakespeare held her at arm's length, locked eyes, and asked gently, "Have you gone as crazy as me then?"

Blue Water Woman pecked his wrist. "In all the years we have been together, you have never wanted anything for yourself. You have seen to my every need, giving me everything I have ever wanted. Mirrors, ribbons, beads, I had only to say I would like something and you provided it. Now you have a need and it is fitting that I do my part to see it met."

"I appreciate the thought, but you're mixing apples and pears. Traveling to the Oregon Country is a far sight more difficult than going to the rendezvous to trade for foofaraw." Shakespeare paused. "And what's this 'we' business, anyhow?"

"Do not even pretend that you will not take me," Blue Water Woman warned. "Twelve moons or more is too many for us to be apart. If you go, I go."

"Sure you didn't take up with some white women while Nate and I were off raising beaver?" Shakespeare responded. "I swear you've got the knack of acting just like one."

"I will take that as a compliment."

"Tactful wench, I'll grant you," Shakespeare grumbled. Her agreement meant more to him than he could possibly convey, but it also bothered him terribly. He wasn't trying to scare her when he mentioned the hardships in store. If anything, he was grossly understating the case. It would make their trip to Santa Fe a while back seem tame by comparison, and they'd tangled with Apaches on that one.

"So we go?"

"I'd like to sleep on it a day or two. It'll take Nate another week to get here so we have plenty of time to talk this out some more."

He slept around the clock. He didn't mean to; it just happened that once his head hit the pillow he was out to the world, and Blue Water Woman made a point of not disturbing him. When Buffalo Horn and the hunting party arrived, she insisted that they camp a stone's throw away.

Shakespeare was flabbergasted on learning how long he had slumbered. The cabin had been tidied, meanwhile, and he sat at the table he had built from a tree that once stood right outside and slowly sipped the hottest, blackest coffee any man had ever tasted. Smacking his lips, he said, "Damn good, gorgeous. Makes me glad to be home."

"Is that the only reason?" Blue Water Woman asked. "And kindly spare me the swear words."

"I never should have let you talk to that missionary woman," Shakespeare complained. "You've been a stickler about proper behavior ever since."

Blue Water Woman brought a fresh baked tray of biscuits to the table. "These will have to tide you over until I fix a meal."

"No hurry," Shakespeare said, raising one to his nose and savoring the smell. Mouth watering, he took a bite. "Bake two dozen more of these first."

Ordeal

The tray was polished off in no time. Shakespeare smacked his lips and fondly watched his wife prepare supper. Although he hadn't told her yet, he knew what his decision would be. He could only hope—he could only *pray*—that his childish notion didn't get them both killed.

Chapter Four

Among the Shoshones it was widely conceded that Winona King was one of the loveliest women in the tribe. Her beauty had more to do with her vibrant personality than the luxurious black hair that cascaded past her slim shoulders to the small of her back, more to do with her strength of character than her comely face or the fullness of her figure.

That Winona had taken a white man for her husband was not held against her by her tribe. The Shoshones had long been friendly to the whites, and the trappers regarded them as staunch allies in the never ending war against the Blackfoot Confederacy.

Winona had done no differently than a score or more of Shoshone women who had found themselves drawn romantically to the strange newcomers whose quirky behavior and rowdy lust for life were irresistibly fascinating. And she had no regrets, save one.

Indian women were accustomed to their mates being gone for long periods. Sometimes the men would be gone for weeks at a time on raids against their enemies or when off hunting.

But white men often stayed away twice as long, especially during the two trapping seasons when they had to catch as many beaver as they could while the fur was at its prime.

Winona didn't like Nate's long absences. Two or three weeks she handled easily. Four weeks bothered her a lot. Six or more left her distracted with worry, hardly able to eat or sleep. She knew she was being childish. Mature women did not let worry get the better of them. But no matter how hard she tried, she couldn't stop herself from fretting.

It took a rare event to take Winona's mind off her anxiety, and on this day such an event took place thanks to her oldest boy, a bubbling cauldron of energy and curiosity.

Winona had risen before daylight as she almost always did. After preparing breakfast, she had tended to chores until the middle of the morning. Then, her infant daughter bundled in a cradleboard on her back, she had taken a short stroll down toward the lake, a daily ritual she greatly enjoyed.

The King cabin lay nestled in a remote valley high in the central Rockies, near a mountain known as Long's Peak, named after an explorer who had visited the region years before. It was a sheltered paradise rife with wildlife. Cool in the summer and spared from the worst of the heavy snows in the winter by a ring of encircling peaks, the valley was so far off the beaten path that few even knew of its existence.

The most prominent landmark was the large lake, a body of water so sparkling clear a person could stand on the shore and see the bottom yards out. Teeming with fish and waterfowl, it was the lure that brought creatures from miles around to slake their thirst. Black-tailed deer came every morning and evening. Elk could be found along the shore at first light. Bighorn sheep sometimes showed up at twilight. And at any given hour throughout the day and night other wild beasts might appear. Including mountain lions, an occasional lynx, foxes, coyotes, wolves and bears.

On this particular sunny morning Winona was nearly to the west shore when she observed a moving black patch of fur in the brush to her left. Instantly freezing, she thought of her rifle, propped in a corner of the cabin, and wished she had brought it as Nate frequently reminded her to do.

The black patch broadened and took on the dimensions of a full-grown black bear. A female, it lumbered to the water's edge, its nose twitching as it scented the air.

Winona stayed where she was. The bear hadn't noticed her and would be unlikely to do so unless it should turn and come straight up the path. She would wait for it to move off, then continue her stroll.

A few ducks swimming close to land quacked and paddled off as the bear dipped its muzzle and drank with delicate lapping movements that contradicted its size and bulk. It must have seen a fish because it abruptly took a stride into the lake and swatted with a powerful front paw. Spray speckled the surface but no fish appeared. Grunting, the bear waddled onto terra firma and shook itself.

Winona crouched in case the bear should gaze in her direction. It bent to the water again and she heard the lap-lap-lap of its tongue once more. Another few minutes, she figured, and it would amble into the forest.

That was when Winona saw something else move in the high weeds behind the bear. Imagine her shock on seeing the head of her eldest pop into view and then disappear. It happened so fast that for a few seconds she actually wondered if she had imagined seeing him. Seconds later, though, the boy reappeared, this time closer to the unsuspecting bear.

For the life of her, Winona had no idea what Zachary was up to. The boy owned a rifle but he was under strict orders to leave the deadlier predators alone. Painters, and bears, were to be carefully avoided.

Yet there Zach was, creeping forward as silently as a ghost. He wore a wide grin, as if he were playing some sort of game. At the end of the weeds he stopped and curled his legs under him.

David Thompson

Winona wanted to shout, to warn him to get out of there before the bear discovered him. But her yell might only make matters worse should the bear whirl and spot Zach. Helpless, she looked on, her heart leaping to her throat when the boy unexpectedly stepped into the open, within inches of the bear's rump. He was unarmed save for a knife at his hip.

Winona began to straighten. She would wave her arms to get Zach's attention, then motion for him to sneak away immediately. But she was not quite erect when her son did the last thing any sane person would do; he hauled off and slapped the bear's behind.

The result was predictable and harrowing. With a bestial bellow, the black bear spun. It saw Zach, who was in full flight toward a nearby tree, and promptly gave chase, exhibiting speed that rivaled the gait of a horse.

Zach bounded like a jackrabbit, weaving and swerving to present an elusive target. Three times the enraged bear swung, three times it missed, but each miss was by a narrower margin.

Winona scarcely breathed. She was terror-stricken, afraid her son would be ripped to shreds. She saw him pull ahead when the bear slowed to avoid a prickly bush, and for a fleeting interval she believed he might gain safety. Suddenly, however, the boy tripped and fell, sprawling onto his stomach. Zach glanced back, realized how close the bear was, and pushed to his feet.

The boy was not going to make it. Intuition told Winona that, and no sooner did the insight dawn than she sprang into action. She ran a few feet, waving and whooping at the top of her lungs to attract the bear, hoping to distract it long enough for her son to climb beyond its reach.

In this Winona succeeded all too well. The black bear veered toward her the moment it laid eyes on her. Like a hairy steam engine it plowed through a wall of bushes to reach her that much sooner. Since she'd acted on the spur of the moment to save Zach, she hadn't given any thought to the consequences of her deed, and now *she* was the object of the brute's wrath. To complicate things, she had the infant on her back.

"Ma!" Zach cried as Winona fled up the path with 500 pounds of raging hulk huffing and chuffing in her wake. The cradleboard slowed her, rendered her balance awkward. Frantically she cast about for a convenient tree, but there were no branches low enough to be of any benefit.

Little Evelyn cooed and gurgled the whole while, enjoying all the activity. Her squirming threw Winona off balance even more.

The bear closed in rapidly. Winona glanced over a shoulder to see exactly how close it was but the cradleboard shifted, blocking her view. She felt something nip at the hem of her dress and had her answer.

A tall fir tree hove into sight on the left. Winona darted to it and ducked around the trunk. The black bear halted on the other side, growling horribly. It shifted to one side, so Winona shifted to the other.

"Hang on, Ma!" Zach shouted encouragement.

He was out of the pine and running toward her.

"No!" Winona found the voice to yell. "Get to the cabin! Fetch my rifle!"

Zach picked up a busted limb and brandished it like a club. "I won't leave you!" he responded. "I'll draw the critter off so Evy and you can high-tail it!"

"Do as I say!" Winona commanded, continuing to circle the fir to keep the bear from reaching her. It was flustered by the shouting and kept looking from her to Zach and back again. But when they stopped, it charged, sweeping past the trunk before she could slide aside. Desperately Winona back-pedaled, her hands raised to protect her face and belly. The bear slowed, elevated a hairy paw to swipe at her.

From out of nowhere a horse and rider materialized. The buckskin clad frontiersman rode his sturdy stallion right into the black bear, the impact bowling the bear over. It rolled several times, scrambled onto all fours, then tried to rear onto its hind legs as bears are wont to do when up against a creature their own size. The rider never hesitated. Cutting the stallion, he rode so close to the bear he could have reached out and plucked hairs from its hide. Then, whipping downward, he smashed the stock of his Hawken into the bear's upturned muzzle.

Emitting a howl of agony, the black bear hit the ground running and never looked back. The undergrowth crackled to its passage, and soon it was gone.

Winona straightened, her bosom heaving from

her exertion. She gazed up into the piercing green eyes of her rescuer and felt her heart melt as it always did. No words were necessary. They both knew how near she had come.

After a bit Nate spoke. "One of these days you'll surprise the living daylights out of me by listening when I give you advice."

"I know," Winona said contritely. "I will never forget my rifle again."

Nate slid from the saddle, and she molded her body to his. Their kiss lingered and might have gone on indefinitely had Nate not cracked his eyelids and seen the smirking boy. He lowered his arms and said in mock sternness, "Don't you have chores you should be doing?"

"Welcome home, Pa," Zach said, offering his hand in manly fashion. "For a while there I figured Ma was a goner."

"Don't tell me that you forgot your rifle too?" Nate said. "What is the matter with this family? It's not as if we live in New York City."

"I left mine inside on purpose," the boy declared.

"Why would you pull a fool stunt like that?" Nate demanded irritably. He was disappointed in the both of them. Wilderness living demanded constant alertness and exercising basic common sense. To venture outdoors without a rifle was akin to committing suicide.

"I needed my hands free—" Zach began, but broke off, as if he had said too much.

"Tell your father," Winona prodded.

"Tell me what?" Nate said.

"Why he needed his hands free," Winona said, and related the bear smacking incident.

Young Zachary withered under their twin glares. He held his palms out and said meekly, "There's a perfectly good reason for what I did."

"This I've got to hear," Nate said.

Zach shuffled his feet. "Well, you see, you're always going on about how important it is for a young coon like me to learn what matters most in life and to set myself to doing those things that will make a man out of me. Remember?"

"I seem to recollect a talk we've had along those lines," Nate admitted, at a loss to foresee where the boy's trail was leading.

"You're always saying how there are special qualities a man has to have to be worthy of the name."

"True," Nate said.

"Such as always being honest, always looking to help folks in need, always being true to yourself."

Nate was amazed his son could recite his words so correctly. Evidently Zach had a selective memory. When it came time for book learning, the boy showed all the intelligence of a chipmunk. "I've said all that."

"You also told me that a man has to have courage or he'll never amount to much. He has to be able to look danger in the face, and even though he's scared plumb through, be able to do what has to be done."

"So what does all this have to do with you swatting a bear? That wasn't brave. It was dumb."

Ordeal

Zach scrunched his face into a knot. "Are those Indians dumb, then?"

"Which Indians?"

"I can't recollect whether it was the Cheyenne or the Apaches. But I do remember you telling me about the boys in the tribe, about how they prove whether they're brave or not. They track down a bear, and when it's not looking they sneak up and thump it on the backside. Isn't that what you told me they did?"

"Yes, but—" Nate began to explain, but Zach went on in a rush of words.

"You told me they had contests to see who could stand behind a bear the longest before it noticed them. You went on about how the bravest boy was held in the highest regard by everyone else. You said that you liked the idea even though it was a mite risky."

Winona turned to her husband. "A *mite?*"

Nate didn't quite know what to say. He half wanted to throttle Zach for somehow turning the incident around so he was the one in hot water. "Just because I mentioned the practice doesn't mean I wanted you to go out and try it," he scolded. "A harebrained stunt like that could have gotten you killed." He gestured at his horse. "We'll talk about this some more later. Right now there are ten pack horses at the cabin waiting to be stripped and fed and watered. Hop to it."

Sulking, the youth dutifully obeyed.

Nate waited until Zach was out of sight, then

61

snuggled against Winona again and went to kiss her. She put a finger on his lips.

"This is important. How many times have I warned you to be careful what you tell him? A boy his age is too reckless for his own good."

"I'll be more careful in the future," Nate promised, and planted his mouth on hers. She kissed stiffly at first, but warmed as his hands roamed.

Winona grinned when they broke for air, her dark eyes twinkling. "There is one part about your being away so long that I like."

"Which part, as if I can't guess?"

"The part where you come home to me."

Their next embrace lasted long enough to bake a cake. Hand in hand they walked along the narrow path, shoulders brushing, hearts in tune. Winona was jolted back to reality by the sight of the ten pack animals.

"Five of those are Shakespeare's. Did something happen to him?"

"He's as healthy as an ox," Nate said. "He asked me to cache his plews here so the river rats wouldn't know where they were hid and steal them."

"River rats?" Winona repeated. Despite her mastery of English, this was a new expression to her. It conjured mental images of a pack of aquatic rodents making off with bales of beaver. Ridiculous images.

In detail Nate imparted the encounter with Cyrus Porter. He filled her in on the attempt to make off with the pack train and the fate of the four responsible.

Ordeal

"And Blue Water Woman? She was not harmed?" Winona queried anxiously, for they were the very best of friends.

"She wasn't hurt," Nate reiterated. "When I left their place, she was being bored to death by Porter's account of his childhood."

Unwittingly, they had slowed. Winona looked up to see the cabin door in front of them. "How long do you have to decide?"

"They leave in five days. Shakespeare doesn't much like the notion of those rivermen going along. But they all swore they had nothing to do with stealing the pack horses, and Porter took them at their word. He even offered them more money since they'll have more work to do with four less to help out."

"Do you think the river rats swore with two tongues?"

"I honestly can't say," Nate replied. "Four bad apples don't mean the whole bushel is rotten to the core."

"Yet you suspect they will cause more trouble?"

"I do, yes."

"So you want to go."

"I have to go."

"Because of Shakespeare?"

"And Blue Water Woman." Nate held the door for her. "Let's say I'm right. If I don't join the expedition, and something happens to those two, I'll never be able to live with myself."

"It will be a very long journey."

"There are few longer."

"Perhaps my cousin will check on our cabin from time to time while we are gone."

Nate clasped her hands and stood nose to nose. "You could stay. It would be a damned sight safer."

"Without you, my life is empty. I could not stand an entire year of emptiness."

"We'll go, then." Nate kissed the tip of her nose. "And if we get rubbed out, you can kick me with your dying breath."

"It is not us I am most worried about. It is our son."

"Him? He wallops bears on the butt for fun. This trek will be a picnic as far as he's concerned."

Winona's throaty laugh was chopped short by a strident whinny outside. More horses neighed in fright as Nate bolted from the cabin and raced to the southeast corner. Around it stood the corral. Zach was hemmed in among the panicky animals, striving to shove past to the fence.

The cause of the commotion reared on two squat legs beside the south rails. It was the black bear. Mouth agape, saliva dripping from its lower jaw, it roared and pawed at the top rail.

Nate ran to the last post and took aim. He'd rather drive the bear off than slay it, but that had failed once and he couldn't risk his stock by trying again. Bears were notional creatures. Now that this one knew where to find prime horseflesh, it might return sometime when he wasn't around.

The black bear swiveled, eyeing Nate. It dropped

onto all fours and slowly advanced, growling fiercely.

Nate bellowed to no avail. He quickly cocked the hammer, pressed his finger to the trigger, and squeezed. There should have been a booming retort, a cloud of gunsmoke. Instead, there was a loud click.

Nate realized the jarring blow he had delivered to the bear's muzzle had fouled the rifle. He set it down with one hand while his other stabbed at a pistol. The bear was almost upon him. He cleared his belt, leveled the flintlock. His thumb pulled on the hammer.

In a spurt of speed, the black bear was on the trapper. A lashing paw struck the pistol and sent it sailing.

Nate retreated, tried to draw his other flintlock. The bear swung again, forcing him to leap to the right or be torn asunder. For a moment the corner post was between Nate and the Bruin, and he availed himself of the precious seconds he had to whip out the smoothbore.

Snarling, plodding methodically, the bear stepped past the post.

Nate sighted precisely and fired, planting the ball above and behind the bear's ear. The beast recoiled, roared louder, and surged at him with its claws flying. Nate resorted to his Green River knife, stabbing ineffectually as the bear drove him steadily backwards. Blood flowed from the head wound, but the bear was hardly fazed.

Suddenly Nate accidentally backed into the corner of the cabin. He tried to dart to the left but the bear moved first, blocking him. Its maw yawned wide.

Two shots rang out, one from the corral, one from the vicinity of the cabin door. Two balls thudded into the bear's head and it sagged, yowling. Its legs kicked a few times, then it was still.

Winona walked from one direction, Zach another, both bearing smoking rifles.

"Thanks," Nate said simply.

"It is fortunate we are going along," Winona said, trying to make light of the occurrence. "You are the one who will need someone to look after him."

Nate stared at the bloody bear, hoping it wasn't an omen of things to come. For all of their sakes.

Chapter Five

On a fine day in late May the Porter-Clark Expedition, as it subsequently became known in the press after Porter supplied the papers with his personal account, left the rustic cabin of Shakespeare McNair bound for the Oregon Country.

Included among the members were McNair and Nathaniel King, free trappers referred to by the newspapers in the States as "illiterate vagabonds," and their wives, simply labeled "squaws." Young Zachary King fared better; he was usually mentioned as the "wild cub" when he was mentioned at all.

The self-proclaimed leader fared best of all. Cyrus Oldfield Porter of the highly respected Hartford Porters was a "distinguished gentleman noted for his unimpeachable courage and indomitable spirit," as one journalistic wag put it. His "protegé," Adam Keel Clark, was eulogized as "an enterprising young man of means whose boundless energy inspired all who knew him."

Receiving shortest shrift were the rivermen from St. Louis, called simply "the workers." Only one of them was ever named, LeBeau, their leader, and that in passing. An injustice if ever there was one.

Neither Chavez, the tracker, nor Brett Hughes, the blond man who kept to himself so much, were referred to even indirectly. This was another injustice, but of a different sort, since one of them played a critical part in the expedition's success.

At the outset of the expedition 12 additional riders tagged along. Buffalo Horn, one of McNair's oldest friends, and the rest of the Flatheads traveled with the party for the first five days.

Initially Shakespeare led the expedition eastward to the foothills, then northward to a low pass that brought them to the west side of the Rockies. It was shortly thereafter that Buffalo Horn had to veer off to the northwest in order to return to his village. During the whole time the Flatheads rode along, Cyrus Porter was conspicuous by his silence. He never remarked that he disliked or mistrusted the Flatheads, yet his attitude smacked of both.

The St. Louis crowd were equally aloof. They hung together, suspiciously eyeing the warriors, refusing to associate with any but their own.

Ordeal

From the pass Shakespeare bore westward to Sandy Creek. Water would be his main consideration on the journey, since without it the stock would swiftly perish. He had to locate streams, rivers and lakes by memory, and not once did he fail them.

Sandy Creek took them to the Green River. A short jog westward for several days brought them to Ham's Fork of the Green, and here they camped two days to give the pack animals a rest.

Nothing of note took place until they stopped. Shakespeare spent most of his time with Porter and Clark. Nate and Chavez rode in advance of the column in order to forewarn them should hostiles appear.

Nate grew to like the tracker a lot. Chavez was a man of few words but undeniable competence. His skill with pistols was demonstrated to the satisfaction of all not long after the Flatheads left.

The column had stopped for the midday break on the bank of a nameless creek, a ribbon of a waterway that invariably dried up during the hot summer months. Here the ground was dry and barren, littered with boulders and large rocks.

Cyrus Porter and Adam Clark walked along the creek a score of yards to stretch their legs. At a gravel bar they removed their boots and waded in a shallow pool.

Nate and Chavez happened to ride up as the two New Englanders moved to the bank to replace their footwear. It was Nate who spotted Porter starting to climb a short section of rock-covered bank.

"Be careful there," Nate called out. "There are a lot of rattlers hereabouts."

"We haven't seen a one," Porter responded. He lifted a foot to step over a rock and abruptly turned pale when a loud rattling sound filled the air.

The snake slithered into the open, tongue flicking as it tested the air. It was less than a foot away from Porter's leg when it coiled, head rising, fangs exposed.

The others all heard, but none were close enough to act. Porter stood petrified with fear, his upraised leg shaking uncontrollably.

Nate snapped the Hawken to his shoulder. Out of the corner of an eye he caught a blur of motion. A pistol cracked, and the serpent's head was smashed to the ground by a heavy lead ball.

Chavez had drawn and fired from the hip without aiming. Most men would have missed. But the Mexican's accuracy had been uncanny; he'd put the ball smack between the rattler's eyes, and at a distance of ten yards.

Porter scooted to the gravel bar and stood quaking. Anyone else would have been thankful for having his life saved. All Porter did was glance at the tracker, then say, "I think a bonus is in order. You're worth every penny I'm paying for your services."

"Gracias, señor," Chavez said, opening his bullet pouch.

Disgusted, Nate turned away. He'd never met a man quite like the New Englander. Porter measured everything by its monetary value, including his daughter's husband and his own life. Some folks, evidently, got so wrapped up in money they forgot about *living*.

It was at Ham's Fork that Nate finally got to say more than two words to one of the rivermen.

LeBeau and his men were in charge of the pack train. Feeding, watering, packing and unpacking—all were under their supervision. They did their jobs conscientiously, if not always expertly.

Then two of the pack horses turned up missing. Nate and Chavez searched but found nothing to indicate the animals had been stolen. It was assumed they had broken loose and wandered off, and Porter appointed LeBeau to go find them.

"And I'd be grateful if you would go with him, Mr. King," Porter added. "He's not much of a tracker and could use your assistance."

The horses had strayed to the southwest. Nate had the lead, his gaze riveted to the soil. The countryside was very mountainous, broken by lush bottomland along the streams. Both horses had paralleled Ham's Fork for several miles, then taken a branch leading northward.

Typically, wild animals were bountiful. Elk and mountain buffalo could be seen grazing wherever there was enough forage. A number of times Nate startled small herds of antelope into flight, the sleek animals racing off in mighty bounds no other creature could rival.

Approaching a bend, Nate bent lower to verify that the vagrant animals had gone around it and not off into the underbrush.

"Hold up there, *honnete homme*," LeBeau said quietly.

Reining up, Nate looked at him. "What's wrong?"

"*Ours*," LeBeau said, pointing.

In a thicket beyond the bend a vague shape moved, an enormous animal twice the size of the black bear Nate had slain. "A grizzly," he said softly. "I'm obliged for the warning."

Loud grunting emanated from the thicket, along with the crackling of branches. Presently the beast lumbered from sight, but Nate was in no rush to move on immediately. He preferred the bear to be long gone to avoid a clash.

"*Ours* grow big out here," LeBeau commented with a trace of awe. "That one, it looked big as a house, *non?*"

"Grizz grow bigger," Nate informed him. "And they're as tough as nails. I saw one take eight balls once and it still wouldn't drop. If one comes after you, aim for the heart or the eyes. Their skulls are so thick and layered with so much muscle it's next to impossible to blow out their brains. A lot of good men have died trying."

"I will remember. *Merci.*"

Nate did not know what to make of the riverman. LeBeau acted friendly enough, but Nate still felt a lingering distrust spawned by the attempted horse theft. To pass the time, and to get to know LeBeau a little better, he commented, "The mountains are a far cry from St. Louis. They take some getting used to after living there."

Ordeal

"Very true." LeBeau gazed wistfully eastward. "Many times I long to be back on a Mississippi riverboat. My body not be made for all this riding."

"What's stopping you from going back?" Nate casually asked.

"The same thing that brought us here. *Argent.* Money." LeBeau doffed his blue cap to scratch his curly brown hair. He was in his early 20s and had handsome, chiseled features and a roguish tilt to his mouth that must have had a dazzling effect on the ladies.

"I thought as much," Nate said.

"*Oui.* This crazy Yankee, this Porter—" LeBeau pronounced it *Poortieer*—"he came into the grog shop where I was drinking, and he say for all to hear that he need good men to go west with him. Most laugh at him behind his back. But he offer more money than I make in two years. So I think it over, and I think, how can I say no? At last I maybe save money. One day I might want a family."

One mystery had been cleared up. St. Louis was the jumping off point for travelers venturing across the plains but there were few seasoned frontiersmen available to act as guides or to handle everyday tasks. Porter had hit on a clever way of hiring those he needed. It helped tremendously that money had been no object.

"That is how all of you were hired?" Nate asked.

"*Oui.*" LeBeau's face darkened. "Some of us should not have left St. Louis."

David Thompson

Nate took a gamble. "Those who tried to take the pack horses were fools."

"Dupree never be one for deep thinking," LeBeau said. "I wonder why he so eager to have his friends join. Now I know. He was a big idiot, Dupree."

"Too bad you didn't have a clue what he was up to. You might have stopped him."

LeBeau's eyes narrowed. "We make our beds, we lie in them, yes? Dupree was a grown man."

Nate loped on. The riverman's thick accent and poor English were terribly hard to understand at times, but enough of LeBeau's personality came through to convince Nate the riverman was truthful in all he said. He would have to share the insight with McNair.

The bottomland widened into a valley. Grazing near a wooded slope were the missing horses. Nate swung wide to come at them from one side while LeBeau approached from the other. They needn't have taken the precaution. Both horses ate on as if they didn't have a care in the world.

Nate slipped a rope over the neck of a middling mare and headed back. So intent had he been on the horses that he'd neglected to pay much attention to the trees bordering the grass. A snort from the mare caused him to shift in the saddle to discover the reason and his mistake.

A huge shadow had detached itself from the pines and moved into the open. Other shadows moved deeper in the forest, but they were smaller. They were cows. The bull vented a challenge and pawed the ground with an iron hoof.

Ordeal

LeBeau jerked around at the bellow. *"Mon Dieu!"* he exclaimed, bringing up his Hall's rifle.

"No!" Nate cried. Mountain buffalo weren't as temperamental as their prairie kin and wouldn't charge unless greatly provoked. The riverman, not knowing this, hastily fired, but as he did, his horse, spooked by the buffalo's scent, broke into a gallop, throwing LeBeau's aim off and him from the saddle.

The bull charged.

LeBeau scrambled to his feet with the agility of a cat. He darted after his mount, which raced on across the valley. The pack animal LeBeau had been leading had stopped dead and resumed feeding, unaffected by the onrushing behemoth.

When Nate saw the riverman go down, he flung the lead rope from him and wheeled the stallion. He had to cover more ground to reach LeBeau than the buffalo did but he made the attempt anyway.

The bull wasn't choosy about its target. Provoked by the rifle blast, it automatically went after the first thing it saw. And its eyesight being what it was, the bull went after the grazing pack horse.

Not until the very last second did the horse lift its head. Nostrils flaring, eyes wide, it tried to flee, taking a long bound that would have carried it beyond the reach of an ordinary predator. The buffalo, being neither, overtook the horse in a twinkling and plowed into it with all the brutal force of a battering ram. Squealing and kicking, the horse slammed onto its side. Had it been able to rise quickly, it might yet have escaped. But its legs thrashed thin air, unable to find purchase. The bull, hooking downward, sank a horn into the soft underbelly of the horse and wrenched.

Nate saw the animal's innards spill out, listened to its whinny of anguish. As the bull gored again, Nate pulled alongside LeBeau and extended an arm. "Swing on!"

Hearing the cry, the bull glanced up. Hooves flying, it came after them.

"Hurry!" Nate urged, firming his leg muscles to bear the added weight as LeBeau jumped and caught hold. Gritting his teeth against the strain, Nate swung LeBeau up behind him, then lashed the stallion into a breakneck gallop. To his rear, ominous thunder rumbled. The bull was hot on their heels, snorting like a bellows, its driving hoofs throwing up clods of dirt in its wake.

"Faster, *mon ami!*" LeBeau coaxed.

Nate was going as fast as the stallion was capable of going. A backward look showed the buffalo 15 feet behind them. Dark eyes blazing, horns bobbing with every stride, the monster gained bit by bit. Nate wished he had a quirt. Not thinking, he lashed the reins harder without result. It was no use.

The bull drew closer and closer, and was on the verge of smashing into the stallion when the stallion's greater stamina paid off. The bull tired and slowed ever so gradually.

Encouraged but prudent, Nate sped on until he was at the end of the valley. The buffalo was moseying back toward its harem, its dignity appeased.

LeBeau exhaled loudly. "You ride well, *Monsieur* King. Another few seconds and it be all over for us."

Rather than chide the man for firing, Nate said, "If that ever happens again, freeze until the buffalo loses interest. They seldom charge if they don't see something move."

"I remember this also. Maybe I stick close to you, eh? I learn all there is to know about these beasts. Then I live long enough to see the Mississippi again."

Nate scanned the valley for the second pack horse, which apparently had run off during all the excitement. "We have to fetch the other one," he said.

"Maybe it will find its way back to camp without our help," LeBeau said.

"It's dragging a rope," Nate reminded him. "Liable to snag and strand the horse unless we find it."

LeBeau grinned. "Where you go, I go, *non?*"

A large gray squirrel chattered at them as they rode into the forest and swung parallel to the timberline. When close to where the mountain buffalo were passing the afternoon, Nate swung wide to the west. He sought sign and soon picked up fresh hoofprints.

The horse had been running, no doubt frightened by the gory death of its fellow. Through the pines and up into a ridge of aspens Nate rode. A jay squawked at them and a rabbit fled for dear life.

"So many animals," LeBeau said. "Everywhere one looks. Around St. Louis there are not so many anymore. Too many people. Kill them off."

Nate had seen the same happen in New York. As more and more immigrants flocked into the state, game grew scarcer and scarcer. Shakespeare claimed that one day the same would happen to the vast prairie and the sprawling mountains, but Nate regarded that as unlikely. Most Easterners hated the frontier, thought it too savage, too primitive. Thank God. So long as they had an attitude like that, Nate's cherished mountains were safe.

The aspens ended in firs. Here the trees were farther apart, the going easier. Nate avoided logs and boulders and reached a needle crest offering a magnificent panorama of the wilderness.

"*Magnifique!*" LeBeau enthused. "I have no idea! This is almost as beautiful as Lady River."

"Almost?"

"All right. As beautiful." LeBeau shook his head in wonder. "I think I see why you live here, my friend. I think I see that you trappers not as crazy as we rivermen like to think."

They sat for a while admiring the spectacle. Nate would have liked for Winona and Zach to share the experience. Thinking of them made him eager to find the missing horse, so he climbed higher.

LeBeau took a deep breath. "The air up here is so fresh, so pure. Makes a man dizzy, like good wine." He chuckled. "My friends hear me talk like this, they want to throw me in a river so I come to my senses."

"What sort of work did you do in St. Louis?"

"You mean on the Mississippi," LeBeau corrected. "Anything and everything. I start when twelve, swabbing decks, empty pots. Then work my way up to riverboat, to steamboat. The work is hard, the pay low, the life, it is grand."

"Sounds like mine," Nate said. "We have more in common than I figured."

Off to the left something moved. Nate reined up, ready to employ the Hawken. He spotted the missing horse trying to sneak back around them. "Tricky devil," he muttered, trotting to intercept the animal. The horse nickered, then fled, able to outdistance them handily until, without warning, it drew up short and nearly lost its footing.

"What happened?" LeBeau asked.

"The rope," Nate said.

It had caught in the fork of a small pine and looped tight. The escape artist was doing its best to tear loose, but the rope was too strong.

Nate stopped and watched the animal's antics. He waited for the animal to tire, then dismounted and untied the lead.

"All this trouble over a pesky *cheval*," LeBeau muttered. "Steamboats never run off on you."

"And steamboats can't keep you warm on a cold winter's day, or let you scratch them behind the ears or give a listen when you have no one else to talk to."

"*Touché.*"

79

David Thompson

Nate remounted, tugged, and almost lost his balance when the pack horse refused to budge. "This crock head is lucky I'm not an Apache," he remarked.

"Why?"

"Apaches eat contrary horses."

"You would never catch me eating one."

"You'd be surprised. If you're hungry enough, you'll eat practically anything. Take my word for it. I know."

"You have eaten horse meat?"

"Several times. I've had rattler on occasion. And dog more times than you can count."

"How horrible," LeBeau said. "I would rather eat my own foot than a harmless little *chien*."

"Most Indians consider dog a real treat. What you would call a delicacy back in the States. Except the Comanches, of course. To them eating a dog is the same as eating your own mother."

"Your wife's people. They are . . . ?"

"Shoshones."

"Do they eat dog?"

"All the time. The plumper, the better."

"I think I will pass on supper tonight."

Grinning, Nate rode next to the stubborn pack horse, leaned down, and struck it a resounding blow on the head with the Hawken. The startled horse staggered a few feet, and while it was disoriented Nate hauled hard on the rope and descended.

As before, Nate avoided the buffalo. In due course they had left the valley far behind and were striking off across the bottomland. The day was warm, a sluggish breeze stirring the waist-high grass.

The pack horse behaved. Nate rode slowly so as not to tire the stallion. A man never knew when an emergency might require a sudden getaway, so it was best to conserve a mount's strength.

Nate estimated they had half a mile to cover when he heard something that sent a tingle of apprehension down his spine.

The mountains rang with gunfire.

Chapter Six

Shakespeare McNair had looked forward to the stop at Ham's Fork. He would be spared Porter's ceaseless chatter and have time to spend alone with his wife and the Kings. He counted on enjoying some peace and quiet, not on the fool New Englanders traipsing barefoot over prime rattler breeding ground, nor on a pair of pack animals deciding the grass was greener elsewhere. But it was the antics of the rivermen that proved most troublesome.

Nate and LeBeau had gone off after the strays. Porter and Clark were sipping coffee, seated in folding chairs brought along so Porter wouldn't have to "soil expensive clothes with common dirt." Chavez was cleaning his pistols, a task he did every day whether the flintlocks needed cleaning or not. Blue Water Woman, Winona, and Zach were munching pemmican in front of a lean-to Nate had built.

For the moment all was tranquil. Shakespeare moseyed toward his wife, his stomach growling, and happened to notice Brett Hughes watching him. Of the entire party, Hughes was the one man Shakespeare had yet to talk to. And now that he thought about it, Shakespeare would have sworn that Hughes had deliberately been avoiding him. Why this should be, Shakespeare had no idea.

The next moment bedlam erupted.

East of the campsite a tremendous din heralded the appearance of scores of frightened antelope. The herd was being chased by a pack of wolves, and on reaching the bank, the antelope plunged in. Poor swimmers, many floundered, the young and the old having difficulty keeping up with the rest. The wolf pack halted at the water's edge. Averse to water, they padded back and forth, yipping and howling in frustration.

All this happened within fifty yards of where Shakespeare stood. The animals were so preoccupied that neither the antelope nor the wolves realized there were humans close by.

Shakespeare was content to watch. He'd witnessed many similar tableaus, part of the constant struggle for survival in the wild.

To the rivermen, the drama was novel, more so because one of them saw a way of obtaining meat for the cooking pots and took off lickety-split toward the spot, shouting to his fellows to follow his lead.

They dashed past McNair before Shakespeare quite surmised what they were about. "No!" he shouted after them. "Don't!" But they wouldn't heed. Hunger and circumstance had combined to override caution.

The boatmen fired on the run. At the first ragged volley only one antelope keeled over. The wolves melted away, gray streaks blending into the undergrowth.

"Stop shooting!" Shakespeare bellowed in vain, running.

The excited rivermen fired rapidly, at random, more missing than scoring but enough scoring to fell more than a dozen antelope. In the river, the adults had gained the far shore while the small ones and the aged struggled.

"Damn it all, stop!" Shakespeare ordered, frowning as the blasts echoed off the surrounding mountains. He caught up with a straggler and batted the man's rifle down. "No!"

The man glared at him, not comprehending.

"The shots can be heard for miles!" Shakespeare explained, racing on. He passed two more who were reloading. "No more firing!"

At the bank five of the river rats were shooting just as fast as they could reload and aim. Shakespeare pushed through them and whirled. "That's enough! You've done enough harm already!"

Confused by the intervention, the five looked at one another. A stocky man who had a habit of swaggering when he walked gestured impatiently. "Out of our way, old one. Tonight we will have a feast fit for a king!"

Ordeal

Shakespeare grabbed the man's rifle to prevent the barrel from rising. "Didn't you hear me?"

"Gaston doesn't like being manhandled," the man snapped. He tried to jerk the rifle loose.

"Listen to the echoes," Shakespeare said. "The sound will carry into all the neighboring valleys."

"So?" Gaston challenged.

"So think of all the Indians who might hear."

"I'm not scared of miserable Injuns," Gaston declared. "Now let go of my gun or else."

Shakespeare purposely held on. During the journey from his cabin he'd been afforded ample opportunity to study the expedition members, to note how well they worked together, to decide which were reliable and which weren't. Of the lot, Gaston was the most hotheaded, the one most likely to take offense when none was intended, and the one least respectful of authority. Shakespeare had foreseen an eventual clash. This, he figured, was as good a time as any to put the man in his place.

Gaston tried again to yank the rifle from the trapper's grasp. "I don't warn a man twice," he said. Shifting, he kicked, driving his foot at McNair's belly.

Shakespeare pivoted, snatched the riverman's ankle, and surged upward. Gaston slammed onto his back, losing his hold on the rifle, and lay there, wincing. "Had enough?" Shakespeare asked.

"You joke, old man."

A snap kick caught Shakespeare on the shin and doubled him over. His shirt was gripped, and the next he knew he sailed head over heels to crash onto his side. He regained his feet to find Gaston crouched and waiting, a glittering dagger held low to thrust.

"Now I gut you, pig!"

The other rivermen had backed off to give them room to fight. Shakespeare dropped his Hawken and slipped his knife free of its sheath. "It'll take more than you to put me under," he announced.

"We shall see."

Gaston took a step, but only one. He changed to stone when a loud metallic click warned him someone else had a stake in the outcome.

Blue Water Woman had her own Hawken leveled. In a cold tone she said, "Cut my husband and the wolves will have something other than antelope meat to feed on tonight."

Whether Gaston would have called her bluff was never resolved, for with a drumming of hooves Nate King arrived on the scene and launched himself from the back of the stallion. His shoulder hit Gaston flush in the chest and they both went down, Nate to pounce on the boatman and punch in a flurry. Gaston, caught unawares and dazed, could do no more than feebly raise an arm to protect himself.

A skinny onlooking riverman took a step and was taking a bead when a friendly but stern admonition stopped him.

"*Non, mon ami,*" LeBeau said. "This is their affair. Gaston, he is a grown man, yes?"

Nate blocked a blow to the groin, then delivered a pair of punches that would have shattered a plank of wood. Gaston slumped, blood seeping from a corner of his mouth. Mad as hell, Nate cocked his arm to jab but a hand seized his wrist.

"That's enough, Horatio," Shakespeare said softly.

"I should beat him senseless."

"If anyone has earned that privilege, it's me. And I don't beat a man when he's down." Shakespeare hauled his friend erect. He was touched that Nate had leaped to his defense but disappointed by the interference since it had left the issue unresolved and Gaston would probably act up again later on. He didn't mention this to Nate.

Cyrus Porter was a study in outrage. Chest puffed out, jowls quivering, he loomed over the prone riverman and shook a thick finger. "How dare you, sir! I hired Mr. McNair to guide us, and it behooves us one and all to heed him when he gives advice. If this were the Navy, I'd have you flogged."

It was doubtful Gaston heard. Groaning lightly, eyelids fluttering, he tried to rise but couldn't.

"What do you have to say for yourself, mister?" Porter went on.

Gaston slowly recovered. Placing a hand on his jaw, he sat up and stared at McNair.

"Did you hear me?" Porter demanded. "I want an explanation for your outrageous conduct."

"I have nothing to say," Gaston grumbled.

"You damned well better or I'll have you sent packing," Porter threatened. "I will not tolerate insubordination on this expedition, either toward myself or anyone in my employ."

Shakespeare scanned the rivermen. From their expressions he gathered that some sided with Gaston. Casting the troublemaker out would create a rift with potentially dire consequences. "I say we let bygones be bygones," he proposed. "Gaston is used to life on the Mississippi, not the wilderness. He didn't know he was making a mistake."

"I don't know," Porter said uncertainly.

"Let's leave it up to him." Shakespeare stared at the riverman. "What will it be? Do you behave yourself and go on with us, or do you saddle a horse and head back all by your lonesome?"

"A lone man would not have much chance of making it across the prairie," Gaston said.

"He might if he knew how to live off the land. Do you know how?"

"You know I don't."

"Not much of a decision, then, is it?" Shakespeare remarked, and was given a withering look of such burning hatred that he knew Gaston wasn't the only man who had made a mistake that day.

"I will go with you," Gaston told his employer. "And from here on out I promise to watch what I do and say very carefully."

"Apology accepted," Porter said.

Several of the boatmen helped Gaston stand. Shakespeare picked up his Hawken, and as he did he saw Brett Hughes beaming like a kid who had just been given a new horse for his birthday. Hughes then glanced guiltily around and moved off. How strange, Shakespeare mused.

Ordeal

The rivermen spent the remainder of the afternoon and long after the sun had set dragging antelope from the river and carving up the carcasses under Shakespeare's direction. He showed them the best way; how to slit the hide open down the back of each hind leg, then to cut a straight line down the middle of the belly to the chin and slice up the inside of the front legs. Once done, peeling the hide was accomplished by cutting ligaments and muscles as the hide was rolled back like a worn stocking.

Porter and Clark watched for awhile. Clark turned several shades of green and hurried elsewhere. Porter, though, was intrigued by every little detail and took a turn skinning a small doe.

That night, after the camp quieted and guards had been posted, Shakespeare walked hand in hand with Blue Water Woman to a flat boulder a hundred feet distant. In silence they gazed on the celestial spectacle for a while.

Blue Water Woman stroked her husband's temple, then commented, "I am worried, husband."

"No need to be."

"You are a poor liar. I saw how that man looked at you. He will make trouble."

"And I'll deal with it when the times comes."

"I should have shot him. Nate had the right idea."

Shakespeare draped a hand on her shoulders. "Never realized how blamed bloodthirsty the two of you are. Maybe you should switch tribes, become a Blackfoot."

"Why must you always joke at times like this?"

"What else would you have me do?" Shake-speare smiled. "If people gnashed their teeth and pulled out their hair every time life dealt them a bad hand, most folks would be bald and toothless by the time they're forty." He leaned back and quoted, "Let me play the fool. With mirth and laughter let old wrinkles come."

"You are hopeless."

"O speak again, bright angel! For thou art as glorious to this night, being over my head, as is a winged messenger of heaven unto the white-upturned wondering eyes of mortals that fall back to gaze on him, when he bestrides the lazy-pacing clouds and sails upon the bosom of the air."

Blue Water Woman folded his fingers in hers. "That one is easy. You've read the play to me a hundred times."

"Try this one," Shakespeare said, and quoted once more, "All is whole. Not one word more of the consumed time. Let's take the instant by the forward top. For we are old, and on our quickest decrees the inaudible and noiseless foot of Time Steals ere we can effect them."

"I don't know."

"All's Well That Ends Well."

"And all your clever words will not stop me from worrying. As you have pointed out, you're not a young man. Gaston is."

"Fiddle-faddle. I'd like to get my hands on the author of the lie that once you pass fifty your life is over. I'm more than a match for that dunder-head."

Ordeal

"He has friends."

"I have my trained tiger."

"Nate?"

"Do you know anyone else who will beat a man to a pulp for looking at me crossways?"

"You cannot fault him for loving you as much as he does."

"Hush, woman. It's not seemly to speak of another trapper that way. Someone might hear and start nasty rumors."

"Joke, joke, joke."

"I really must give you more English lessons. You're not supposed to say the same word three times."

Her light laughter was carried by the cool breeze to the ears of the nearest sentry and beyond to the lean-to where a robust young man rolled onto his back and propped his head on his hand.

"What is bothering you tonight?" Winona asked sleepily. "You toss more than Zach does."

"I have a sour feeling, is all."

"It comes of eating three helpings at supper."

"Not that kind of feeling. I think we're in for some hard times, real hard times, and I wish I hadn't brought you along."

"You worry too much."

"About the three of you, yes. Zach and you and Evelyn are all that matter to me."

"What about Shakespeare and Blue Water Woman?" Winona interrupted. "I should think they matter after the many winters they have been our best friends."

Nate shifted once more so they were eye to eye, or almost, since hers were closed. "Of course they do. But not the same way." He paused. "Family is special. When a man truly loves a woman, she means more to him than life itself. He'd do anything, defy anyone, to make her happy. Her welfare is all he cares about. Which is why I won't let anything happen to you if I can help it."

Nate gently touched her cheek. "You had no notion of the difference you made in this coon's life. Before meeting you I sort of rambled through life doing what I pleased and not accomplishing a thing. You gave me purpose, brought me out of myself so that I try to be better than I'd be otherwise. Thanks to you, I found meaning. Some say only oafs fall in love. If so, I'm glad to be the biggest oaf this side of the Divide."

Nate waited for her reply, but all he received was the caress of her breath on his face as she breathed in the rhythm of deep sleep. Smiling, he kissed her forehead and snuggled against her warm body. "Serves me right," he muttered. "No wonder some men would rather talk to their horse than their wife."

Soon Nate drifted off. It seemed he had hardly closed his eyes when the crack of a shot snapped him awake and he sat bolt upright, his hand automatically sliding to the Hawken.

The camp was in turmoil. Horses whinnied. Men ran toward the string and shouted back and forth.

Ordeal

Winona and Zach also sat up, rifles in hand.

"Stay put," Nate said. "I'll see what all the fuss is about." He spotted McNair running toward the horses and fell into step beside him. "Maybe hostiles heard those shots after all."

"We'll soon know."

Cyrus Porter stood at the center of a ring of onlookers, brusquely interrogating a riverman. "—see anything, anything at all?"

"No, *Monsieur*," the river rat said. His accent was thick, but he spoke English a bit more fluently than LeBeau. "I looked and looked but it ran away too fast. And my eyes are not so good in the dark."

Shakespeare stepped forward. "What's all the ruckus about? What got the horses so agitated?"

"Tell him," Porter commanded.

The swarthy riverman glanced nervously at the benighted terrain. "I was on guard duty when the horses, they began stomping and prancing. I came right over and heard something off in the woods, something big."

"How do you know?" Shakespeare asked.

"I heard branches break, *Monsieur*, and much *grunir*, much growling." The man imitated the sounds he'd heard, a guttural rumbling that might have been a big cat or a bear. "When I got close to the trees, it stopped. I heard it run off with much noise."

"You did well," Porter complimented him. "Evidently you scared off whatever it was."

The men moved among the horses, calming the animals. Several made bold to go a short

93

way into the woods and returned to report they had seen nothing. Porter dismissed everyone but added two more guards, who were instructed to stay close to the string at all times.

"What do you think?" Nate asked as he walked to the lean-to with his mentor.

"Damned odd that a painter or a grizzly would make so much noise. Growling, yes, but breaking limbs and such?" Shakespeare surveyed the trees. "I'm going to search for sign come sunup."

"You'll have company."

The camp was barely astir when the two trappers stealthily stalked among the pines, their moccasins soundless on the thick carpet of needles. They found where the three men had entered and surmised that they'd gone 20 feet before turning around.

"Mighty brave of them to go this far," Shakespeare joked.

"They would have gone farther, but they forgot to take a torch."

Spreading out, they hunted in an ever wider pattern. Nate was the first to see the figure squatting by a log. He raised his rifle, then saw who it was. "Chavez?"

"I have found something," the tracker said.

In the soft soil at the base of the log was a print, a *human* footprint, the impression undeniably that of a boot such as the rivermen wore. The man had jumped over the log when running off, leaving deep prints on both sides.

"Let's see where the trail leads," Shakespeare suggested.

Ordeal

The footprints curved in a wide loop that brought them into the camp from the east, at a place where the shadows had been darkest during the night. Here they lost the tracks among the slew of jumbled prints already made by their party.

"What do you make of it?" Nate asked.

"One of us made the noise," Chavez answered. "Perhaps as a prank of some sort."

"A damn stupid one if that's the case," Shakespeare said.

The trapper shrugged. "I was curious. Now I know." He ambled toward the fire.

Shakespeare stepped to the river so no one would overhear. "Prank, my ass! Someone tried to scare the horses off but got cold feet when he thought the guard might take a shot at him."

"Who would be that dumb?" Nate asked skeptically.

"Don't put anything past this outfit. If brains were gold they'd all be paupers," Shakespeare groused.

"Chavez is a good man. LeBeau too."

"Do you buy that line about Chavez just being curious?"

"What else would he have been doing there?"

"Maybe he planned to erase the tracks but we showed and spoiled it. He had to show us or we would have been suspicious."

Nate shook his head. "I've ridden with the man for days. He's the one I trust the most."

"Don't trust any of them," Shakespeare advised. "Not yet, anyhow. Somebody is up to no good, and until we discover who, and why, we have to keep

95

one eye on our backs every minute of the day or someone is liable to stick a knife into us when we're not looking."

Nate had never known his friend to be wrong. Never, ever. Which added weight to his premonition and promised to turn their Pacific odyssey into an ordeal none of them might survive.

Chapter Seven

Young Zachary King was in his element. Born and bred to the wild, the boy could never get enough of the majestic mountains, the pristine valleys, the myriad of animal life. Nature was not only his passion, it was his school, and he was an apt and enthusiastic pupil. In keeping with his inquisitive nature, Zach loved to explore. New Territory always presented a feast of new sights and experiences on which he happily gorged.

The journey to the Oregon Country was heaven on earth. Zach got to see uncharted regions practically daily, and along the way encountered more wildlife than he'd ordinarily come across in a month.

The leg of the trek from Ham's Fork to a huge lake was no exception. Across a high range of hills they traveled, always bearing to the northwest. Herds of buffalo grazed unconcerned along the bottoms. Elk and deer showed no fear, and in fact were so ridiculously easy to kill that the rivermen seldom had to go more than a few hundred feet from camp to bring down all the game needed.

There were moments the boy would never forget, such as the rare spectacle of a pair of playful otters frolicking in a river, their sleek bodies cleaving the water like living arrows. Zach rode closer for a better look, and the otters promptly stopped cavorting to boldly return his delighted stare. One then snorted and both swam downriver, twisting and spinning in a dazzling acrobatic display.

Another scene Zach would never forget was that of the buffalo kill. At the base of a sheer cliff overlooking the river lay hundreds of mangled carcasses. The stench was almost enough to make Zach sick. Covering his mouth and nose with a hand, he goaded his reluctant paint nearer so he could study the skeletal rib cages and other bones jutting from the surface. A flock of buzzards were gorging on the grisly remains, and at his approach the ungainly scavengers took to the air with a loud flapping of their large wings.

Zach didn't need to ask about the cause of the mass death. He knew how Indians sometimes drove whole herds over precipices, accomplishing in an hour a job that would otherwise require many weeks of patient stalking. He did inquire if there was any way to determine the tribe responsible, and his father waded in the reddish-brown water, searched for a while, and came out holding part of an arrow. From the markings, the Crows had been the culprits.

An event the boy found noteworthy but which none of the adults gave more than idle notice to was the discovery of a den of young wolves. The pups barked at Zach when he walked up to the opening, then retreated uttering frightened yips. He tried to coax one out, but the bravest of the litter would only crawl close to his fingertips, sniff a few times, then scoot back into the shadows.

The pups reminded Zach of the wolf he once befriended, which had long since left him for the company of its own kind. Periodically Blaze returned for short spells and they would romp around the cabin and tussle as in days of yore. But the wolf always drifted away after awhile, leaving Zach sadder for the reunion.

Convinced those in the den were never coming out, Zach straightened and was surprised to see his father a few yards off, watching him. "A wolf litter, Pa," he disclosed cheerfully.

"Don't get any notions, son," Nate advised. "We're not about to wet-nurse a pup all the way to the Pacific and back."

"I know better than that," Zach assured him.

"When I was your age, I didn't," Nate said, and rode on.

Little else of interest took place until they reached a lake approximately 60 miles in circumference with an outlet into a river on its north side.

"Is this the Great Salt Lake, Pa?" Zach inquired, thinking he had at last set eyes on the unique body of water he'd heard so much about from various trappers.

"No," Nate said. "The Great Salt Lake is even bigger." He gestured at the glassy surface. "Some call this Snake Lake. Some know it as Sweet Lake. Myself, I say it's Black Bear Lake."

The expedition camped along the eastern shore that night. Zach spent a restful hour skipping flat stones, then went for a short walk. After so many hours spent in the saddle, he was restless, anxious to let off some of the boundless energy boys his age possessed.

As Zach walked, he daydreamed. Of the many pleasant minutes spent curled up in front of a cozy fire in the King cabin. Of the many hours his father had patiently spent teaching him the art of survival. Of the many days spent among his mother's people, the Shoshones, and the kindness of his kin.

Absorbed by memories, Zach walked to the top of a knoll and started down before he spied the conical structures several hundred feet distant. Stopping in midstride, he saw a tendril of smoke curling skyward.

Only three tribes were partial to making cone-shaped forts of stacked poles, and they all belonged to the Blackfoot Confederacy. The thought sent Zach racing back to camp. He wanted to shout an alarm but feared being heard by the war party. Dashing to where his father and Shakespeare were seated, he sagged to one knee and coughed out, "Trouble, Pa. Big trouble."

"What has you so flustered?" Nate asked, rising.

Zach explained. He stood aside as all the men gathered together and a plan of action was debated. His mother, he noted, frowned when it was decided that Nate would lead half the rivermen directly into the Blackfoot camp.

"Is that wise?" Cyrus Porter asked. "From what I've heard, these Blackfeet are regular barbarians when their dander is up."

"I'm not scared," Adam Clark boasted.

"You should be, greenhorn," Shakespeare said. "A ten-year-old Blackfoot could whip you without working up a sweat." He regarded the deepening twilight. "We were lucky in finding them before they found us. Now we can wipe them out first."

"You're taking a lot for granted," Porter said. "Perhaps violence is unnecessary. We'll send an emissary, offer them a few trinkets to demonstrate we come in peace."

"A fine idea," Shakespeare said. "Just be sure whoever you pick as your emissary has his last will and testament made out, because we won't be seeing him again."

"They'd murder a man without provocation?"

"What you call murder, they call counting coup, and there's nothing Blackfeet love more than counting coup on white men," Shakespeare said. "In their eyes, each and every one of us is a bitter enemy to be slain on sight."

"But that's patently ridiculous!" Porter said. "We've never done them any wrong."

"Won't make no nevermind to them," Nate

spoke up. "They got into a racket with Meriwether Lewis once, and ever since whites have been unwelcome in their country."

"Meriwether Lewis?" Porter repeated. "Why, that must have been thirty years ago! And they've held a grudge all this time?"

"You've got to understand how these Indians think," Shakespeare said. "Some trappers like to say the Blackfeet are no account any ways you lay your sight, but that just isn't so. They live for war, and they're not fussy about who they make war on. Whether it's trappers, Sioux, Shoshones, Flatheads, or any other tribe, it doesn't make a lick of difference. They've been fighters for as long as any of them can remember, and I suspect they'll go on fighting until there isn't a single one left alive."

"You almost sound sorry that could happen," Adam Clark said.

"I am," Shakespeare confessed. "The Blackfeet are a fine tribe. I should know. I lived among them awhile, back in the days before Meriwether Lewis soured them on our kind."

Zach didn't mention that he also knew the tribe extremely well, thanks to a short time spent among them as a captive. He'd been treated kindly, allowed to roam as he pleased, and one of the more prominent warriors had offered to adopt him. The stay had left him with fond memories of the Blackfeet. He'd made up his mind never to do them a wrong if he could help it. Consequently, he advanced and tapped on his father's elbow.

"What is it, son? We're sort of busy."

"You'll spare them if you can, won't you, Pa?"

Nate looked down, pursed his lips. "It means that much to you, does it?"

"Yes, sir."

"I'll do what I can. But don't expect miracles. They're liable to open fire as soon as they set eyes on us."

"I know you'll do your best."

Zach stood to one side as the adults finished making plans. Three of them were to remain behind with his mother and Blue Water Woman to safeguard the horses while the rest crept to the camp. In the bustle and excitement, no one bothered much about him, and he was able to slip off with the men. He glanced back as darkness enfolded them and saw his mother looking all around. She'd be madder than a wet hen when she realized what he had done, but he needed to see it through.

Fifty yards from the forts, the men halted. Shakespeare took half to form a ring around the sheltered inlet. Nate waited an ample interval, then those with him fanned out and, in military order, glided forward along the lake and then turned right, facing the camp. Zach figured out their strategy. If the Blackfeet wanted to do battle, his father's men would have their backs protected by water. If the Blackfeet tried to escape through the woods, Shakespeare would stop them.

Zach had stayed well back so his father wouldn't spot him. As the line cautiously closed on the forts, he snuck next to the nearest man. The thought of being in a pitched battle made the nape of his neck prickle. His knees felt wobbly, and he had to breathe deeply to still the butterflies in his gut.

The forts were quiet, the fire almost out. Zach tensed for the outcry sure to sound once the sentry discovered them. To his amazement, there was none, nor did anyone appear when Shakespeare bellowed in the Blackfoot tongue.

"Ho! Blackfeet! You are surrounded! Come out with your hands empty! We will wipe you out if you do not hold your fire!"

On Nate's cue, the line halted. He moved to the foremost fort, careful to stay to one side. At the entrance he squatted and peeked inside.

Zach gasped when his father went in. He dreaded hearing a shrill whoop and his pa's death scream, but the night wind was all that disturbed the stillness. His father reappeared and smiled in relief.

"There's no one home!" Nate called.

A thorough search confirmed that the Blackfeet were gone. Shakespeare and Chavez took torches and scoured the strip of ground between the forts and the forest. Everyone hustled over at their shout.

Zach was no slouch at reading sign. He could tell that upwards of ten warriors had made off through the trees within the past few hours.

"Eleven warriors, *señor*," Chavez told Cyrus Porter. "Two limped and were helped by others."

"Were they wounded, you think?" Porter responded.

Shakespeare answered. "That would be my guess. They must have been in a fight with someone else within the past day or two and were in no shape to tangle with a party the size of ours." He chuckled. "A lucky break for us."

"Unless their village is close by," Nate said. "Hundreds of them could be after our hair by tomorrow."

"Can't be helped," Shakespeare said. "Our animals are tuckered out. And since we can't travel very fast at night anyway, we might as well rest up and head out before sunup."

"Drat," Porter said, gazing at Black Bear Lake. "I was hoping to do some fishing before we pressed on. In St. Louis I purchased new tackle which I haven't been able to try out yet."

Zach saw his father stare hard at the New Englander and wondered why until it occurred to him that Porter was supposed to be in a ripsnorting hurry to find his daughter. How could the man think of wasting time when she might be in deadly danger? he asked himself.

"Well, if that's the way it has to be, so be it," Porter went on. "Enough adventure for one evening. Let's eat and turn in so we can leave early as Mr. McNair suggested."

The men broke up. Zach cradled his Hawken and turned to go, but a heavy hand fell on his shoulder. He gulped.

"Hold on there, whippersnapper. Your Uncle Shakespeare wants a word with you."

Zach turned, grateful it wasn't his pa.

"I'm disappointed in you, Zachary. I truly am. I thought you were fonder of your head than

105

this. I ought to tell your father and hand him the switch."

"Pa never beats me," Zach said.

"Ever wonder why?"

"He doesn't care to see me in tears, I reckon."

The mountain man sighed. "Thou hast the most unsavoury similes," he quoted, "and art indeed the most comparative, rascalliest, sweet young prince." Lowering his arm, he walked slowly. "No, Zachary, that isn't the reason. Your father doesn't take a switch to you because his father took one to him more times than you could count if you started now and counted all night."

"Grandpa didn't!" Zachary said, trying to cope with the image of his pa being so mistreated. "He never told me about it."

"And he won't because that's the kind of man he is. It's important you know so you won't hurt him by doing something like this again."

"How would I hurt him? I'd be the one shot."

"More of him anon. There is written in your brow, provost, honesty and constancy. If I read it not truly, my ancient skill beguiles me." Shakespeare nudged Zach's shoulder. "In other words, you're not stupid so don't pretend you are. You'd hurt him because he cares for you with all his heart, and it would pain him terribly to have to bury you."

Zach had no argument to offer. Chastised, he gnawed his lower lip as he sometimes did under stress, then said halfheartedly, "I was curious, is all."

"I can't fault you for having an inquisitive

nature," Shakespeare said. "I was the same way when I was your age. Curiosity lured me from Maine to the Mississippi. And once I heard of the marvels to be seen in the Rockies, why, I had to go farther. I wouldn't be here today if I wasn't forever wondering about what lies over the next range."

"Then you understand."

"Yes, young coon, I do. But that doesn't mean I approve. Take it from me. You must learn to control your curiosity."

"Did you ever?"

"Eventually."

"How old were you?"

"Forty-nine."

They shared a laugh which ended prematurely when a pair of long-haired apparitions swooped down on them from out of the night.

"Here you are!" Winona declared, snagging Zach by a whang on his buckskins. "Come with me. Your father and I would like some words with you."

"And you!" Blue Water Woman scolded her husband. "You should know better than to encourage him when he misbehaves. Winona has been worried about him."

Zach heard his uncle protest, but Blue Water Woman gave him an earful. Which is exactly what Zach got on reaching the lean-to. He listened to his folks' sincere warnings about needlessly risking his life, and when they were done and staring down at him, their hurt feelings as plain as the noses on their faces, he pleased them by saying, "I'm truly sorry. I won't ever let it happen again."

"Good," Nate said. "We'll take you at your word, son. You've never lied to us before, and I know you won't start now."

So with a clear conscience Zach partook of a steaming bowl of rabbit stew and settled in for the night. The many hours spent on horseback had tired him more than he anticipated, and within a very short while he was sound asleep. Vaguely, he overheard his folks discussing the next stage of the journey and got the impression his father was a bit worried.

That was the last thought Zach had before being awakened by an uproar that startled him into leaping to his feet. Sluggish and dazed, he failed to remember where he was and cracked his head on the lean-to. The jolt brought him around. He moved into the open, rifle in hand, startled by the commotion, shouts, and whinnies.

The horses were in a panic, this time with reason. The strip of forest bordering the string was ablaze, trees and brush crackling noisily as dancing tongues of flame consumed the growth. Zach saw men frantically untying animals to lead them to safety, and other men toting water to throw onto the fire before it could spread.

Neither of Zach's folks were anywhere around. He assumed they were helping out and ran to do the same. In his haste he nearly collided with someone hurrying several frightened pack horses along.

"Watch it, *mocoso!*" the man said gruffly in a thick accent.

Zach recognized Gaston and recoiled a step.

"Afraid, are you?" the riverman said, smirking. "As well you should be. Your father would be, too, if he knew me better." Gaston flicked out a hand as if to playfully cuff Zach, but the blow was a hard one.

Gritting his teeth, Zach refused to give the bully the satisfaction of seeing him in pain. He forced a smirk of his own and responded, "I'll be sure to tell my pa. Maybe he'll give you a taste of the medicine he gave you back at Ham's Fork."

Gaston fingered the hilt of his knife. "There is nothing I would like more than to see him try, little one."

Further conversation was interrupted by more men hastening stock past. Gaston snickered and joined them.

A cold wind seemed to blow down Zach's spine. He shivered as he jogged closer to the heart of the bedlam. His father was there, helping LeBeau untie horses. There were few left. He assumed most had already been tended to when the two men from Hartford spoke.

"How many have run off, Cyrus?"

"Sixteen."

"We can't afford to lose that many."

"Tell me something I don't know," Porter said. "We'll have to organize a search party at dawn."

"What if the Blackfeet show?"

"We'll cross that bridge when we come to it."

A lone mare had straggled from the rest, over-looked in all the confusion. Zach spied it twenty yards down the lake and ran to fetch it. To his annoyance, the mare kicked up her heels and trotted another 20 yards when he was steps away from grabbing the lead rope dragging on the ground.

"Hold still, darn you," Zach said. He went slower this time so as not to scare her, but the mare took off again, going twice as far.

Zach pursued. The light from the fire no longer penetrated the veil of gloom, and he moved in near total darkness. He could barely see the water ten feet to his right, while the pines to his left formed an inky wall.

Slowing, Zach held out a hand and spoke softly to assure the mare he was harmless. She chomped at grass, as tame as a kitten until he reached for the rope. He was prepared, however, and leaped, grabbing hold. The mare tried to tear free but he held on, digging in his heels. She bobbed her head and swung her head, then apparently realized the futility of her effort and quit resisting.

Zach stood with his back to the lake, rubbing her neck. He glanced over her shoulders and was taken aback to see something move in the woods. Thinking it was another horse, he kept quiet so it would wander over and be easy to snare. The thing in the woods stepped into a small clearing and paused to scour the vicinity. It had two legs.

Zach ducked low so only his eyes were above the mare. He couldn't imagine who would be skulking about while the camp was in turmoil and everyone was needed to lend a hand. He went to call out, to ask who it was, when he was bothered by the thought that it might be an Indian.

The figure took several steps toward the lake, then abruptly wheeled and ran into the trees.

Perplexed, Zach conducted the mare back. The fire still burned but had been contained to a small area. Men swatted flames with blankets, threw dirt, or tossed water at a frenzied rate. Among them were his father and Shakespeare. He would have joined them had his mother and Blue Water Woman not found him and told him to stay close to them.

It took over an hour of strenuous labor before the fire was put out. The men were exhausted, their clothes smudged, their faces grimy.

Zach smiled as his pa and McNair trudged over. "That was something!" he enthused. "You saved the whole forest from going up in smoke."

"Not thanks to whoever started it," Shakespeare complained. "I'd like to get my hands on the varmint."

"It was set on purpose?" Zach marveled. "Who would be so addlepated?" Suddenly he recollected the figure in the pines, and he was set to tell them when a harsh cry rent the cool morning air.

"Yonder! On that hill!"

To the east, an orange band heralded the dawn. Under the band reared a hill barren at the top, and across the crest moved a small army of men.

"Who are they?" Cyrus Porter wanted to know.

"Who do you think?" Shakespeare said.

Zach knew, all too well.

They were Blackfeet.

Chapter Eight

Nate King was not one to bemoan bad fortune. While others cried out or gestured in alarm, he faced the New Englanders and said, "It'll take the war party two hours to get here. Which gives us an hour to find our missing stock and another hour to be well on our way."

"Will an hour give us a big enough lead?" Porter asked.

"It should," Nate said. "They're on foot, we have horses."

Porter wasn't satisfied. He swung toward McNair. "Do you agree?"

"I taught Horatio everything he knows. His words come out of my mouth."

"Let's get cracking, then."

Leaning close to his mentor, Nate whispered, "You'll take care of things at this end?"

"We'll be packed and ready."

"That's not what I meant. If we're not back—"

"I'll drag them off by their hair," Shakespeare said, grinning at Winona and Zach, who were just a few yards away. "Promise."

Nate picked LeBeau and Chavez to go with him. A circuit of the burn area revealed that the horses had run off in two directions. Ten had gone southward, six eastward—toward the Blackfeet.

"The smaller bunch first," Nate said.

At a gallop they sped through the woodland for over two miles. From a convenient bench they saw the horses grazing in a lush basin. Nate sent the tracker to one side, the riverman to the other. He took the direct route, walking the stallion so his companions would have time to get into position.

The moment Nate showed himself, the horses fled. They'd tasted freedom and found it to their liking. In a compact mass they cantered across the basin, only to stop in confusion when Chavez and LeBeau hurtled from the brush. A sorrel cut to the right, launching into a gallop that would have insured its escape had Chavez not wheeled in close, whirling a long rope overhead.

Nate had witnessed *vaqueros* at work on his visit to Santa Fe. Masters at *la reata*, they could do tricks that bordered on the miraculous. Chavez was in the same class. From 30 feet out, he threw a small loop, hard and fast, aiming ahead of the fleeing sorrel so that the horse ran into the noose and the rope fell around its neck in a smooth motion. Then, taking a quick turn of the *reata*

113

around his saddle horn, Chavez snubbed the rope so the sorrel couldn't pull it loose. His superb bay, trained for the job, dropped onto its haunches, anchoring the rope tight.

The sorrel bucked and yanked but was helpless. Chavez let it weary itself, then took up the slack and brought the horse over. "Reminds me of my younger days, *señor,*" he remarked, smiling. "Days I dearly miss."

"You did this for a living, I gather," Nate said as he shooed the runaways toward Black Bear Lake.

"*Si.* South of Tucson. My three brothers and I worked hard to make our ranch a success. Our *padre* was very proud." Chavez became melancholy. "Leaving them was the hardest thing I have ever had to do. One day, soon, I will go back and take up my life where I left off."

The revelation sparked Nate to say, "Sounds to me as if you never should have left in the first place."

"Sometimes our decisions are made for us." Chavez tilted back his sombrero. "I drifted to San Antonio de Bexar, and then north to St. Louis where a cousin lives. But the city did not agree with me. I was ready to leave when I saw a poster on a wall saying that Señor Porter wanted to hire a good tracker for high wages. So I applied. Just as soon as he pays me, I am off for Tucson."

"Your family should be happy to see you again."

A shadow flitted across the tracker's face. "Perhaps. One can never tell."

Ordeal

Forty minutes had elapsed when Nate placed the six horses in McNair's keeping and turned to go. "Remember your promise," he said.

"We'll take the river north. I'll have a signal fire made each night."

"You'll do no such thing. The Blackfeet have eyes too." Nate gazed at his wife and son, who were busy packing and loading supplies. "I'll find you on my own account."

"Keep your eyes skinned."

"Always."

The trail to the south lay along the lake shore. Where the lake ended, the hoofprints turned westward, into a long valley containing more antelope than Nate had ever seen in one place at one time. LeBeau was agog at the sight of hundreds upon hundreds of the sprightly animals bounding off with prodigious leaps. Chavez, accustomed to enormous herds of cattle, was unimpressed.

The delay in catching the first six had given the larger bunch a considerable lead. Nate restlessly marked the ascent of the sun, and as the minutes combined into an hour and the hour became two, he grew increasingly anxious to catch the stock and rejoin his family and friends.

They were almost to the end of the valley when their way was barred by a small herd of buffalo. Nate skirted to the north, crossed a dry wash, and discovered a notch that brought him out on the plain beyond. In the distance rose puffs of dust.

"The *caballos*," Chavez guessed.

"*Oui*," LeBeau said.

At a brisk walk Nate pursued. Their mounts had already been ridden hard and had to be conserved. In due course he made out the shine of sweaty hips, then the full outline of the horses. The animals were tired, heads low, legs plodding. "They'll stop at the next water," he predicted. "We can take them without much fuss."

A line of cottonwoods marked the course of a stream. Scenting moisture, the runaways trotted to the bank, then drank greedily.

The three men advanced in a line, each spaced 20 feet apart. The rambunctious horses were making so much noise drinking that none noticed.

Nate had a rope in hand and slipped it over a big brown with no difficulty. Chavez and LeBeau followed suit. All went well, and soon nine of the ten were reclaimed. Nate moved toward the last, a gray gelding, and the horse lifted its dripping muzzle, snorted, and fled up the opposite bank.

"Damn!" Nate groused. He started to go after it, but Chavez beat him to the bank.

"Should I help?" LeBeau asked.

"He doesn't need any," Nate said.

No sooner were the words out of his mouth than a tremendous roar caused all the horses to shy and prance. Nate had heard such roars many times before. "Stay with these," he shouted, and flew across the stream and into the brush.

A gunshot sounded. Another. The roaring grew louder, seeming to shake the trees. Nate burst into a clearing and there was the gray, down on its side, its entrails spilled out over the ground, while astride the stricken horse reared a slavering grizzly, one enormous paw on the gray's chest. Chavez had emptied both pistols and was bringing his rifle into play.

"No!" Nate bellowed. "Leave it be!"

Chavez glanced at him. "I must finish it off."

The bear took the matter out of their hands by charging the tracker. Chavez, distracted, would have been caught unawares if not for his bay, which spun and bolted.

Grizzlies were fast but only over short distances. This one came within a claw's breadth of ripping open the bay's flank when the horse swerved to avoid a thicket and a paw nipped at its tail.

Chavez applied his spurs. The bear went faster, snarling horribly, gaping jaws wide to bite. Twice its huge teeth clamped shut, gnashing air.

Nate, meanwhile, attempted to overtake them. He tried to get a bead on the grizzly but the many twists and turns thwarted him. The bear began to lose ground and Nate relaxed a little, sure that Chavez would escape. Then he spied what lay ahead.

Directly in the tracker's path lay a wide gully. Twelve feet from rim to rim, it spelled certain death for Chavez if he slowed or swung wide to go around. The bear would be on him in a flash.

Nate raised the Hawken again, convinced he had to shoot to distract the bear long enough for Chavez to reach safety. He saw Chavez bend forward, saw the tracker lash his reins and pump his legs.

The bay marshaled more speed. Hoofs pounding, it swept to the very brink of the gully and jumped, hurtling skyward in a magnificent arc. For a heartbeat it seemed to hang in midair, the outcome in doubt, Chavez's life in jeopardy. But it landed evenly, well clear of the rim, and Chavez reined up in a spray of dust.

The baffled grizzly halted at the edge and roared its anger. It looked down, apparently decided the walls were too steep to negotiate, and turned. It saw Nate.

So concerned had Nate been about Chavez's welfare that he had neglected his own. He was only 30 feet from the bear when it came after him, and he knew that even if he put a ball into the beast it would still reach him. Accordingly, he reined the stallion to the left and fled.

The brush was thick, some thorny. Nate was nicked and scraped, the stallion suffering worse. Rending of limbs told him the bear had taken a beeline and was almost upon him. He dared a glance and saw the monster within feet of his horse. It was going to catch him!

Nate brought up the Hawken, then glimpsed a cottonwood directly ahead. Instead of swerving, he galloped right at the trunk and, at the last possible instant, cut to one side, missing the tree by inches.

Grizzlies were massive brutes. Once they got up steam, they needed space to slow down. They couldn't simply stop dead, as a cat might do. This one tried, though, when it saw the cottonwood, digging in its hind paws and pushing at the ground with its front ones. But it was hopeless.

Ordeal

The impact shook the tree from roots to treetop. Nate heard a resounding crack and looked back to find the grizzly reeling as if drunk while shaking its head over and over. He continued on until he could no longer see it, then he slanted to the right and soon reached the gully.

Chavez had paralleled his course on the other side. "That was a close one, *amigo*," he said, smiling. "For both of us."

"I figured you for a goner," Nate agreed. He peered down at the bottom, 40 feet below. "That was some jump. I never could have made it."

"I refuse to end my days in the belly of a dumb brute," Chavez said. "Not when I have so much to live for." He paused, went on wistfully. "Anita is her name, and a prettier *señorita* can't be found. She promised to wait for me. I will not let myself die until I have held her soft hands in mine and gazed into her lovely eyes."

Many questions presented themselves, but Nate wouldn't pry. "I hope you get to see her again," was all he said.

From the brush rumbled a savage token of the bear's fury.

"Do you think it hunts us?" Chavez asked.

"Yes." Nate scoured the slopes for a spot to cross, but there was none. "Let's go east a spell. Maybe the gully will end."

Abreast, they rode briskly, both keeping an eye on their back trail. The cracking of undergrowth dwindled, and soon Nate judged they had gone far enough to resume talking. "Porter will have a fit over his horse, but it couldn't be helped."

"The bear came out of nowhere," Chavez related. "The horse was down before I could lift a finger."

"It happens."

Chavez motioned at the mountains. "This wilderness of yours is *muy grande*, but it is too savage for my taste."

"You have bears in your neck of the woods."

"Black bears, *si*. Which usually run rather than fight, and which do not grow as big as carriages."

"We have grizzlies, you have Apaches. I reckon we're even," Nate said, only half in jest.

Chavez chuckled. "It is said that if you were to put an Apache and a hungry bear in a locked room, the Apache would be the one who came out."

"You must have fought them a few times, growing up where you did."

"Many times. But not all Apaches are so wild. Some are friendly." Chavez wore that wistful expression again. "One worked for my father. He was an old White Mountain Apache, and he could track better than anyone I have ever known."

"He taught you?"

"*Si*. I took a liking to him when I was small. Used to bring him cookies and things my *madre* made. So in return he took me under his wing, as you would say, and shared all he knew with me." Chavez's voice dropped. "It was a sad day when I buried him."

"Old age?"

"No. Some Chiricahuas raided our *rancho*."

120

Nate reined up. The gully wall on the other side had buckled long ago, and erosion had worn a groove to the bottom. Unfortunately, his side was as steep as ever. "Think you can cross here?"

"Does a bird have wings?"

The tracker rode a dozen yards from the rim. Then, with a slap of his sombrero, he flew like the wind. He galloped into the groove at breakneck speed, the bay sending dirt and small rocks flying. A bound brought it to the near side, where, muscles rippling, it surged clear to the top without losing its footing once.

"That's a fine animal you have there," Nate complimented him. "Did you raise it from a colt?"

"No. I took it from a man who had no further use for it."

The meaning was obvious, and while Nate would have liked to learn more, he refrained from prying a second time. They rode to the stream in silence.

LeBeau paced the bank, his brow furrowed. On beholding them he grinned and clapped his hands. "There you are! I was getting worried, *mon amis.*"

"We wouldn't run off and leave you," Nate assured him.

"But you be killed, *non?* I heard shots, and roars." LeBeau stepped into the stirrups. "Without you, I think maybe I not find the others, and I do not care to be stranded in this harsh land."

"First Chavez, now you. It's not all that bad once you grow accustomed to the way things are."

"Maybe, friend. But on the Mississippi I need not look over my shoulder every minute of every *jour* for Indians, bears, or cougars. The worst that happen to you on a riverboat is you fall overboard. And I be a good swimmer."

The pack horses in tow, Nate retraced their route through the valley and into the high mountains bordering the lake. He changed course to come up on it from the southwest. On spying the shimmering surface, he stopped, tied the stallion, and moved forward alone to reconnoiter.

As Nate expected, the expedition was long gone. Swarming over the camp site were dozens of Blackfeet, over a hundred painted for war. A half-dozen were huddled near the lake, no doubt the leaders, mulling their next move. Nate did not have long to wait for them to make up their minds. A muscular warrior sporting a pair of eagle feathers in his hair spoke at length in their tongue, then the entire war party loped north along the shore.

Nate sprinted to the horses. LeBeau and Chavez were waiting tensely, rifles in hand.

"Well?" LeBeau said.

"The Blackfeet are after the expedition," Nate stated, mounting.

"What do we do? Maybe get ahead of these devils?"

"No. We'll follow for the time being."

The riverman shifted in the saddle. "Is that wise, my friend? I not know these Indians as you do, but I know they kill us if they catch us. We should be with our friends to help."

Ordeal

"Ever tried to push hard through heavy timber with a string of horses? Can't hardly be done." Nate responded. "For another thing, we'd make a godawful racket, which the Blackfeet might hear. And we could wind up straying far off the trail. Then what good would we be to anyone?"

Neither man liked the proposition, but they fell in behind him as Nate went around the southern tip of the lake and up the east shore. By all rights the Blackfeet should be too absorbed in the chase to notice anyone dogging them, but to be safe Nate never strayed from cover.

The war party jogged tirelessly for half an hour. When it dawned that they wouldn't be able to overhaul their quarry anytime soon, they slowed and walked.

The morning dragged. Nate stopped every now and then to scour the woods for stragglers. His foresight saved their lives, for shortly after noon he halted and distinguished eight or nine Blackfeet standing by an aspen grove.

Nate had nearly blundered into the open. He sat stock still, wondering what the Blackfeet were up to. They were gathered around a warrior seated on a log who appeared to have something wrong with his leg. After a few minutes two Blackfeet helped the hurt man to his feet, and the group departed.

By late afternoon the Blackfeet had slashed their pace in half, leading Nate to conclude they were about to give up. Then he saw a column of smoke rising from a hill, saw the war party fanning out, and his heart sank.

"What has happened?" LeBeau asked. "Did McNair stop?"

"Looks that way," Nate said, at a loss to understand why his friend would have done so. He slid off the stallion and studied the nearby trees. "I need to see what is going on," he declared, walking to a pine.

The bark was rough and dotted with sap which clung to his fingers. Nate gained the upper terrace without mishap. From there he could see the expedition encamped on the hill. Breastworks were being hastily erected in a gigantic circle, the men scurrying about like so many ants. He eased a leg to a lower limb to descend but changed his mind on seeing figures *beyond* the hill.

Suddenly Nate comprehended. Another party of Blackfeet were closing in from the north. The distance made counting them next to impossible, but he estimated there must be 50. The wily Blackfeet had executed a pincer movement to catch Porter's expedition between the two groups, and it had worked admirably.

Quickly Nate descended to inform the others.

"*Mon Dieu!*" LeBeau exclaimed. "One hundred and fifty against twenty! They are doomed, yes?"

"Not so long as I'm still breathing," Nate vowed.

"What can we do?" Chavez asked. "The three of us would throw our lives away if we attacked so large a force."

Nate pondered deeply. They couldn't stand there twiddling their thumbs while their friends and loved ones were wiped out. There had to be something they could do. But what?

Ordeal

Nate recollected hearing once about a small party of trappers surrounded by a Blackfoot band that outnumbered the trappers two to one. The whites had faced imminent death but were spared by a timely display of the northern lights that persuaded the superstitious Blackfeet to call off the attack.

Which didn't help Nate much. It was broad daylight. And supposing the Blackfeet held off until the next day. There was no guarantee the northern lights would be visible that night. No, he had to think up a strategy the three of them could put into effect.

"When the leader of an Apache raid is killed, they call off the attack. Would the same work with these Blackfeet?" Chavez asked.

"Sometimes it does," Nate said. "Usually when the war parties are small and there is no one to take the leader's place." Unconsciously, he fingered the trigger of his Hawken. "A war party this big is bound to have two or three who can fill the leader's moccasins at a moment's notice."

"Maybe we draw the Blackfeet off, *non?*" LeBeau suggested. "We ride half a mile, then shoot our guns."

"Wouldn't work," Nate said. "We'd draw off half, at the most. The rest would keep the expedition pinned down. All we'd do is get ourselves killed."

"I hate to be helpless," LeBeau said.

"Not half as much as I do," Nate told him. Having his wife and son up on that hill and knowing he was powerless to save them tore him apart inside. He hurried back to the tree and climbed

125

to his roost. Little had changed. The defenders worked furiously on their breastworks while the Blackfeet were in the act of completely encircling the hill.

Nate noted the lay of the land, seeking an advantage there. North and east of the hill grew forest. To the west lay the placid lake. To the south, the shore, a bare strip 60 feet wide. He figured the three of them might be able to sneak close to the base of the hill from the east and dash to the breastworks when the time was ripe.

Evidently the Blackfeet were in no hurry to launch an assault. Nate saw several dragging limbs from the woods and others busting the limbs into pieces to use as firewood. It was the sight of a particular warrior that gave Nate a flash of inspiration and sent him clambering downward so rapidly he nearly lost his handhold twice.

"What has gotten into you?" Chavez inquired.

"I had a brainstorm," Nate declared. "If it works, we'll send those Blackfeet scurrying off like a spooked herd of buffalo."

"And if it does not?"

Nate smiled grimly. "Then the three of us will wind up looking like porcupines."

Chapter Nine

Shakespeare McNair had been in a lot of tight spots during his many years in the wild. Not that he sought trouble. Rather, danger was a daily part of the life he had chosen to lead. And none knew better than he that the survival rate for mountaineers, as the trappers liked to call themselves, was abysmally low. Few precise records were kept, but it was known that in one year alone, 1826, 116 daring men had gone boldly into the mountains after beaver; 16 came out at the end of the season.

Shakespeare had almost been put under more times than he cared to recollect. Notable among them was the time a war party of Bloods backed him to the edge of a 500-foot-high cliff. And the time a grizzly had cornered him in a cave, blocking the only way out.

Now McNair had a new situation to add to his list. As he stood on the crown of the hill and watched the Blackfeet prepare to make an assault, he felt in his bones that his time had finally come to meet his Maker. Despite the brush breastworks hastily erected at his command, the Porter party had a snowball's chance in hell of living through the day.

Shakespeare looked around him. The men were spaced at regular intervals around the perimeter, each one with a rifle and a brace of loaded pistols. At the center, tending the fire Shakespeare had instructed be built, were the women and young Zach. Cyrus Porter had balked at starting one, saying it was a waste of time and wood since nightfall was hours off. Shakespeare had to explain that if it appeared the Blackfeet were going to break through the breastworks, he would have burning brands tossed on the barrier to keep the warriors out just a little longer.

Shakespeare wished he had been brought to bay with a party of seasoned trappers instead of greenhorn rivermen and uppity snobs. The rivermen were brave enough, but they would prove no match for the Blackfeet, who were bred to warfare from the day they were born. To be as fierce as an Indian, one had to live as an Indian.

Shakespeare had another regret. He would have liked to spare his wife and the Kings from the savagery about to unfold. If the women didn't take part in the battle and meekly submitted to the Blackfeet, they might be spared. But Shakespeare knew them too well. Both would rather die than give in. These were strong, independent-minded women who would pull their own weight, not prissy puppets such as those who often graced parlors with their coiffured presences back in the States. Blue Water Woman and Winona stood on their own two feet and made apologies to no one for their actions.

There were only two bright spots in the whole predicament. One was that Shakespeare had had the foresight to send a pair of riders ahead as a precaution. Thanks to them, the second war party had been spotted when it was yet a long ways off, giving him time to prepare.

The second bright spot was Nate King's absence. It comforted Shakespeare considerably to know that the man he looked upon more as a son than a friend would live on. Nate would be heartbroken for a few years, but eventually he'd recover and go on to make something of his life.

Commotion among the Blackfeet shattered Mc-Nair's reverie. He stepped onto a stump for a better view and saw a muscular warrior who wore two eagle feathers moving along the line, girding the warriors for the clash.

Smiling, Shakespeare raised both arms to the heavens and bellowed as would a professional orator, "Friends, Romans, countrymen, lend me your ears!"

Every last Blackfoot stopped whatever he was doing to stare upward.

"In the reproof of chance lies the true proof of men," Shakespeare quoted on, "the sea being smooth, how many shallow bauble boats dare sail upon her patient breast, making their way with those of nobler bulk! But let the ruffian Boreas once enrage the gentle Thetis, and anon behold the strong-ribbed bark through liquid mountains cut, bounding between two moist elements, like Perseus' horse—"

Shakespeare would have continued, but Porter and Clark ran up to him, the former shaking a finger as if in accusation.

"What in God's name are you doing? Those heathens will think you're crazy."

"That's the general idea," Shakespeare said.

"I beg your pardon?"

"Indians have a special regard for those whose brains are in a whirl," Shakespeare explained. "Convince them you're addlepated and they won't lay a finger on you."

Clark glanced at the Blackfeet. "Will it work this time?"

"Afraid not," Shakespeare said. He pointed at the warrior with the two feathers. "See that big one there? His handle is Raven Beak. He and I go back a long ways, and we never did cotton to one another. I was putting on a show for his benefit."

"You're a strange man, McNair," Porter said.

"I'll take that as a compliment."

The Blackfeet broke out in a chorus of blood-thirsty yells, many shaking their weapons overhead. Raven Beak stepped in front, a fusee in his brawny hands.

Shakespeare faced around. "They're working themselves into a killing frenzy," he announced to all and sundry. "In a few minutes they'll charge. Hold your fire until I shoot, then cut them down just as fast as you can. If they reach the barricade and we can't hold them, fall back so I can set it alight."

Some of the rivermen were pale, others glaring defiance. Brett Hughes and Adam Clark both looked ready to bolt. Alone among them, Zachary King stood straight and calm, a credit to his parents and their upbringing.

A strident war whoop rang out. Shakespeare looked and saw Raven Beak leading the warriors up the slope at a trot. Since every shot had to count, Shakespeare fixed a bead on Raven Beak himself. He would let the Blackfoot get a lot closer, then put a ball between his eyes.

A heavy air of dread hung over the top of the hill like thick fog. The men had their rifles ready, the women and boy too, their features etched in somber lines.

Shakespeare saw Raven Beak stop and wave the fusee, exhorting the others. The Blackfeet howled. Raven Beak half-turned, beaming confidently at his warriors, then he froze, the smile dying on his lips.

A moment Shakespeare waited, resisting an urge to squeeze the trigger sooner than he should. When Raven Beak didn't move, he glanced up and blinked in surprise. The cries of the Blackfeet on the south side of the hill faded as more and more became aware of the new element that had been added.

A huge, swirling cloud of dust swept toward

the hill like an undersized whirlwind. It raced along the shore of Black Bear Lake, billowing and flowing as if a thing alive. It was the sort of cloud a big group of horsemen might make. Indeed, moments later lots of riders did appear, vaguely visible in the midst of the dust. Rifles and pistols spat lead to a chorus of fiery shouts.

Shakespeare jumped to the conclusion that a body of trappers had heard the racket and were coming to the aid of his beleaguered party. He let out a lusty whoop. The rivermen, taking his cue, did the same.

Between the dust cloud and the reaction of the defenders, the Blackfeet were thrown into confusion. A few fired at the oncoming horsemen, the range too great for their inferior trade rifles.

Shakespeare realized the lives of those with him hung in the balance. Few trapping brigades contained anywhere near as many men as the Blackfoot war party. So whoever had rushed to the rescue was relying on the shock of being unexpectedly attacked to compel the Blackfeet into flight. So far the warriors were holding their ground, although many looked uncertainly to Raven Beak for guidance.

An extra nudge would do the trick, Shakespeare reflected. He saw that the Blackfeet on the north side of the hill had stopped their assault as word of the newcomers spread like wildfire from man to man. Most hurried around to see for themselves. They had lowered their weapons and were completely off guard.

Shakespeare seized the bull by the horns, in a

manner of speaking. Spinning, he yelled at the expedition members, "If you value your hair, follow me! We have to convince these cussed devils that they're dead if they stay!"

With that, Shakespeare shoved part of the breastwork aside, barreled through, and charged down the slope screaming like a banshee. Behind him streamed the others.

Raven Beak glanced up in consternation. He began to run up the slope, then hesitated and looked at the dust cloud. Just at that moment one of the riders fired a rifle. Raven Beak twisted, his shoulder rupturing outward. He staggered, yet didn't go down. Some warriors rushed to help him but he pushed them off, threw back his head, and shouted: "Many more whites come! With many guns! We must go or be destroyed!"

The message was relayed from warrior to warrior. In concert, the Blackfeet sped eastward, a few firing arrows or rifles. A riverman was transfixed through the thigh and fell groaning. In retaliation, Porter gave the command to fire and a neat volley tore into the retreating Blackfeet, blasting eight of them off their feet. Added to this was another, smaller volley from the horsemen.

The Blackfeet needed no more incentive. With the wounded being helped along, the war party fled pell-mell. In the time it would take to count to ten, they were bobbing stick figures among the pines and diminishing every second.

Shakespeare shook a fist at them. "Stuff that in your pipes and smoke it!" Grinning, he faced the riders, who were slowing. "You!" he blurted in surprise.

"Me," Nate replied. He spat dust from his mouth, then swatted dust from his sleeves. "Who were you expecting? Jim Bridger? Or Carson, maybe?"

Shakespeare had no answer. He was irritated because he'd failed to guess who it would be when it should have been obvious. He saw the weary, sweaty pack animals, all trailing ropes to which had been lashed two bundles of brush and limbs. He saw that the horses of the three men had pulled single bundles, saw the streaks in the dirt behind them. And he threw back his head and cackled.

The two New Englanders came up, their mouths dragging. "What a clever ruse!" Cyrus Porter exclaimed. "Which one of you was genius enough to think of it?"

"Señor King," Chavez answered.

"*Oui*," LeBeau added. "He turned we three into an army."

Winona and Zach stepped close to the black stallion, neither saying anything. They didn't have to. Their eyes spoke volumes. Nate swung down, embraced each briefly. His voice was throaty when he turned to Porter and said, "I reckon we have an hour at the most before those Blackfeet figure out we skunked them and come back thirsting for our blood."

"How would they guess?" Porter said blandly. "We're safe enough, I should think."

"They're not stupid," Nate said.

Ordeal

"He's right," Shakespeare threw in. "I want everyone mounted and set to go in fifteen minutes."

For once the rivermen obeyed without grumbling. The wounded man was tended by Blue Water Woman, who applied an herbal poultice. The man could ride, although he suffered severely.

Shakespeare had a destination in mind. By late afternoon they reached a river and bore northward. Five miles from the lake they passed mineral springs, some giving off the stench of sulfur. Shakespeare rode close to one to observe it bubble and boil.

Toward sunset Cyrus Porter and Adam Clark rode alongside the mountain man. Porter cleared his throat. "I don't mean to be critical, but we're not proceeding as swiftly as I would expect. Is it safe to hold to a walk when the Blackfeet might be after us?"

"No," Shakespeare allowed.

"Then why are we?" Adam demanded.

Shakespeare focused on the older man. "Didn't you tell me that the last anyone knew, your daughter and those other settlers had decided to put down roots in the Bear River region?"

"So?" Porter rejoined.

Shakespeare pointed at the river. "There it is."

Porter sputtered, then flushed red and snapped, "Why didn't you inform me sooner? We should be alert for evidence of where they stopped."

"What do you think I've been doing?" Shakespeare said. "And why do you think I told Chavez

135

to stay half a mile behind us? He's keeping his eyes peeled for the war party."

The information was relayed. Until dark the entire expedition scoured the lowland adjoining the river. No trace of a settlement was found, not so much as the charred remains of camp fires.

At a small plain Shakespeare called a halt. He directed that the horses be tethered but the packs left on in case they had to make a quick departure in the middle of the night. Four guards were posted, with four more to relieve them at midnight and another four later.

Blue Water Woman had coffee on and was preparing antelope for supper. Shakespeare sat with a grunt, then tiredly filled his battered tin cup. "Been a long day," he commented.

"By tomorrow night we will be at the Snake," Blue Water Woman said. "We will be safe from the Blackfeet once we are past it."

"You hope," Shakespeare said. He sipped loudly, then pivoted as a rider trotted to their fire. "Any sign of them?"

"No, *señor*," Chavez said. "I waited a long time, as you told me. They are not chasing us. I would stake my life on it."

Later Nate walked over and accepted a cup, taking his black. "We need to talk," he said after several swallows.

"About the daughter?" Shakespeare guessed.

Nate nodded. "We might as well be hunting for a needle in a haystack."

"We tried telling Porter that before we left, but he wouldn't listen. Since he's the captain of this outfit, until he's ready to quit we continue searching."

"He's wasting his time."

"Would you feel the same if it was Evelyn who had gone missing? Or Zach?"

"No. And I'm not saying we should stop looking so soon."

"Then cut to the bone."

"How long do we stick with him? He was just jawing with my family, and he mentioned to Winona that he'll look for two or three years if need be before he'll accept never seeing Hestia again."

A branch popped in the fire, inducing Shakespeare to pick up a stick and feed it to the flames. "He hired me to do a job, so I'm obliged to help him for a year or so. Any longer than that and he'll be on his own." Shakespeare was going to elaborate, but he saw someone standing in the shadows a dozen feet away, apparently eavesdropping, so he said loudly, "You there, friend! Plunk yourself down and make yourself comfortable."

The man started to back away. "No, thanks," he said with a hint of an accent. "I'm just stretching my legs before I turn in. I didn't mean to disturb you."

"I insist, pilgrim," Shakespeare said, putting on a false smile of welcome. He glanced at Nate, who had a hand draped on the butt of a pistol, and gave a barely perceptible shake of his head.

The man came forward slowly, almost apprehensively, firelight highlighting his blond hair and rugged countenance.

It was Brett Hughes. Shakespeare had hardly shared ten words with the laconic loner the whole journey. On inquiring of Porter, he'd learned that Hughes had been hired to handle the supplies and to maintain a meticulous record of all expenses incurred. Shakespeare didn't think it strange that a man as wealthy as Porter would keep track of every expenditure. Some rich men were so miserly they couldn't stand to part with a single cent.

Nate leaned back, his hand drifting from his pistol. He lifted the coffeepot and said, "Care for a cup? Blue Water Woman makes coffee strong enough to curl your toes."

"I suppose it can't hurt," Hughes said, hunkering on the other side of the fire. Although the night was warm, he rubbed his hands together as if cold and held them near to the flames.

Shakespeare did the honors, passing the cup and asking, "Care to have it sweetened?" He noted that the blond man's hands were large and calloused, hardly the hands of someone who made a living scribbling in account books.

"No, thanks," Hughes said.

"This your first trip into the mountains?" Shakespeare casually asked.

"Yes."

"How do you like it so far?"

"Rather exciting," Hughes said. "Of course, you must be used to this sort of thing, living in the Rockies as long as you have."

"Heard about me, have you?"

Ordeal

"Who hasn't? It's rumored you've been out here longer than any other mountain man, that you were here before Lewis and Clark." Genuine respect marked Hughes's statement. "I can't begin to imagine the things you've seen and done, the hardships you've endured."

"It would fill a book," Shakespeare conceded.

Hughes drank and smacked his lips. "You're right, Mr. King. This is delicious. Almost as good as tea."

Shakespeare grinned. "I wouldn't have taken a hardy sort like you for a tea-drinker."

"Been drinking it all my life," Hughes said. "Once a day, like clockwork." He gave the impression of being about to say more, but instead he drank some coffee.

"Tea is hard to come by on the trail," Nate remarked. "Or did you bring a supply?"

"I'm traveling light," Hughes answered. "Which is just as well. Mr. Porter keeps me busy as a beaver from sunrise to sunup."

"He does like to get his money's worth," Nate said.

"And he's always so quick to fly off the handle," Hughes said. "You'd think a man of his social standing would have more patience with those who work for him."

"Money doesn't have a thing to do with it," Shakespeare said. "Some folks are just so soured on life they can't get the acid out of their systems."

"True, but he's worse than most," Hughes said. He leaned forward and spoke in a conspiratorial whisper. "He's so bad I'm downright afraid to mention what I saw the night of the fire for fear he'll go after the man without proof."

Shakespeare's good humor evaporated. "You saw who started it?"

"I might have."

"Care to share with us?" Nate prodded.

Hughes acted reluctant to say anything. He sat there swishing the coffee in his cup while peering thoughtfully into space. "I suppose I can trust you. And it might help to have someone else know, just in case the man tries something else. If he is the blinking culprit, that is."

"What did you see?" Shakespeare asked.

"Well, it was like this." Hughes looked over his shoulder, and when assured they were alone, he went on, saying, "I couldn't sleep very well that night so I'd gotten up to take a walk. As I was nearing the string, I happened to see one of the rivermen going into the forest. I figured he was heeding Nature's call and went on with my stroll." Hughes paused. "Not five minutes later the fire broke out. And when I ran to help douse the flames, I saw the same riverman come out of the trees at the far end of the camp."

"He could well have been the one," Nate said.

"My thinking exactly. But I must stress I have no proof, and without it we can't accuse him."

"So who was this coon?" Shakespeare goaded.

"Gaston."

Nate arched an eyebrow. "Why would Gaston want to run off the horses? It's a long walk back to the Mississippi."

Ordeal

"You'll have to question him," Hughes said. "All I know is what I saw." Depositing his cup, he rose. "I'm grateful for the chat. By nature I'm a solitary man who likes to keep his own company, but I don't mind having friends. Consider me one of yours." Smiling, he walked into the darkness.

"Interesting," Shakespeare said, partly to himself. "What did you make of it?"

"I pegged Gaston as hotheaded, not stupid," Nate responded. "We'll have to watch him closely from now on."

"You believe Hughes?"

"What reason would he have to lie?"

Not having one to give, Shakespeare fiddled with the fire, a habit of his when in deep thought. Just because he didn't know of a reason didn't mean Hughes didn't have one. As much as he'd like to believe that bastard Gaston had been to blame, a nagging suspicion gnawed at his innards, a suspicion that there was more to Hughes than the man let on. Then, too, he'd never been one to trust men who offered friendship as readily as some preachers offered salvation. Both, in his opinion, had to be earned.

Nate rose to go with a parting remark. "It's not bad enough we have hostile tribes and grizzlies to worry about, we also have to be on guard against a renegade in our own camp. Things have been rough so far, but I have a feeling the worst is yet to come."

"You and me, both, Horatio," Shakespeare said. "You and me, both."

Chapter Ten

Fort Hall on the Snake River was built in 1834 by an American named Wyeth. The enterprising type, he'd hoped to set up a trading empire but floundered and was forced to sell the fort to his British rivals, the Hudson's Bay Company.

To say no love was lost between American trappers and the HBC would be an understatement. They were in constant competition for furs, and nowhere was that competition more intense than in the Oregon Country.

Under a treaty signed in 1818 and renewed in 1827, citizens of both countries were permitted to settle and do business in the region. This created a powder keg, with both sides suspicious of the activities of the other and each seeking to win an advantage that would prove their claim to the territory more valid.

Ordeal

Nate King knew all this from conversations with free and company trappers who had been there and back. So when he first set eyes on the high adobe walls, he felt edgy over the reception the expedition would receive, not relieved at reaching one of the few fortified outposts between the Mississippi and the Pacific.

Shakespeare McNair was likewise aware of the loyalties of the fort's occupants, and he felt it prudent to make mention of the facts to Cyrus Porter, adding, "You'll have to keep a tight rein on your men. We have to be on our best behavior the whole time we stay here."

"Do these Hudson's people have the authority to throw us out if they wish?" Porter inquired.

"They do. And they can refuse to sell us goods or trade things we need."

"We have plenty of supplies left. Why not keep on going?"

"Because if your daughter's party passed by, odds are they stopped. Maybe they mentioned where they were headed."

Porter fidgeted in the saddle. "Very well. I leave this to your discretion."

Shakespeare rode on ahead with Nate at his side. The gates to the fort were wide open, and a regular stream of Indians passed in and out. To the northwest lay a Nez Percé encampment totaling over 200 lodges.

A lone sentry, the picture of boredom, stood atop the front wall. He straightened as the mountaineers drew rein below and stared at the column with open disgust. "Just what we need," he declared. "More of you bleeding Yanks to raise our beaver."

"Sorry to disillusion you, friend," Shakespeare said, "but we're not on trapping business."

The sentry leaned low over the parapet and sniffed loudly. "Could have fooled me, friend," he shot back, "unless you grease yourself with castoreum for the hell of it."

It never ceased to amaze Nate that his friend could stay so calm when provoked. He had a sharp retort on his lips but McNair merely grinned and gave a little shrug.

"You've a keen nose, mister, and I trust your wits are just as keen. We're acting as guides for a man trying to find his daughter. She came west to the Promised Land and hasn't been seen since."

The sentry gazed toward the column, eyes narrowing. "Your employer may be in for a letdown, mate. A heap of settlers have lost their hides on this trail, yet more keep coming every month."

"Greener pastures. It will cure you or kill you every time."

Chortling, the sentry beckoned. "Feel free, mister. And later, if I should see you at the sutler's store, feel free to treat me to a whisky. The name is Pearson."

"McNair," Shakespeare said. "My friend is Nate King."

Pearson gripped the edge of the wall. "Did you say McNair? Not Shakespeare McNair, who used to live with Two Humps's tribe?"

"The same."

"Hell, man. Two Humps claims the two of you explored every nook and cranny from Vancouver Island to San Diego."

"Pretty near." Shakespeare gazed into the fort. "Is he here now?"

"Just left. That's his village yonder."

Nodding, Shakespeare entered, drawing curious stares from HBC men and Nez Percé alike. His flowing white hair and beard were enough to warrant study, since few lived long enough in the wilderness to see their hair turn gray, let alone white.

"Who is Two Humps?" Nate asked.

"A chief. He and I were blood brothers back when the Oregon Country was a gleam in Thomas Jefferson's eye. We traveled some, fought some, swam in the surf when we could. Later I'll introduce you."

A bustling commerce existed at the sutler's store. HBC men were exchanging trade goods for hides at a wide table set up just inside. A long line of patient Nez Percé waited their turn, each bearing an armful of prime furs.

"Look at all them plews," Nate said as he tied the stallion to a post. "Were they ours, we'd be millionaires like old John Jacob Astor."

"And what would you do with so much money?"

"I've never given it much thought," Nate admitted. "No one in my family has ever been rich, although my father came close. The Kings have always been content to live by the sweat of their brows, and when times are lean to make do as best we can." He tucked his rifle in the crook of his elbow. "You might think this strange, but I've never had any great hankering for a lot of money."

"Good thing you married a Shoshone," Shakespeare quipped. "There are some white women who are as partial to dollars as they are to breathing. If one of them had sunk her hooks into you, she'd push and nag until you installed her in a nice mansion or dropped dead from too much work."

Shakespeare headed for a short, squat building and rapped on the closed door. A guttural voice bid them enter.

Seated at a polished desk was a man in a suit, a quill pen poised in hand. His bulldog features were heightened by bushy sideburns running to his lower jaw, which clenched at the sight of the two trappers. Setting the pen down, he smoothed his jacket and said, "Americans, I'd wager. I'm Andrew Smythe-Barnes, in charge of this post."

McNair made the introductions and briefly explained their presence, concluding, "We'd like to make camp west of the fort while we ask around about a party of settlers who must have passed this way within, say, the past six months."

"Permission granted. And it might interest you to learn that I keep a record of every group that stops," Smythe-Barnes revealed. "Does Cyrus Porter know the name of the leader of these settlers?"

"I never thought to ask," Shakespeare said.

"Why not bring him around this evening? Say about six? I'd be honored if you gentlemen would join me and a few of my men for supper."

Nate was surprised by the invite; Hudson's Bay men were notoriously unfriendly to Americans. He wondered if Smythe-Barnes had an ulterior motive and mentioned as much once Shakespeare and he stood outside.

"Could be," the mountain man said. "But more likely you're seeing enemies behind every tree when there's nothing but shadows."

Porter, Clark, and Hughes waited at the head of the column. On hearing McNair's report, Porter smiled. "Lord, it will be wonderful to sit at a table and eat like a civilized human being again. This Smythe-Barnes sounds like a true gentleman."

"I can't wait to have a drink," Adam Clark said, then glanced at Porter to add icily, "that is, if it's all right with you?"

"A few, yes," Porter said. "Just don't go overboard and get drunk like you did before we departed Hartford."

"I wasn't drunk," Clark responded testily. "I was tipsy."

"A delicate distinction," Porter said. "When a man has had so much to drink that he can't stand on his own two legs without help, then in my book he's drunk."

Nate made a show of surveying the mountains so as not to appear interested in their conversation, but he was. A drinking problem explained a lot about Clark's behavior and attitude. It also compounded the potential problems awaiting them up the trail, since the hardest part of the journey still lay ahead.

Shakespeare was more interested in the reaction of Brett Hughes. The blond man put a hand over his face as if to stifle a yawn when actually he smirked in secret glee. Why the man would do such a thing, Shakespeare had no idea.

Clark slumped in the saddle, sulking like an oversized child. "Never fear, Cy. I will watch myself this evening so I don't embarrass you," he told Porter.

The whole group drifted toward the campsite. Brett Hughes moved his mount next to their leader and commented, "There are a few supplies we're short on. Perhaps I'd better go into the fort now and buy what we need before the Nez Percé empty the sutler's shelves."

"An excellent suggestion," Porter said. "Off with you. And if you need more money, you have only to let me know."

Shakespeare saw the New Englander pat his coat as Hughes nodded and trotted off.

"I hope the supplies won't be expensive," Porter remarked. "I don't have more than five thousand left, and it has to last me until I get home."

Glancing back, Shakespeare observed Gaston and two other rivermen within earshot. "It's not my business to tell another man how to run his own affairs," he said quietly so they wouldn't hear, "but I wouldn't advertise the fact you're carrying a lot of money, were I you."

"I don't see any reason to keep it a secret," Porter said. "It's not like there are footpads lurking behind every boulder." He chortled. "Besides, money breeds influence. The more a man has, the more others look up to him."

"Money can also breed a knife in the ribs if the wrong parties learn you have it," Shakespeare mentioned. "So don't say I didn't warn you if someone tries to separate you from your five thousand."

Porter patted the twin pistols under his belt. "No one would dare. Appearances to the contrary, I'm a crack shot, Mr. McNair. Practiced weekly at my club in Hartford."

"Shot at a lot of moving targets, did you? Bears and painters and varmints and such?"

"Don't be silly, Mr. McNair," Porter said. "We shot at clay targets on occasion. Most of the time we used stationary targets. What difference does it make?"

"A big one," Shakespeare said. "Clay targets don't duck and weave when you're shooting at them. And they don't shoot back."

Camp was set up in short order. The rivermen erected a large red tent for the New Englanders and a score of Nez Percé children came to watch, giggling in fascination, a few making bold to rub their hands on the canvas.

Gaston was one of those putting the tent up. He glared at the youngsters, shooing them away when they came too close to suit him. And when one accidentally bumped into him, he spun, gripped the little boy's shoulder, and barked, "*Arretez!* That will be enough, you brat! Run along to your squaw before I take my boot to your bottom!"

The boy grimaced in pain and went to run off but tripped over his own feet and sprawled in the dirt.

"Idiot," Gaston snapped, drawing back a heavy foot.

Nate had witnessed the incident but had been too far off to get there sooner. He darted between the river rat and the child, his hands on his pistols. "That will be enough out of you," he warned.

Gaston backed up a step, glowering. "Or what? You will beat me again? I think not, bastard. The last time you took me by surprise."

Nate almost tore into the man but held himself in check.

"Or maybe you will ask your friend, LeBeau, to help you?" Gaston mocked him. "He thinks he is so high and mighty now because Porter picked him to be our *patron!*" He sneered. "Yet LeBeau does not speak English as good as I do!"

"It's not LeBeau or me you have to worry about," Nate said through clenched teeth, jabbing a thumb at the frightened boy. "It's the men in his tribe. If they hear how you've mistreated him, they're liable to want your hair."

"You're trying to scare me but it won't work," Gaston said. "All I did was squeeze his shoulder."

"Even that's too much," Nate said. "Some tribes don't believe in laying a finger on children, no matter how bad they misbehave." He watched the young ones scurry away. "I knew a trapper once, name of Prost, who had gone on a visit to the Crows. He took a batch of hard candy for the sprouts. After he ran out, a boy kept pestering him for more, and he lost his temper and slapped the boy."

"What happened?" Gaston asked, not sounding so sure of himself.

"We found Prost later, wandering the prairie. They'd taken all his fixings, stripped him buck naked, and cut off the hand he'd slapped the boy with."

The riverman cocked an eye after the fleeing children. "Damn, King. I didn't mean no harm. If the Nez Percé come after me, will you talk to them for me?"

"Why should I?" Nate retorted, turning to go.

"Because you may be a smelly, son of a whore trapper who doesn't have the brains God gave a flea, but you're not the kind of man who can stand still when someone else is being hurt without cause."

Nate had pivoted at the insults, his fists rising. Then he saw that Gaston was smiling, if slightly. "Think you have me all figured out?"

"*Oui.* I've known men like McNair and you before. Men of honor. You have your own code that you live by. Believe it or not, so do I."

Nate didn't know whether to believe the boatman or not. For the moment he decided to give Gaston the benefit of the doubt, and said, "If they show up, I'll see what I can do. But I'm not making any promises."

Gaston grinned, albeit slyly. "*Merci.* I thank you."

Walking off, Nate heard footsteps, and someone fell into step next to him.

"You handled that well, *mon ami*," LeBeau said.

"Did I? We'll see," Nate said. "I might have been better off pounding some sense into his thick skull."

A clatter of hooves foreshadowed the arrival of Brett Hughes, who galloped through the camp and reined up in a spray of dirt in front of Nate and LeBeau. "King, you'd best come quick!" he exclaimed. "Your wife needs you."

"Winona?" Nate said, recollecting that the last time he had seen her was shortly before the two women took Zach into the fort to purchase a few articles.

"Some of those Hudson's Bay crowd are giving her a hard time," Hughes said. "They made some remarks that upset her, so she called them a few names and now they won't let her leave. I came as fast as I could."

"Get down," Nate said.

"What?"

Unwilling to waste more time, Nate reached up and swung Hughes to the ground. The clerk went to protest but Nate ignored him, gave the horse a slap, and vaulted into the saddle on the fly. He thought he would have to go into the fort to find his wife, but she was just outside the gates, Zach and Blue Water Woman behind her, three HBC men in front, a crowd of Nez Percé watching. A heavy-set HBC man was poking Winona's shoulder with a thick finger and leering at her, daring her, by his expression, to resist.

Nate hauled on the reins and leaped off the horse. In four bounds he was behind the trio of buckskin-clad troublemakers, who had heard him and started to turn. Like lightning he struck. His fist caught the man on the left in the pit of the stomach and staggered him. A jab sent the trapper on the right stumbling.

The man who had been poking Winona drew back a pudgy fist to strike, but Nate beat him to the punch in more ways than one, ramming a series of blows into the man's face. Lips split and cartilage crunched. Furious, Nate waded into the retreating trapper, delivering punch after punch, showing no mercy, giving no quarter. Grunting, the man fell onto his backside and sat rigid in a benumbed stupor.

"Look out, Pa!" Zach shouted.

The trapper on the right had straightened, his hand sweeping to a flintlock on his right hip. The trapper on the left was going for a butcher knife.

Nate drew without realizing he'd done so, both pistols at once, the guns leveling of their own accord. The men froze when he pulled back the hammers.

"No, husband!" Winona cried, leaping to his side. She would not have minded if he shot all three, but she knew it would embroil him in a clash with the British authorities, and she didn't want him jailed, however briefly.

In that suspended moment of time when the trio stared down the twin barrels of eternity, there was a flurry of movement in the fort, and the Nez

Percé parted to allow Andrew Smythe-Barnes and several other of the Hudson's Bay crowd through. All were armed, Smythe-Barnes with a fine shotgun.

"What have we here?" the head of the post demanded. "Having a bit of a row, are we?"

"This bleeding Yank started it, guv," said the trapper with the knife. "He jumped us without cause."

"You lie, white man," Blue Water Woman said. "My friend and I were trying to leave but you would not let us. You insulted us, put your hands on my friend."

Smythe-Barnes placed his own hands on his hips. "Is this true, Dinkus? Were you forward with these squaws?"

"As the Lord is my witness, no sir," Dinkus said. "Just ask Rafe and Charlie, here. We was mindin' our own business, true and proper."

Nate took a half-step. "Like hell you were!"

"Here, here," Smythe-Barnes said. "That will be quite enough of that, Mr. King. Put those guns away and conduct yourself in a civil fashion. I won't tolerate ruffianism at my post, and I have a stout barred room waiting for anyone who won't take me at my word."

Reluctantly Nate complied, but he kept one hand on a pistol. He rested the other on his wife's shoulder and asked, "Are you all right?"

"Fine, husband. They did not harm us." Winona deliberately chose not to relate the fleeting fear she had felt when the three men first blocked her path and suggested she entertain them in a back room, fear not for herself but for her son, who would have lashed out had she not stopped him.

"Since no one was gravely hurt, I see no need for a formal investigation," Smythe-Barnes was saying. "Unless one or the other of you prefer to press formal charges? In that case I'll have to take statements so I can call witnesses."

Dinkus scratched his stubbly chin and drew a circle in the dirt with a toe. "No need to go to that much work, guv. We'll chalk it up to a misunderstandin' and let it go at that if the blooming Yank will do the same."

"How about it, King?" Smythe-Barnes said.

"I'll let it drop but I won't forget," Nate said. "And if there is a next time, I'll let my flintlocks do my talking for me."

"There's no need for threats," Smythe-Barnes said. "We're all gentlemen here."

"Are we?" Nate said, staring at the trio of company men.

Smythe-Barnes faced the crowd that had gathered. "Be about your business, people. The excitement is over. Just a minor disturbance is all it was."

"Wrong," Nate said, still so mad his temples pounded. He loved Winona more than life itself, and he'd be damned if he was going to let any man, white or red, lay a finger on her with impunity. "There's one more thing, postmaster."

"What might that be?"

"Don't call my wife a squaw. Ever." Nate looped an arm around Winona, took the reins to Hughes's horse in hand, and marched toward camp. "Damned John Bulls! From now on you don't go into the fort alone."

Winona gave her man a hug, relieved he had showed when he did. Zach wouldn't have been able to keep from interfering much longer, and then blood might have been shed. "How did you know?" she asked.

"Hughes fetched me."

"That was nice of him," Blue Water Woman said sourly, "since they were friends of his."

"You know that for a fact?" Nate said, looking at her.

"I saw him talking to those men a short while before they came up to us," Blue Water Woman detailed. "They laughed and slapped one another on the back."

"Hmmm," was all Nate said.

"There was something else strange," Winona commented. "When they walked over, they acted like they had been drinking. Their legs were unsteady, and when they spoke they sounded as if their mouths were full of flour."

"Why was that so strange? You've seen drunk men before."

"Because, one I love, they did not smell of whiskey. Not a little. And when you arrived they were able to talk and act just fine."

Nate mulled the information, puzzled over its significance. It sounded as if the men had staged the whole thing, yet their motive eluded him. And another thing. There had been plenty of Nez Percé women at the fort. Why hadn't those three picked on any of them?

The clerk, Porter and Clark were hastening anxiously toward the fort but stopped to await the returning party.

"We came as soon as we heard," Porter said. "Were there really men giving your wives a hard time?"

"We almost spilled blood," Nate said, his gaze on Hughes. "No thanks to your friends."

"My—?" Hughes said, and laughed, a brittle tinkle as of glass breaking. "Where did you ever get such a notion? I never set eyes on those men until today."

Nate handed over the reins, saying, "You were seen talking to them, so don't try to deny it."

"No need to," Hughes said good-naturedly. "They stopped me to ask questions about our expedition, and then had the gall to ask me to lend them money so they could go on with their debauchery."

The excuse was plausible. Lacking grounds to press the issue, Nate let it drop and faced Porter. "A word to the wise, as they say. Tell everyone to tread lightly in the fort and to shy away from the HBC crowd. They like to throw their weight around every chance they get."

"I'll give orders to that effect." Porter looked toward the woodland to the west. "How unfortunate Mr. McNair is off hunting with Chavez. We could use his expert advice at a time like this."

What's wrong with mine, damn you? Nate nearly said, but didn't. His family and Blue Water Woman tagging along, he walked to where they had piled their belongings and reclaimed the rifle he had negligently left behind in his rush to protect Winona.

Zachary hunkered down and said, "I wanted to teach those vermin a lesson, Pa. I sorely did. But Ma wouldn't let me tangle with them. She said she didn't want to make a fuss with Evelyn on her back."

"Your mother and you both did fine."

The boy accepted the praise but was still upset. He'd seldom seen anyone be so rude to his mother, and his anger had about choked him. "I suppose. Yet I can't help thinking that I should have put a ball into the gut of that fat one. You should have seen him running his fingers through Ma's hair, treating her like she was a horse he was looking to buy."

"I'm glad I didn't see that," Nate said severely.

"You are?"

"I would have shot him dead and been thrown into the coop."

"Then I would have sprung you."

Nate saw that his son was serious. Smiling, he clapped Zach on the arm. "I know I can count on you when things are tough. Always remember this, though. It's not enough to be willing to defend yourself or those you care for. You also have to know when to act and when to let things sort of drift along. There's a time for shooting and a time for using your head, and it's a smart man who can tell the difference."

"I didn't see you letting things drift," Zach said.

Nate grinned. "I couldn't. I wanted to put a ball into them so bad I could taste it."

Ordeal

Father and son laughed, sharing a special moment. Winona took a seat, Evelyn in her arms, and nonchalantly opened the top of her dress so the child could breast-feed.

"What is your secret?" she asked her son.

"Ma?"

"Knowing how your father is, I thought he would be upset for days, growling at everyone like a bear that has just come out of hibernation. How did you cheer him so fast?"

The boy glanced at his father, then did that which showed he stood on the brink of young manhood; he winked and answered, "We had us a man-to-man talk, Ma. Men stuff. Only a man would understand."

"Most interesting," Winona said in her precise English, a fluency stemming from years of hard study and practice. She took great pride in her ability, as did Blue Water Woman, and it was generally conceded among the trapping fraternity that of all their Indian wives, Winona and Blue Water Woman knew English the best, even better than many of the trappers.

The banter ended when Brett Hughes appeared and told Nate, "I'm glad none of you were hurt. I guess I should have said something on Winona's behalf, but I figured you'd rather take care of it."

"I'm in your debt," Nate said, uncomfortable about confessing an obligation to someone he hardly knew.

"No, you're not," Hughes said. "I told you the other night that I'm honored to have McNair and you as my friends, and there's never a debt between friends." Waving, he cheerfully left.

"Is he your friend, Pa?" Zach asked.

"He figures he is."

Winona reverted to her Shoshone tongue. "My people have a saying: Beware a man who shows you his teeth but not his heart."

"Your people, as always, are wise," Nate said in the same language. His inflection and pronunciation were not always right, but he could speak Shoshone better than any other white man. "I wish we had some of them with us. Touch The Clouds, Drags The Rope, and your uncle, to name just a few. Then I would not worry so much about you."

"What is meant to be, will be. The men of my tribe do not worry half as much as you, my husband. You must learn to worry less. It cannot be healthy for you."

Nate smiled. "They don't fret because their womenfolk are always telling them not to."

From out of the forest rode Shakespeare and Chavez, each with several grouse dangling from his saddle. They separated. NcNair studied his wife and friends closely and said as he dismounted, "Something happened while I was gone. What?"

Nate let the wives tell the story. He became curious about a man standing on the west wall of the fort, staring in their direction. Was the man spying on their camp? he wondered. Or simply keeping his eyes peeled for hostiles?

Shakespeare squatted and folded his arms across his knees. "It could be coincidence that those HBC men pestered you," he said to the women. "But I'm not a big believer in coincidence. And from what you tell me, they acted darned peculiar."

"The farther we go, the more peculiar this whole thing becomes," Nate said.

"Bad medicine," Blue Water Woman said.

"Or just bad men," her husband responded.

Young Zach, who rarely got to take part in their discussions and wanted to prove he fit right in, ventured, "There's something I've been wondering about and maybe one of you can set me straight."

"What is it, son?" Nate replied.

"Mr. Porter. He says he's all upset about his daughter who went missing, and he keeps saying how much money he's spending to track her down, and how cost is no object."

"What's your point?"

"I've never seen him look very sad. Mostly mad."

Nate glanced at Shakespeare, who glanced at Blue Water Woman, who in turn glanced at Winona. "Go on," she urged.

"Haven't you noticed?" Zach said. "Mr. Clark and him are supposed to be all upset that Hetty is nowhere to be found. But not once have I seen either of them look as miserable as I know that you, Pa, and you, Ma, would look if I went missing. Mostly, they act angry." The boy paused, his face mature beyond its years. "I might be all wrong, but sometimes I think that maybe Mr. Porter doesn't love his daughter as much as he claims, or he'd be a darned sight more upset more often. Wouldn't he?"

Nate slowly nodded.

"Out of the mouths of babes," Shakespeare said.

"I'm not no baby," Zach scolded. "If my notions are dumb, say so. Don't call me names."

"Your notions aren't dumb," Nate said.

"Really?" Zach swelled with pride.

"Not in the least," Shakespeare said. "And that's what has me asking myself if maybe we made a mistake, if maybe there's more to this so-called expedition than meets the eye."

"And if maybe we're going to live to see it through to the end," Nate said. No one argued, not even his wife.

Chapter Eleven

The Nez Percé had long been friendly to whites. When Lewis and Clark made their historic odyssey, they noted in their journals that the Nez Percé were as helpful as could be.

Which was all the more remarkable, given that the Nez Percé were a powerful tribe who controlled a vast area of the Plateau region and could have resisted the white tide as fiercely as the Blackfeet, had they wanted to. Eventually they did, but by then it was far too late.

Two Humps of the Nez Percé was an honored warrior, a respected chief, and one of those who had long pushed for friendly relations. Not out of any noteworthy kinship of spirit. Rather, Two Humps, and many like him, saw the whites as a limitless source of the material goods the Nez Percé so highly valued.

It had not always been so. Once, the tribe had been like every other in the region, living simple lives in small scattered villages, subsisting as plain fisherfolk who dwelled in unadorned mat-roofed dwellings.

Then came the white invasion. The whites had guns and steel knives, steel traps and fire steels and tinder boxes and axes of superior make and so much more it dazzled the minds of the simple Nez Percé. They couldn't get enough trade goods to suit them, and soon they found themselves unwittingly depending on the whites for many of the things they had once gone without or had made themselves.

To be fair, not all the blame could be placed on the whites. For another factor in the great change that had come over the Nez Percé was their decision to live as did the warlike Plains tribes. They started counting coup. They wore shirts and leggings of buckskin, decorated with beadwork. They forsook their plain lodges for tall buffalo-hide tepees.

In so doing, the Nez Percé were no longer the Nez Percé of old. They were just like the Blackfeet, the Crows, the Shoshones. They were powerful, yes, but they had paid a price for their power: the loss of their simpler life.

Of late there had been grumbling among some that the tribe had erred in cutting ties with the old ways and taking up the new. These tiny voices of protest were smothered by the greater greed. But they did not go unnoticed, and one of those who did notice, much to his own surprise, was Two Humps.

164

Ordeal

For several moons the old chief had been deeply troubled. He knew the old ways well, and when he parted the fabric of time to peer at the life once led by his people, it seemed that they had, indeed, been unwise. They were so caught up in owning horses and *things* that they had lost sight of some of the greater values that had once bonded them as a people.

Two Humps wanted to share his troubled heart with another. But not with his wife, who was perfectly happy with the way they now lived, with all her utensils and parfleches and brightly colored European-made blankets. Certainly not with any of the other prominent warriors who, like him, had been largely responsible for the changes and would laugh at the suggestion that they had done wrong. Nor could he talk to those who were complaining, since they would take his interest as evidence he accepted their argument and use his good name to further widen the rift between those who yearned for the old days and those who did not.

Two Humps was left with no one to talk to until the morning that a commotion in the village drew him outside to see a square-shouldered white man with hair and beard like driven snow and a younger one with the bearing and aspect of a big mountain cat.

Hurrying forward, Two Humps made the sign for friendly greeting and called out, "Wolverine! My friend! My heart sings to see you again!"

Shakespeare McNair gripped the chief by the shoulders and said sincerely in the Nez Percé tongue, "Your heart sings no louder than mine, old friend!" Turning, he indicated Nate and said, "This is another one whom I cherish. They call him Grizzly Killer."

Two Humps regarded the younger trapper. "He has an honest face. And he kills silver-tips. If he is not married, I have a pretty granddaughter who might interest him. She cooks and weaves well, but I hear she snores."

"Grizzly Killer has a wife," Shakespeare said.

"He could have two. Some do."

"Not him."

"It is just as well. I have always been happy with one, myself. Men who want more must be able to close their ears at will."

Nate was scanning the busy village, which reminded him in every respect of those of his adopted people. Laughing children played various games. Women at one spot had deer hides stretched taut on stakes and were scraping off hair and tissue. Elsewhere other women were gossiping gaily while mending a torn buffalo hide. Men worked at making arrows or sharpening knives or other crafts of war.

Horses, of course, were everywhere, as well they should be, since the Nez Percé were noted as the finest horse breeders west of the Mississippi. They had developed a special stock, which some called the Palouse because the animals were bred in the Palouse River region, and others had recently taken to calling the Appaloosa.

Nate had once owned a fine Palouse, a gift from another Nez Percé chief, given after Nate saved the chief's camp from an enemy war party. It had been the finest animal Nate ever owned, and one day he intended to trade for another.

Now, gazing on the idyllic scene, on the abundance of horses and decorated lodges and fine clothes of the inhabitants, Nate remarked, "Your people are some of the happiest I've ever seen, Two Humps. It looks like you have prospered over the years." He spoke English because McNair had informed him the chief spoke a little.

Neither Nate nor Shakespeare understood why a fleeting sadness lined the old warrior's features. "Yes, Grizzly Killer," he said haltingly, "we rich people now." The sadness deepened. "Much rich." He motioned at his lodge and addressed them in his own language. "You would do me honor by smoking a pipe."

"We will be glad to," Shakespeare said. Since he knew the warrior well, he knew Two Humps was greatly aggrieved and was curious to learn why.

The subject had to wait until after they were formally escorted inside and had passed the pipe around. Two Hump's wife, Blanket Woman, brought them pemmican in a bowl. They sat munching for awhile, waiting for their host to speak as etiquette dictated.

When Two Humps did turn to them, he used sign language as a concession to Nate. "It is a sign that you have come when you have, Wolverine. An omen. My spirit has been troubled of late. I have looked for answers and not found them.

167

Now the answer walks into my lodge."

"How can I be an answer when I do not know the question?" Shakespeare signed.

"The question is you. The answer is you," Two Humps responded.

"My friend tries to confuse me," Shakespeare said.

"I speak with a straight tongue." Two Humps lowered his hands a moment. "For many moons now my people have lived by the new ways. Some say this is not right. Some say the old ways are better. I was of two minds. At times I would think the new is best. At other times I would think the old was better."

Shakespeare thought he understood. He spoke in Nez Percé, "People change as they grow, my friend. A young man is ruled by his feelings. A man in his middle years by his thoughts. An old man is ruled by his regrets, unless he has learned to use his thoughts to control his feelings." He paused. "A warrior like you should have no regrets. You have lived a full, long life. Most Nez Percé would give anything to have done as well."

"These things I know," Two Humps said. "The question that has bothered me does not concern the stages of my own life but the course of all my people."

"As Grizzly Killer said, the Nez Percé have prospered. I remember the first time I set eyes on them, when they lived along the river in small, dirty lodges. They have come far."

"At what cost?"

Ordeal

Shakespeare saw into the depths of his friend's tortured soul, and made no answer.

"I have asked myself why many times," Two Humps continued. "Why did we do as we did? Was it only for finer lodges, finer clothes, finer belongings?" He mustered a wan grin. "There was another reason. It was you, and friendly whites like you. We wanted to be as our friends were. That is why you are the answer to my question. That is why I thank you for coming when you have."

Nate had listened in a fruitless effort to get the drift of their talk. He saw his mentor and the chief clasp hands, and was surprised to see a glistening sheen in the old warrior's eyes. Since it was improper for a younger man to speak unless invited to do so by an older warrior, he contented himself with chewing more pemmican.

"I am glad I could help you," Shakespeare said, "although I still do not know quite how I have done it."

"What matters is that you have." Two Humps patted the mountain man's knee. "Now tell me. What has brought you to our country? It must be important. Too many winters have gone by since last you visited."

In barest detail Shakespeare related the journey to date, ending with, "Last night we ate with the chief of the whites at the fort. He told us that at one time there was a small group of settlers on the Bear, but that they went westward four months ago."

"This is so," Two Humps said. "I visited them

twice when we were in the vicinity of the Bear. Most of them were nice and offered me food or drink."

"Do you remember one named—" and here Shakespeare had to resort to English—"Oliver Davin?"

"Sorry, Wolverine. None of them told me their white names. The one I remember best was a beautiful young woman with hair like the sun and eyes like Black Bear Lake. She always had a smile for me."

"Hestia Davin," Shakespeare said.

"What's that?" Nate asked, forgetting himself.

"From the description Porter gave us, Two Humps met his daughter a few times. You'll be glad to know she isn't anything like her pa."

"Does Two Humps know why the settlers left?" Nate asked. "Smythe-Barnes had no idea."

"It was the point men," Two Humps answered when the question was relayed. By point men, he referred to the Hudson's Bay contingent at the fort, a nickname the traders had earned because of the point system used to rate the worth of their trade blankets. "They drove the pretty woman and the others away."

Shakespeare translated for Nate, the two mountain men sharing flinty looks.

Two Humps went on. "I know because I was out hunting with my nephew one time when we saw a line of riders to the south. We went to see who it was, thinking it might be enemies. But it was the pretty woman and her people, leaving. She did not look happy. One of them had learned a little sign. He said the point men would not trade with them, would not sell them goods. He said the point men did not want them here."

Nate involuntarily clenched both brawny fists. He recollected how Smythe-Barnes had played the innocent the night before, remembered the HBC man claiming he'd done all in his power to help the settlers out. It had all been a bald-faced lie.

"Did this man tell you where the pretty woman and the others were going?" Shakespeare asked.

"No, Wolverine. He did not." Two Humps scrutinized the two men. "You will try to find them, will you not?"

"Yes."

"Good. I am going with you."

Shakespeare had been about to make excuses so he could inform Porter of the news. The chief's offer, like a bolt out of the blue, rooted him in place. "You want to come along?"

"I do."

"May I ask why?"

"It has been too long since we rode together. I want to do so one more time before I go to meet my ancestors."

"These people I am with are not my people. I have put myself under the man who leads them. He is chief, not I. He must make the decision."

"Take me to him."

Shakespeare could readily imagine how Porter would react; the man despised Indians. But he was loathe to flat-out refuse his friend's request out of respect for the many grand times they had shared when young men. So he tried another approach. "I have no idea how far we are going, or how long we will be gone."

"It will be like the old days when we went where we wanted, when we wanted," Two Humps recalled fondly.

"We might go through the country of your enemies."

"Since when has an enemy stopped a Nez Percé from doing as he pleased?"

Shakespeare had one last argument, a statement he bit off before making it. You are not as young as you once were, he almost said, and inwardly laughed at his audacity, for neither was he. "If I cannot change your mind, meet us west of the fort when the sun is straight overhead. We leave soon after."

"I will be there."

Nate was amazed when he heard, and made no bones about it as they walked back. "Have you gone plumb crazy? You know how Porter feels about Indians. The rivermen hate them even more. They're likely to try and make wolf meat of your friend."

"They'll try."

"I wouldn't do it if he was someone I'd ridden the mountains with."

"Yes, you would."

"What makes you so sure?"

"Because we think alike. We know that true friends come few and far between. They're as rare as hen's teeth, more valuable than diamonds. A person can go a lifetime and not have more than two or three deep friendships." Shakespeare hooked a thumb in his belt. "Two Humps and I were like peas in a pod once. I'd do anything for him."

"In that case, you can count on me to back you."

The Nez Percé village lay close to the east wall of the HBC outpost. As the two trappers rounded the southeast corner, they beheld Cyrus Porter in a heated exchange with Smythe-Barnes. Behind Porter stood Clark, Hughes, and Chavez. Behind the HBC man were the ruffians who had given Winona a hard time.

Porter was practically raving. Livid, gesturing angrily, his bellows could have been heard in Canada. "—formal protest with my government when I return! You'll learn that you can't treat American citizens this way and get away with it!"

"I am in charge," Smythe-Barnes sniffed, "and I can do as I damn well please! If I don't care to sell goods to Americans, that is my prerogative."

No one, as yet, had noticed the mountain men. Shakespeare startled everyone by stepping up to Smythe-Barnes and giving the Englishman a shove that sent him tottering into the ruffians.

"McNair!" cried one, and went for his flint-lock.

Instantly there was a loud metallic click. A pistol had blossomed in Chavez's hand as if out of thin air. "I would not do that were I you, *señor*," he warned, "or you will have a hole in your head the size of a walnut."

The Hudson's Bay men froze, Smythe-Barnes in the act of rising, his knees half bent. "Now hold on, Mex!" he said. "We don't want any killing!"

Cyrus Porter turned to McNair. "This son of a bitch has been playing us for fools! When Hughes went to buy supplies yesterday, he was told the sutler was too busy with the Nez Percé and to come back today. They assured him they had plenty of goods on hand and could fill our order." Porter glared at Smythe-Barnes. "But when we showed up, he told us they had changed their minds and had no intention of selling us a damn thing!"

"He did the same to your daughter and those settlers," Shakespeare revealed.

Porter reacted as if struck. "How do you know?"

"I know," was all Shakespeare would say. To identify Two Humps by name might reap dire consequences for the Nez Percé. "My guess is that when the settlers first showed, Smythe-Barnes acted as if he was their friend, led them to believe they could buy all the supplies they needed. That's why they settled on the Bear instead of going on to the Oregon Country. They figured they could get everything they needed right here."

Smythe-Barnes had straightened, his expression defiant. "You're making idle conjecture," he snapped.

"Am I?" Shakespeare sparred. "I've been wondering why a bunch of greenhorns set down roots in the middle of nowhere. I knew they had to have a good reason. And they did. They believed they could get everything they needed for their homesteads from your post. They thought they could trust you, that you were a godsend. Little did they know that you were deceiving them."

"You have no proof," Smythe-Barnes said.

Shakespeare seemed not to hear. "I'm curious. How did you do it? Did you wait until their guide had left and then showed them your true colors, thinking they would have to go on back to the States without someone to show them the way to the Oregon Country? And what happened to their wagons and household goods? They didn't take them, because I know for a fact they went westward on horseback."

"I refuse to dignify your accusation with an answer," the HBC man said.

Porter was distraught. He appeared about to hurl himself at the head of the trading post. "In God's name, why would you do such a thing? There were women in that party! How could you have let them go on without a seasoned guide?"

Smythe-Barnes smoothed his jacket, saying nothing.

"I can tell you," Shakespeare offered. "He did it because he's British and the settlers were Americans."

"So?" Porter said.

"So sooner or later the two governments will get around to working out who gets the Oregon Country. And the one who has the most settlers living there will have the better claim."

Shock made Porter's mouth drop. "Is that the truth?" he demanded of the Englishman. "You want to discourage Americans from settling there?"

Smythe-Barnes squared his shoulders. "I don't have to answer any of your questions. And I'll thank you to leave the vicinity of my fort while you still can."

"You pompous ass!" Porter roared. Lunging, he seized Smythe-Barnes by the front of the shirt. "Thanks to you my daughter might be dead!"

"I had my bloody orders!" Smythe-Barnes roared back.

It was Nate who pried the two apart before they came to blows. He no sooner held Porter at arm's length than all the fight drained out of the New Englander and Porter slumped dejectedly.

"My poor, poor girl," he mourned.

"Don't chalk her off yet," Shakespeare said. "With a little luck they might have made it by their lonesome. There's plenty of game, so they wouldn't have starved if any of them could shoot half straight. And water wouldn't be a problem once they reached the Columbia."

Adam Clark took hold of Porter's arm and gave it a shake. "Did you hear him? Cheer up, Cy. At least we know she was alive when she left here, which is more than we knew when we left St. Louis."

Porter nodded dully, repeating, "My poor, sweet Hetty."

"Take him to camp," Nate advised Clark, and as the shattered father and the hopeful suitor departed, he wheeled on Smythe-Barnes and the ruffians. "The more I hear, the more I suspect that what you did to my wife was done on purpose. If I can ever prove it, I'll be back, gents. And I'll come loaded for bear."

At a gesture from the indignant Smythe-Barnes, the Hudson's Bay men marched into Fort Hall. The gate slammed shut behind them, and from within wafted snide laughter.

"For two cents I'd burn the place to the ground," Shakespeare muttered.

"Their government would be outraged. The British might label it as an act of war," Hughes said, alarmed. "Washington would call for an official inquiry, and we all could find ourselves facing charges."

"It was just wishful thinking," Shakespeare pacified him, then changed the subject. "How bad is our supply situation?"

"We're very low on flour, almost as low on salt. And Mr. Porter ran out of oats for his horse. He insists it must have a portion daily."

"We can make do without bread and cakes. I've lived on a strict meat diet for weeks at a time with no problem. The salt won't be missed after awhile. As for the horse, it can eat grass like the rest."

"I suppose we can get by," Porter agreed.

Shakespeare squinted at the sun. "We have two hours to pack up. So let's get cracking."

Porter had secluded himself in his tent. Shakespeare oversaw their preparations to leave, and he was directing a pair of rivermen in the loading

David Thompson

of pack horses when someone hailed him from a corner of the fort. Looking up, he recognized Pearson, the sentry he had spoken to upon their arrival.

"I've got to make this short," the man said when Shakespeare went over. "Smythe-Barnes would have my head if he knew I was talking to you." Pearson nervously glanced at the rampart. "I heard about what happened, and I'm mad. It wasn't right. Not all of us who work for HBC agree with company policy. If I was in charge and not that horse's ass, Americans could buy whatever they wanted."

"I'm grateful for your honesty."

"There's more," Pearson said, lowering his voice. "I've heard you're hunting for those settlers from Bear River. One of them mentioned that they were headed for the Willamette Valley. Hope that helps you."

"It does," Shakespeare said, since it eliminated California and saved them a lot of searching. "You were here when they left. Do you know why they went on horseback instead of in their wagons?"

"Sure. They sold them to Smythe-Barnes, and the oxen that pulled them," Pearson disclosed. "He swindled those pilgrims good, he did, and made a hefty profit."

"How?"

"It was like this." Pearson paused. "When they first arrived, he sold them things. A few goods here and there. Then, after Fitzpatrick had gone and they were about to begin building their cabins, Smythe-Barnes told them they weren't welcome at the fort anymore. It left them stranded and short on supplies."

"The bastard," Shakespeare said.

"They protested, but there was nothing they could do." Pearson moved close to the wall. "They claimed they wanted to go back to the States, but they didn't think they could manage the wagons by themselves, since none of them knew the route well enough to find their way back again. Smythe-Barnes offered them a way out. He bought the wagons and their household goods at pennies on the dollar, then turned around and offered the horses and a few piddling supplies at twice the going rate."

"I'm surprised they took him up on the offer. They must have known he was playing them for fools."

"They knew, but they had no choice. The Blackfeet were on the prowl. Raven Beak's bunch. Those greenhorns had to move on or be wiped out." The Hudson's Bay man chuckled. "But they had the last laugh. When they'd bought their horses, they headed west, not east. Smythe-Barnes was fit to be tied."

All the pieces to the puzzle fit.

Pearson peeked around the corner. "I'd best be going before I'm spotted. But there's one last thing you should know."

"What?"

"One of the men in your party is a spy working for the American government."

Impressed by the HBC man's sincerity, Shakespeare had been willing to accept everything, until this. "What bill of goods are you trying to sell me? We're out to find a missing woman, nothing more."

"So you think, McNair," Pearson said. "But I overheard Smythe-Barnes and Dinkus talking. They never mentioned a name, but they're certain one of the men with you was sent to spy on British operations in the Oregon Country." He took a step. "Now I must be off. If you ever make it back this way, we'll share that drink."

"I'm in your debt," Shakespeare said absently. He was greatly troubled by the news, for it changed everything.

Pearson touched his hat. "Good luck, mate. I reckon you'll be needing lots of it before too long."

Chapter Twelve

The expedition left Fort Hall without further incident. As they were about to leave, Two Humps arrived, resplendent in his best beaded buckskins, a pair of parfleches hung over the back of his Appaloosa.

Shakespeare expected a bitter argument when he approached Cyrus Porter. "I'm sorry to bother you," he said, "but a friend of mine wants to come along with us, and I told him he could if it's all right with you."

Porter didn't so much as glance up. He was seated on a stump, his elbows on his knees, his chin in his hands. His face was a study in human misery. "Whatever you want," he said forlornly.

It was plain to Shakespeare that all of Porter's pent-up feelings were finally being let out. He was glad to see it, for it proved Porter did care about his daughter. "We'll find Hestia," he pledged. "In a few more months you'll be together again."

"Makes you wonder, doesn't it, McNair?" Porter said, more to himself than to the trapper.

"What does?"

"Why do we bother? We raise them, lavish them with everything money can buy. We make great plans for their future, and we do everything in our power to insure they will succeed." Porter's head drooped lower. "Then they go and run off with a nobody the first chance they get. Why did I bother all those years? Why is she putting me through this nightmare?"

Shakespeare held his peace and left. It occurred to him that a selfish disposition and a shallow brain went well together. The more he learned about the father, the more he pitied the daughter. It wasn't hard to see why she had gone off on her own. There were more ways to smother a person than most realized.

The expedition stuck to the Snake River for the next stage of the journey. The nights were cool, the days increasingly hot. A wide plain bordered the river on both sides to a distance of 20 to 40 miles, and here game was scarce. Nate, often accompanied by Two Humps and Chavez, had to range farther and farther afield to find any.

Cyrus Porter gradually recovered from the doldrums. On the third day after leaving Fort Hall, he rode up to McNair and stated bluntly, "Why the hell did you bring an Indian along?"

"You gave your permission."

Ordeal

"You said it was a friend. I assumed he was white."

"Two Humps *is* my friend." Shakespeare looked at him. "And you can't blame me for the conclusions you jump to." He clucked at his horse. "Before you get to acting contrary, keep in mind that if Two Humps can't tag along, this old coon won't be going another step."

"This is blackmail."

"Call it what you like. What's it to be?"

Porter puffed out his cheeks like an irate chipmunk, then exhaled so loudly his horse looked back to see what was making so much noise. "Since you leave me no choice, your Indian friend can stay. But he had better not cause us any trouble along the way."

"He won't," Shakespeare said, and couldn't resist having some fun by saying, "I just hope you don't make a liar out of me by not acting your age when he's around."

"What on earth are you talking about?"

"I told him you're the chief of our little caravan. To an Indian, a chief is someone special. Most warriors have to earn the title by proving their courage in battle and showing they care for their people by helping the sick and the poor." Shakespeare skirted a bush. "Think you would qualify?"

"For your information, mister, I've given more money to charitable causes than you've made in your whole life," Porter stated. "As for my courage, I stood my ground when we were surrounded by Blackfeet, didn't I?"

"We were trapped, but I won't quibble. Just do me a favor and pretend you're half as noble as Two Humps and I'll be grateful."

"Sometimes, Mr. McNair, you try my patience," Porter said, and trotted toward Adam Clark.

Grinning, Shakespeare scanned the southern horizon, then gazed at the mountains rearing to the northwest. They had to reach those mountains swiftly. In the middle of the plain they were too exposed. He hadn't warned the others yet, but they had new dangers to face now that they had left Blackfoot country behind. Dangers every whit as deadly. He thought of Nate and the other two, off hunting again, and hoped they'd make it back safely.

Unknown to McNair, three miles to the south Nate King led Chavez and Two Humps into a narrow, arid valley in search of game. They had found deer sign earlier. The tracks had brought them to where they now sat staring in astonishment at other prints that bisected those of the buck and four does.

"*Estrano*," Chavez said. "Very strange, *señor*. What do you make of them?"

"They weren't kids," Nate answered, dismounting. "The feet are too big."

What made the new tracks so intriguing was that whoever made them had been barefoot. The prints overlapped because those responsible had been walking in single file, but Nate was able to distinguish seven different sets. He looked at the Nez Percé and signed, "Who are they?"

Ordeal

"Earth eaters," Two Humps signed, his face screwed in contempt.

Nate had heard of them. Diggers, the trappers called them. A tribe as different from the Nez Percé and the Shoshone as night from day. Those who had encountered the Diggers claimed they were little better than animals, a wild, savage people given to running around naked and living off the land as best as their wits allowed. They were as poor as dirt but as crafty as wolves. And while they shunned well-armed parties of whites, they were not averse to springing an ambush if they thought they could get away with it.

"We must tell Shakespeare," Nate proposed, moving to his stallion. To his understanding, the Diggers never settled in one spot for long. They were wanderers by nature, roaming an extensive area throughout the year, and always traveling in large packs. Where one was found, usually many more were nearby.

"*Señor!*" Chavez exclaimed, pointing.

Nate turned. The tracks crossed to a steep hill and climbed to the crest. Silhouetted against the pale blue sky were seven smallish, dark figures, all armed with bows and arrows.

Two Humps hefted his lance. The Nez Percé had no fondness for the Earth Eaters, with whom they had been fighting since time out of mind. He was more than willing to give the scrawny ones a fight if they wanted one.

The figures descended partway. The stoutest of them handed his bow to a fellow and walked slowly into the valley. Judging from his posture, he was ready to bolt at the first inkling of a threat to his life. He came within 20 feet and regarded them through eyes the color of coal.

Nate clasped his hands in front of his body, with the back of his left hand pointing down, to demonstrate they came in peace. He studied the Digger, a short, hairy specimen who wore a loincloth of rabbit skin. When the warrior didn't react, he repeated the sign language.

The Digger raised his hand. "Question. You three alone?" he asked.

"No," Nate answered. "We are with a big party of white men. A big party," he emphasized.

Brow knitting, the Digger gazed past them toward the plain. "I see no one else," he signed.

"They are out there," Nate insisted, and immediately wanted to kick himself for stupidly telling the Digger where to find the expedition. To persuade the Digger to leave well enough alone, he added, "You would do well to stay away from them. They have many rifles that shoot far."

"Our bows shoot far," the Digger signed. "And we have many of them."

There was a challenge in the hairy warrior's tone that Nate disliked. "How many of you are there?" he asked, wanting an idea of their numbers.

"Many," was all the Digger signed. He glanced at the Nez Percé, grunted like a wild boar, then turned and jogged off.

Chavez had a hand on one of his dueling pistols. "What was that all about, Señor King?"

"He was taking our measure," Nate said,

swinging into the saddle. He rode down the valley, glancing over a shoulder once to see the Diggers disappear over the crest. They were fetching more warriors. Nate felt it in his bones. He also felt trouble loomed.

The three miles to the Snake were made at a gallop. Their horses lathered with sweat, they drew rein at the head of the column where McNair rode with Porter and Clark.

"Tarnation," Shakespeare said. "Was the Devil himself after you, or were you trying to ruin three good horses?" He was cheerful, but he suspected the truth and made no comment until Nate was done. "It was dumb luck and can't be helped. They call themselves the Shoshokos. I've had dealings with them before. In their own way they're as bad as Apaches. We have to find a place we can defend."

Which wasn't easy to do in the middle of a high plateau plain. There were gullies and gorges galore, but none were suitable. Most had no outlet, or were too steep, or too narrow. The sun sank lower and lower to the west, their shadows rippling over the ground in their wake.

"I was afraid of this," Shakespeare said. "We'll have to camp in the open and pray for the best."

Just as the mountain man spoke, to the northwest reared a knoll with a flat top. Twenty feet high, sheer on three sides, it was as likely a spot as they were going to find. The horses were herded into the center and contained within a rope corral. Spare guns were passed out, extra ammunition to those who wanted it.

No fires were lit at Shakespeare's orders, a wasted precaution, as it turned out. Supplies and saddles were stacked at the top of the slope. Behind these the men waited, except for rivermen posted at intervals along the rim.

Nate found it hard to sleep. Frequently he checked on his family, who slept fitfully nearby. The distant wail of wolves, the wavering yip of coyotes, the snarls of painters, they all took on new, ominous meaning. Toward the middle of the night, as he fought off a wave of drowsiness, yet another coyote added its cry to the bestial chorus, and he heard Shakespeare stir beside him.

"They're coming."

"That was one?"

"Be my guess."

"Sounded like an ordinary coyote to me," Nate said.

"Whose ears are you going to trust? Yours, which are still lined with peach fuzz? Or mine, as sharp as an owl's and the envy of Indians everywhere?"

Nate would have laughed had the darkness not come alive with furtive sounds; rustling, stealthy padding, and faint scuffling. He jabbed Chavez with an elbow and the tracker woke up. "We have company."

The word passed along the makeshift wall. Flintlocks were readied, pistols laid out within easy reach.

Porter and Clark were on McNair's right. They made the most noise, the younger man coughing loudly, the older announcing when no announcement was needed, "Hold your fire, men, until we give the signal."

Shakespeare pivoted. "Yell a little louder, why don't you? There must be someone down to Mexico who didn't hear you."

Presently the horses set to nickering and stomping their hooves, as they did when they smelled something they didn't like. Shakespeare snapped his fingers, said "Damn me for an idiot!" and dashed off toward the rope corral. "Follow me, Nate."

Nate did automatically. He didn't know what they were doing, but long ago he'd learned to trust his mentor implicitly. It never occurred to him to waste time asking questions that would shortly be answered anyway. They ran to a point northwest of the corral.

The horses were acting frightened, milling about with nostrils flaring, ears pricked.

"Those crafty coons," Shakespeare said.

"Who?"

"The Shoshokos. They're trying to stampede the herd. Probably have themselves a painter skin or grizzly hide, and one of them is upwind waving it around so the wind carries it to our stock."

Nate thought of the consequences should the Indians succeed. The horses would burst through the rope and down the slope, trampling anything and everything in their path, which would include the barrier and all those lined up along it who didn't get out of the way in time. "What can we do?"

"Fight fire with fire."

"How?"

"Live and learn, Horatio," Shakespeare said. Bending, he picked up handfuls of loose dirt and tossed them into the air. Again and again he did the same. The dirt fell just outside the rope, but puffs of dust were blown among the horses by the stiff breeze.

Nate comprehended, and snickered. The scent of the dust would deaden the smell of the painter or grizzly. He joined in, throwing handful after handful, covering 20 yards northward and then reversing and going southward again. It took a while, but the horses quieted.

"You're a genius," Nate said.

"Being savvy is a matter of how old you are," Shakespeare responded. "The longer a man lives, the more experience he has under his belt. A hos my age, why, I've enough experience to fill a book as big as the works of old William S."

"I'll remember this trick," Nate said.

Before returning to the others they made a circuit of the horses, checking on the four rivermen posted around the perimeter. None reported any movement or sounds.

Back at the barricade, everyone was awake. Winona and Blue Water Woman were passing out jerky to the men. Nate accepted a piece from his wife and sat down. Zach came and squatted between him and Chavez.

"When will they attack, Pa?"

"They might not," Nate said. "Once they realize how many of us there are and how many guns we

190

have, maybe they'll turn tail and make themselves scarce."

"You don't really believe that, do you?" Zach asked. A while back he had learned that sometimes his folks told him things that weren't necessarily so, just to calm his fears.

"No," Nate admitted without hesitation. He figured that if his son was old enough to ask such questions, then the boy was old enough to be told the truth. "I've heard tell the Diggers aren't very fond of white men."

Shakespeare, overhearing, added, "They're not. Haven't been since Joe Walker trekked to California a few years ago. He had about sixty men with him, as I recollect, and they stumbled on some Shoshokos. Before long there were eight or nine hundred dogging his heels. He tried to bluff his way out, and when that didn't work, he had his men charge."

"Gosh!" Zach said. "They must have been awful brave to go up against so many warriors."

"When your back is to the wall, son, you'd be surprised how brave you can be," Shakespeare said. "But yes, they were a courageous bunch, and they licked those Shoshokos fair and square. Killed over thirty, if memory serves." He bit off some jerky and talked with his mouth crammed. "Course, you have to remember that few of the Shoshokos knew what a gun was. All that noise and smoke scared them something terrible."

"Which means these won't be so easy to frighten off," Zach inferred.

"That's about the size of it, I'm afraid."

An hour went by. Two. Nate peered into the darkness so intently his eyes hurt, but he saw no sign of the Diggers. As the night waned and no attack came, he tried telling himself the Indians were gone and the expedition could continue on at first light.

Then pale pink streaks brightened the eastern horizon, streaks that became bands, the bands spreading until the east half of the sky glowed bright enough to reveal the knoll and the adjoining plain.

"*Mon Dieu!*" LeBeau blurted out.

Nate heard similar oaths up and down the line. He would have swore himself had his son not been at his elbow.

"What are we going to do, Pa?" Zach asked.

The knoll was surrounded by Shoshokos. Under cover of darkness they had snuck within bow range and formed a gigantic ring. There were over 200, all kneeling, all armed with bows and arrows. Most were hairy and had small frames. About half wore loincloths; the rest were naked. They stared at the top of the knoll, showing no hostility but no friendliness either.

"We're dead men," Adam Clark said.

"Shut your mouth," Shakespeare chided, glancing at Zach. "So long as we're breathing we have a chance."

"Against that many?" Clark stubbornly said. "Old man, living in the wild so long has scrambled your thinking. All those savages have to do is fire a few flights of arrows, and they'll make pincushions out of all of us."

Ordeal

Shakespeare almost lost his temper. When he was younger he had done so regularly. But he rarely did so anymore, which was fortunate for Clark or he would have bashed the greenhorn in the head with his rifle stock. "Figured that out all by yourself, did you?" he responded. "Maybe it's also occurred to you that if they wanted us dead, we'd already be pincushions. They must want something from us."

"Look," Nate said as one of the Diggers stood and advanced. "It's the same one I talked to yesterday."

The grimy Shoshoko held his arms out from his sides to show he was unarmed. Ten feet from the stacked supplies, he halted and employed sign language. "I am Coyote's Brother of the Shoshokos. I would talk to your chief."

Shakespeare nodded at Nate. "You handle it. Porter doesn't speak sign and wouldn't know what to say if he did."

"The hell I don't," Porter said. "I'd order the heathens to disperse or else."

"Or else they wipe us out?" Shakespeare shook his head. "No-sir-reee. Let us take care of the parlay. We can talk to them on their own terms."

Nate handed his Hawken to his son and rose. "I am Grizzly Killer. Why have your people crept up on us during the night? Why do you block our way?"

Coyote's Brother ignored the questions and posed one of his own. "Are you the chief? Why did you not say so before? Was the white man afraid to say who he is?"

David Thompson

"Does a chief have to tell everyone he meets?" Nate said. "Now you know. So answer me. What do your people want?"

The Shoshoko resented being addressed like a misbehaving child. "We must speak as equals. As friends."

"First you must prove you are friendly. Tell your warriors to go the distance two arrows can fly and stand in the open where we can see them."

"We will later. Now you and I will talk." Coyote's Brother stood on tiptoe to see beyond the barrier. "Your people are very rich. My people are very poor. We would like to trade with you."

"What do you want?"

"One hundred guns. Fifty knives. And half of your horses." The demand was uttered calmly, without malice.

"My fellow chief jokes with me," Nate replied. "He knows we cannot trade so much. Say again, and this time say what is in your heart."

"That is in my heart."

"Then your own heart jokes with you. Would you give up one hundred bows, fifty knives, and half of your horses to anyone who asked for them?"

"We are willing to give you something of equal value."

Nate caught himself before he laughed aloud. "You have just said your people are poor. What could you have to trade that we would want?"

A sly smile curled the Shoshoko's face. His next statement was perplexing in the extreme. "There are women with you."

Ordeal

Neither Winona nor Blue Water Woman had shown themselves. Nate couldn't see how the Digger knew, unless they had spied on the expedition the afternoon before. He didn't answer, waiting to see where the palaver would lead.

"Do not think to deny it," Coyote's Brother signed. "We know. We can smell them." His smile widened and he sniffed loudly. "They are not white."

"Your scouts saw them," Nate said gruffly, irritated by the game the hairy man played. "One is my wife, one the wife of another beaver man." An appalling idea hit him. "And they are not for trade. Not now, not ever."

Now it was the Shoshoko's turn to look as if he was about to split a gut. "We have more than enough women of our own. We do not want yours." He idly rubbed his hard belly. "But perhaps you would like another?"

"I am content with the one wife I have."

"The woman we want to trade is special."

"In what way?"

The warrior's hands stabbed the air. "She is special because she is white."

Chapter Thirteen

For Indians to take white women captive was not uncommon. As more and more greenhorns headed for the Promised Land, more and more encountered hostile tribes and either paid with their lives or were adopted. Women and children, at any rate. Men were usually killed outright, suffering the most devious torture imaginable.

As yet, however, the number of women going west was relatively low. Whenever one was captured, it soon became common knowledge, the word spreading from fort to fort, from camp fire to camp fire, so that all mountaineers would be on the lookout for her.

There had been no reports of missing white women in months. No one at Fort Hall had mentioned a recent abduction, and despite the ill will between the British and the Americans, the HBC men would have made a point of letting the Porter/Clark expedition know.

So it was that Nate King greeted the Shoshoko chief's claim with skepticism. "You have taken one of our women?" he signed. "Why have we not heard of it?"

"You are the first white man we have told."

"Bring her, that we may see for ourselves."

"We will," Coyote's Brother signed, "but first we want to know what you will give for her. We want one hundred rifles, fifty knives, and half your horses."

The demand had come full circle. Nate suspected a trick, but rather than brand the warrior a blatant liar, he signed, "Would you trade for something, sight unseen? No. You would ask to see what you were trading for to be sure it is worth what you would pay. You must let us see this woman, or we cannot make you an offer."

"You will want to trade much for her. She is very beautiful."

Nate signed, "If that is so, why do you want to part with her? Beautiful women are cherished by all tribes. Are the Shoshokos so different that they do not like beauty?"

"She is very beautiful by white standards," Coyote's Brother amended. "She is not so beautiful by ours."

"Explain."

The warrior showed uncertainty for the first time. He bit his lower lip, looked back at the ring of watching Diggers, and seemed to derive courage from their presence. "Our people have dark hair and dark skin. Our women have dark hair and dark skin. This is as it should be, as it has always been. We are happy, and it brings us good medicine."

An inkling of the point the Digger was trying to make caused Nate to stiffen.

"Some white women have dark hair, like ours. But all white women have pale skin, which shows they do not have good health and explains why most are so weak and such poor walkers. They are bad medicine." Coyote's Brother paused. "It is worse medicine when they have pale skin and pale hair."

"Pale hair?"

"Hair the color of the sun. The woman we want to trade has hair this color."

"And her eyes?" Nate asked. "What color are they?"

"Like a lake. A deep lake."

There was a sharp intake of breath behind Nate. He guessed it was McNair, and signed, "Has she told you her name? Can you say it?"

"We call her Good For Nothing, since all she does is sit and cry. We waste food feeding her. She is a burden to our tribe and we want to get rid of her."

Nate pretended to ponder a bit. He knew he must not appear too eager to trade, or the Diggers would hold out for the full price being asked and complicate the trade immensely. "I must talk with my people. We will decide if we want this woman. If she is bad medicine for you, she might be bad medicine for us."

Ordeal

"She is white," the warrior reiterated. "One of your own. She must know how to please white men."

"We will see," Nate signed. Turning his back to the Shoshoko, he slid over the wall of supplies and hunkered next to McNair. "You saw. You know who it is."

"Can't be anyone else," Shakespeare agreed.

Cyrus Porter was listening. "Can't be whom? What was that all about, Mr. McNair? What do those heathens want of us?"

"They want to trade for a captive." Nate paused, dreading how the wealthy Hartforder would take the news. "They have a white woman in their clutches."

"Good Lord!" Porter declared. "Those fiends! Of course we'll do all in our power to rescue the poor woman. Who could she be?"

"Your daughter, would be my guess," Nate said.

Dumbfounded, Porter's lips worked like those of a fish stranded out of water. For a full 15 seconds he sat thus. Then his stupefied look gave way to a mask of sheer rage, and he grabbed his rifle and went to push to his feet.

"No!" Shakespeare cried. He was closest; he looped both arms around Porter's shoulders and held him down. "You mustn't let on that you know her, or the Shoshokos will up their price!"

"Let me go, damn it!" Porter fumed. He was younger than McNair by many years and heavier of build, but he could no more budge the mountain man than he could a mountain. "They'll turn her over to us right this minute or they'll all pay, and pay dearly!"

"You're not thinking straight," Shakespeare cautioned. "Rile them now and you'll only succeed in getting all of us killed. You have to be patient and let Nate and me deal with them on their own terms."

"Like hell!" This came from Adam Clark, not Porter. The young dandy had gaped on hearing the news. Now he, too, snatched his rifle and would have risen had another rifle not been shoved in his face.

"I won't let you get us all killed," Nate stated crisply. "LeBeau, take Mr. Clark's gun from him until he's cooled down some."

The riverman stepped forward, bent low so the Diggers couldn't see him, and reached for the Hall's. Clark held on, eyeing him defiantly. "Tell me, *monsieur*. What good will we do her if we are all dead?"

Clark looked helplessly around for support, but no one came to his defense. Scowling, he let his fingers go limp and the rifle was taken.

LeBeau chuckled. "And they say those of us with French blood in our veins are hotheaded!" He took a post beside Chavez. "It is like the kettle calling the pot black, *non?*"

Nate grasped the furious father's rifle and gave it to Chavez. "I'll do the best I can to get her back quickly," he told Porter. "But you have to remember who we're dealing with. One wrong gesture, any little mistake, could get this woman killed. The Diggers have no use for her. Their chief has said as much. It's probably lucky for her we came along when we did, or they might have killed her before long. We have to be mighty careful."

"And we don't know for sure that it is Hestia," Shakespeare threw in. "The description fits, but it could be someone else. We have to be patient until they bring her here."

"All right! All right!" Porter growled. "I won't make a scene. Do what you have to."

Nate glanced at Winona, who smiled encouragement, and straightened. Coyote's Brother hadn't moved, and from the diamond pinpoints of curiosity lighting his eyes, it was apparent he had heard everything. Nate climbed over and signed, "We have talked your offer over."

"I do not know your tongue, but I heard some of you argue. I can guess why. Your people want the woman but they are not willing to give us what we want."

"You took our words wrongly, Indian," Nate signed, and felt his stomach flutter as he tried his bluff. "We argued, yes. But the reason is that only one of us wants this woman. You keep her and do as you want with her."

The Shoshoko couldn't hide his surprise. Murmuring broke out among the warriors below, who could see the exchange clearly thanks to the rising sun. "Only one of you cares what happens to this pretty woman?" Coyote's Brother signed. "A woman of your own kind?"

"None of us knows her," Nate signed. "What is she to us?"

"If a Shoshoko woman were taken, we would do all in our power to get her back."

"We are not Shoshokos. Our ways our different from yours." Nate hoped his features didn't betray any of the anxiety he felt. He was gambling the woman's life on the Diggers' gullibility.

"So you will not give us anything for her?"

"The man who wants her does not have much to give. He can spare one knife, one axe, one fire steel, and a red blanket. I told him you wanted much more and not to waste your time making an offer."

"Bring this man out so I may speak to him."

"He does not know sign."

Coyote's Brother stared over the boxes at the horses a moment. "I must talk to my people." Wheeling, he hurried down. The Diggers rose, breaking ranks to cluster around him. A dozen voices spoke at once.

Nate walked to a stack of small crates and leaned on them. On the other side crouched Zach. He winked at his son, then said to Porter, "I made them an offer. They're debating whether to accept."

"How much did you say we would trade?" Porter asked.

"A fair amount of goods," Nate fibbed.

"Fair, hell! Tell the bastards we'll give them anything they want. Our horses? They can take them all. Our supplies? They can take everything. Guns? We'll give them however many they want. All that's important is having Hetty safely in my arms again."

Ordeal

Of those who knew sign—McNair, Winona, Zach, Blue Water Woman, and Two Humps—not one told Porter the truth. All of them knew what was at stake, and all of them appreciated the deception Nate was trying to pull off.

The Nez Percé did say, though, in his halting English, "We make mistake. We maybe kill many Earth Eaters. Show them who better warriors."

Nate figured the Shoshokos would spend a long time discussing what to do. He was wrong. Within minutes Coyote's Brother came back, and the first words he signed sent a tiny shiver down Nate's spine.

"We think you lie, white man. We think you do care about this white woman." The Digger pointed at the sun. "When it is there," he pointed at where the sun would be about two in the afternoon, "the woman will be here, and then we will see if you speak the truth."

Nate's bluff had been called. Either he held firm, in which case he wouldn't give a torn plew for the woman's chances, or he showed weakness and gave the Shoshokos the edge they needed. "We are on our way to the big water. We cannot waste half a day waiting for you to bring her."

Coyote's Brother signed, "There are many of us and few of you. I think you will stay until the woman is brought."

"We have many rifles," Nate responded. "So I think we will go when we please. And if your people try to stop us, your women will shake the stars with their wailing tonight." He paused, as if having an idea. "Unless you would agree to a plan that will satisfy us both."

"What plan?" the warrior asked with evident distrust.

"Can you ride a horse?"

"The Shoshokos can do anything whites do."

"Good. Then perhaps you would take some of us to your village to see this woman. On horseback we would get there and back much faster."

If Nate harbored any lingering doubts about the intentions of the Diggers, they were dispelled when Coyote's Brother grinned like a bobcat about to pounce on a quail.

"How many of you would go?" the warrior asked.

"Four," Nate said, thinking fast. "We will lend you a horse to use."

"I must speak to my people."

Nate swung around and found Shakespeare upright and staring at him in amusement. "What's tickled you?"

"Though this be madness, yet there is method in it," McNair quoted with gusto. "I see through your scheme, and except for one small miscalculation, I think it might work."

"What did I do wrong?"

"Not a thing. Weren't you listening?" Shakespeare stared at the buzzing Diggers before elaborating. "I expect you're counting on me to go along, but I have to stay with the greenhorns to get them ready. You can see that it has to be one of us, can't you?"

"I can," Nate said, chagrined he hadn't thought of it himself. "So I'll just take Chavez and LeBeau."

"And Two Humps, in case the plan falls through. He knows the country better than I do."

"And Two Humps," Nate agreed. He faced the tracker and the head of the rivermen. "I've tricked the Digger chief into taking me to his village to see the white woman. What he doesn't know is that I have no intention of trading for her. I'm going to steal her back right out from under his nose. But I can't do it alone. I need two good men willing to give their lives if need be to save this woman. And I can't think of two better men anywhere than the two of you."

Chavez lowered his head, his sombrero hiding his eyes. "I am flattered, *señor*," he said, suddenly hoarse. "I will come. A pretty *señorita* is always worth dying for."

"True, my friend," LeBeau said. "Many times in St. Louis I thought I would." He tweaked his mustache. "Count me in."

Nate looked at the Nez Percé. The old chief simply nodded once.

"Now just a damned minute!" Cyrus Porter barked. "This woman might be my daughter. I can't let you put her life in peril. What if your plan doesn't work? What if these savages turn on you?"

"My sentiments exactly," Adam Clark bristled. "None of you knows sweet Hetty, so you don't really care if she lives or dies, but I, on the other hand—"

He got no further. Nate reached over, grabbed him by the throat, and yanked him nose to nose. "For hundreds of miles I've had to listen to you flap your gums, mister, and I'm mighty tired of hearing you whine. You're a flash in the pan who doesn't have the sense to know when others are doing him a favor. The only chance you have of seeing Hetty Davin again is if we're able to pull this off." Disgusted, Nate shoved.

Clark landed hard on his buttocks. He turned beet red and clenched his fists as if about to spring. Instead, like a sail going limp from lack of wind, he sagged and rested his forehead on a saddle. "I hate this wilderness and everyone in it," he sniveled.

"Watch your back," Shakespeare suddenly said.

Coyote's Brother was returning, a strut in his walk. Showing teeth, he signed, "I agree, Grizzly Killer. I will take you to see this white woman."

Horses were swiftly produced. The Shoshoko acted disturbed on learning that the Nez Percé was going but didn't protest.

Nate hated leaving his family on that knoll, surrounded by hundreds of enemies, with no guarantee he would ever set eyes on them again. He fought an impulse to keep looking back and focused on the sweaty back of Coyote's Brother in front of him. The Digger rode as if drunk, flopping and sliding back and forth, his elbows flapping like bony wings.

The one time Nate did shift in the saddle, he saw the ring of warriors closing in again on the knoll, forming the living wall that kept the expedition hemmed in. A lot of activity was taking place on top as Shakespeare did his part.

The Shoshoko took them to the southwest, toward low hills jutting onto the plain like giant knobby fingers. On reaching the first hill the warrior bore to the right, around its base and past another. In this weaving manner he brought them deeper into the hills, and by the looks he bestowed, he thought he was doing a fine job of confusing them.

Nate glanced at Two Humps. The venerable chief wore a smug smile, and on noticing Nate's glance, he grinned as if to say there was nothing to worry about, he knew exactly where they were. Nate grinned back, grateful Shakespeare had sent his friend along.

It was an hour short of noon when Coyote's Brother took them through a gap between two hills, onto a small plain dotted with brush and small boulders. And something else. Everywhere Nate looked there were small, crude conical structures built over frames of willow poles. They were nothing like the fine lodges he was accustomed to. He was shocked by the poverty of these people.

Any sympathy Nate felt soon evaporated under the harsh glare of reality. They had to cross a dry wash to reach the sprawling encampment, and as they trotted up the opposite slope, a huge swarm of flies rose to their left and swarmed in the air.

Nate turned and drew rein. His stomach churned, reminding him that just when he thought he'd witnessed every sort of atrocity there could possibly be, along came another, newer one to prove him wrong.

Nine bodies lay in a row. All men. They resembled the bloated carcasses of long-dead buffalo more than human corpses. Naked, each scarred by wounds and mutilation, they festered with sores and dirt and more flies. Eyes had been stabbed out, fingers and toes chopped off. Jugulars had been severed, stomachs ripped wide.

LeBeau paled and averted his gaze. He wanted to be sick but refused to embarrass himself in front of the others.

Chavez rode a bit closer and said, "Apaches do the same. Are they who I think they are?"

"The settlers," Nate guessed. A hubbub of voices alerted him to a horde of Shoshokos coming toward them. Most were women, yet there had to be 50 or 60 men still in the village. He fingered the Hawken, his skin crawling as flies droned around him.

"I do not like this, *señor*," Chavez said. "They could pull us from our horses before we get off a shot."

"We go on in," Nate said.

Coyote's Brother had halted and was beckoning.

The Shoshokos parted to form a narrow aisle as Nate King and the others entered the village. Behind them, the swarm of flies descended again to cover their grisly feast.

Chapter Fourteen

"This is insane," Cyrus Porter objected. "We're asking to be slaughtered. Once the barrier is down, they'll swarm over us like a plague of locusts."

"Less talk and more work," Shakespeare directed, hefting a bundle to his shoulders. He would never admit as much, but the wealthy New Englander had a valid point. They were playing with fire, so to speak, the fiery lust to kill evident in the faces of many of the Shoshokos below.

Adam Clark was hefting a saddle. "I hope to high heaven you know what you're doing, McNair. I'd hate to be killed now, when we're so close to rescuing sweet Hestia."

Support for the pair came from an unlikely source, the riverman, Gaston. "*Oui*. I agree. We

David Thompson

have come too far to let ourselves be wiped out by these naked vermin."

"Keep loading the pack horses," Shakespeare insisted. "We have to be ready when they come."

"*If* they come," Gaston said.

"They will. Nate King is too good a man to let the Shoshokos pull the wool over his eyes," Shakespeare said. He carried his burden to a pack animal and lashed it on tight.

Winona was loading another close at hand, and when she noticed him, she walked over. "I heard. If those man knew Nate better, they would not be so worried." Winona took tremendous pride in her husband's ability, both as a warrior and a provider. Among her people those were the two qualities most essential in a husband. Usually a man excelled in one or the other. It was rare for someone to be superbly skilled at both, as was Nate.

Shakespeare refrained from telling her he was as concerned as the greenhorns. Nate was one of the best, but there were limits to what any man could do, and the odds against the young mountaineer were formidable.

"I do not think the Diggers will attack us before their chief returns," Winona speculated.

"That would be my guess," Shakespeare said. "Their plan is to wait until after we've made the trade and our guard is down. Then they count on being able to mingle freely with us and jumping us when we least expect."

"They will be in for a surprise."

Shakespeare fervently hoped so. He worked hard loading up helping those who needed it, rechecking all the knots. When the time came, they wouldn't be able to stop to hitch up a pack that was slipping or to retrieve supplies that fell off. There would be no second chances. They had to be as ready as they were ever going to be and have everything done perfectly the first time around.

Five rivermen were posted at the top of the slope at all times, just in case the Diggers present decided not to wait. The Indians murmured among themselves, seemingly content with the status quo.

That would change soon enough, Shakespeare mused. Frequently he gazed at the southwest horizon for any trace of a dust cloud or riders.

Once the pack animals were loaded, they were lined up in rows of three, each lashed to the next by a short length of rope. Lead ropes were looped around the saddle horns of individual mounts so the expedition could ride out at a moment's notice.

Satisfied all was in order, Shakespeare cradled his Hawken and strolled to the slope. He was taken aback to see one of the Diggers trying to get a point across to Porter and Clark.

"I can't understand you, you silly monkey!" the hopeful suitor was saying. "Quit pestering us and go join your fellow misfits."

"Don't be so hasty, Adam," Porter said. "Maybe he had something important to tell us."

By then Shakespeare was there. "What do you want?" he queried in sign.

"I am Half Moon," the Shoshoko signed, adopting an arrogant attitude. "My brothers and I are hungry. We want food."

The demand galled Shakespeare. Ordinarily he would have booted the warrior off the knoll, but with scores of spiteful eyes fixed on him and scores of bows ready to fly at the slightest provocation, he swallowed his anger and signed, "We have jerky made from antelope. An entire parfleche full."

"I will take it."

Shakespeare had to remember which horse carried the antelope meat. He wasn't about to reveal that there were three more parfleches. Selecting the bag containing the least amount, he gave it to Half Moon, who walked off very pleased.

"That's our food," Porter said. "Who knows when we might need it?" He smacked his mouth distastefully. "Why did you give in to them?"

"To give them something to do," Shakespeare said. "An idle mind is a dangerous thing. They might get a notion into their heads to scalp us and be done with it."

Porter glared at the Shoshokos, then punched his left palm with his right fist. "I hate this waiting! It's driving me to distraction." He watched the parfleche being passed among the Diggers and grew madder. "Thank God none of my peers in Hartford is here to witness my disgrace! Being pushed around by a bunch of scrawny primitives is bad enough as it is."

"I should think your friends would admire our common sense," Shakespeare said, trying to calm the man down. "If we hadn't handed over something to eat, we might be dodging arrows even as I speak."

"There are limits, Mr. McNair," Porter said. "A man of my standing shouldn't stoop to trafficking with heathens."

"You'd do it to save your daughter, but not us?" Shakespeare said. "It's nice to know where the rest of us fit into your scheme of things."

"I wouldn't expect someone like you to understand," Porter said, and huffed off.

Many times Shakespeare had regretted agreeing to serve as guide, none more so than now. For the umpteenth time he lifted eager eyes to the horizon, fervently hoping all went well. If the woman was indeed Hestia Davin, Porter would turn around and head for civilization, leaving Shakespeare and his friends free to make their way to the Pacific Ocean at their leisure.

Come on, Nate! Shakespeare prayed. *Where are you?*

At that moment, Nate King was looking down on a sea of unfriendly faces, the warriors rife with venom and ready to strike should their chief give the word. His pulse quickened as he thought of how easily the Shoshokos could end his life, merely by pulling him off the stallion and driving a dozen knives or more into him before he squeezed off a single shot.

But Nate didn't show his unease. Head high, shoulders back, he behaved as calmly as he would

in a Shosone village. The Diggers chatted excited-
ly, some pushing and shoving to get close to him
and the others. Children pointed in awe, women
pointed and whispered. The men merely glared.

Half the encampment had been crossed, and
Nate wondered if maybe he had let himself be
lured into a trap. Then Coyote's Brother stopped
in front of a dwelling slightly larger than most.
The warrior slid down, stooped, and entered. Nate
heard a scuffling noise and a slap. He started to
lift a leg from a stirrup.

Coyote's Brother reappeared, dragging the captive. He abused her in his tongue and kicked at
her back. She made no attempt to resist, but lay
on her side as limp as a sack of potatoes.

Nate longed to leap to the woman's defense.
For her sake and his he had to act as if
he didn't care that she was being mistreated.
Tearing his gaze away, he looked sternly at
Chavez and LeBeau to insure neither of them
intervened.

The tracker, accustomed as he was to dealing
with Apaches, sat looking bored by the whole
business.

The riverman, however, burned scarlet with
rage and would have pounced on the chief had
he not glanced up.

Nate gave his head a curt shake, then, com-
posed, he turned. Coyote's Brother leered up at
him and gestured.

"Here she is, Grizzly Killer. As I promised. You
can see for yourself that she is pretty for a white
woman."

Ordeal

Pretty, perhaps, but her current state belied her beauty. Her curly blonde hair was disheveled and filthy. Her dress was torn, crumpled, and smudged. The skin of her forearms and lower legs was caked with dirt, as were her bare feet.

Nate couldn't see her face. He signed, "I would like to look at her features. Maybe you have broken her nose or deformed her with your blows."

"I know how to hit a woman without ruining her," Coyote's Brother signed, offended. Snatching hold of her hair, he wrenched, flipping her onto her back and exposing her face for all to see.

She was beautiful. Even with her left eye swollen and black and blue, even with her cheeks puffy from repeated blows, even coated with dust soiled by her tears, the woman was undeniably beautiful. But there was something terribly wrong. Her blue eyes were as blank as an empty blackboard. There was no hint of recognition in them that above her sat another white person.

"What is wrong with her?" Nate signed.

"She is whole," Coyote's brother responded.

"You lie, Indian," Nate accused. "Look at her eyes. You have hurt her brain."

"I did not!" Coyote's Brother was livid. "She has been this way since the day we tired of using the men as slaves and killed them."

Nate put two and two together. The Shoshokos had taken the settlers captive months ago and kept the men alive until just recently. One of those ghastly corpses was the woman's husband. The Shoshokos had likely forced her to witness his mutilation and death, and her current state was the result.

Coyote's Brother made a surprising suggestion. "Talk to her, white man. Maybe she will answer. She never answers me."

Leaning directly over her face, Nate said gently, "Miss, would you happen to be Hestia Davin? My friends and I have come to save you. You can talk if you want. The Diggers won't hurt you bad with us sitting right here."

The woman didn't react, not the least little bit. Her eyes stayed locked wide, her face pale, her breathing so shallow she might have been a corpse herself.

"*Bastardos*," Chavez said.

"I kill them all," LeBeau vowed.

Nate sat back and sighed. He felt the same but he had to continue acting a part or they all stood to suffer. "You tried to trick us, Coyote's Brother," he signed. "You wanted us to trade for this?" He jabbed a thumb at the captive. "She is worthless. We have no need of her."

"She is your kind. You can heal her."

"None of us would bother," Nate lied, and wanted to laugh when doubt marred the warrior's countenance for the first time. "You keep her."

"We do not want her," the chief signed. He was upset and it showed.

Nate had the wily rascal right where he wanted him. He waited, certain the Shoshoko would make another offer to trade only for much less than the last time. Nate would act reluctant, then agree, and they would all head back. His plan was working out nicely.

The very next moment a saddle creaked and LeBeau strode to the woman and knelt. Coyote's Brother took a half-step, as if to interfere, but froze when LeBeau's right hand dropped to a pistol. Coyote's Brother backed up. LeBeau tenderly clasped the woman's head in his hands, saying softly in his heavy accent, "It will be all right, *petite*. I not let him hit you."

Raw rage contorted the chief's face. His hands clenched and unclenched.

Nate hid his own anger. The riverman's rash act endangered them all unless he did something quickly. "Get back on your horse before we join those poor souls by the wash."

"*Non*," LeBeau said, stroking the woman's hair. "This poor *femme*, she has suffered enough."

"Can't you see what you've done?" Nate said. "You can help her all you want once we're shy of this village."

"No."

"Of all the muleheaded—" Nate began, even though he felt the same. He was spared from venting his spleen by Coyote's Brother, who whirled on him and employed sign so fast Nate had a hard time following the drift of the speech.

"Someone tried a trick, but it was not me! You lied! You claimed none of the whites want her, yet it is plain this young one cares for her a great deal. Perhaps I should ask for more than I thought. Perhaps I should ask for twice as much."

Nate kept his composure and replied, "Once again you are wrong. I did not speak with two tongues. I told you that one of our men was interested in her and willing to pay one knife, one axe, one fire steel, and one red blanket. This is the man."

"This one?" Coyote's Brother signed in disappointment.

"He is not a rich man, as I told you," Nate went on. "You would do well to take his offer. No one else would trade so much for a woman who cannot speak or even wash herself."

The chief turned and whispered to several warriors. He scowled the whole while, thunder imminent on his brow.

"I hope you know you nearly got us killed," Nate said to LeBeau. "As it is, I've convinced him that you're interested in her and willing to strike a deal."

LeBeau wore a strange expression. He touched the woman's puffy cheek and said, "Tell him I give all I own."

"Like hell. I do that, and he'll know I've been lying through my teeth," Nate said. "We want him to think he can't get much for her so he'll be more willing to take her back to where the rest are. If he suspects she's valuable, he'll keep her here."

"I do not go without her," LeBeau said, his tone leaving no doubt he meant it.

"What's gotten into you?" Nate asked. "Sure, she's pretty, but you don't even know the woman."

Ordeal

"Do I need to?" LeBeau said. He adjusted the tatters of her dress so that she was decently covered. "Have you known many women, *Monsieur* King?"

"Known how?" Nate said. "There was my mother, but she hardly counts, not if I take your meaning correctly."

"You do."

"Then I can't say as I have," Nate admitted. The truth was, he'd known two, and only two. "I've always been shy around womenfolk."

"Not me," LeBeau said, his eyes on the blonde. "I know many in my time. Very, very many. They are for me—how you say?—the breath of life. I love women. I drink women, sleep women, think women. *Comprenez-vous?*"

"What?"

"Do you understand?"

"I understand it's amazing you're not hitched. Any man who makes a habit of sticking his head in bear traps sooner or later has it caught fast."

The riverman grinned. "You are much like McNair. So far I avoid the steel jaws, but I always have this great fondness for them. More than for anything else."

Before Nate could comment, Coyote's Brother stepped to the stallion.

"It is a poor price your friend is willing to pay, white man. But I would like a new knife and a new axe. Tell your friend I accept his offer."

Nate winked at the riverman. "The chief has taken the bait. I'll have his people rig up a travois so we can haul the woman along."

"She rides with me," LeBeau said. Squatting, he hooked both arms underneath her and lifted her slender form effortlessly. "Help me, my friends. Please."

They had to prop the woman against the riverman's back and tie her so she wouldn't fall off. Her cheek rested on the middle of LeBeau's back, and her arms dangled uselessly at her sides. LeBeau reached back to pat her hand and said, "Soon all will be well, pretty one. You will see."

Coyote's Brother led them to the gully. Once again the Shoshokos pressed in uncomfortably close. Nate expected them to drop behind after the village was passed, but to his dismay a group of 15 warriors showed every intention of coming along. Worse, they formed a circle around the horses, hemming them in. "Are these warriors going with us?" he signed.

As slyly as ever, Coyote's Brother grinned. "They are."

"But they are on foot. We will have to ride slow so they can keep up."

"They can run far when they have to," Coyote's Brother signed. "And we might need them. Two sleeps ago a hunting party saw a Blood war party in the direction of the Snake. A big war party."

It was a lie and Nate knew it. The Bloods, like their Blackfeet allies, never ventured into the region. Yet he dared not argue, dared not tip his hand until the right time. "We are glad to have them along," he signed.

Getting through the hills took twice as long as the ride in. Coyote's Brother rode tall on his horse, showing off for the benefit of his tribesmen.

Chavez rode beside LeBeau. Neither spoke. Every so often Chavez would stare long and hard at the woman, and when he looked away he had a vaguely haunted aspect to his gaze, as if she stirred memories he'd rather not recall.

Nate rode by himself until the plain hove into sight. He had forgotten all about Two Humps until the Nez Percé came abreast of him.

"When?" the old warrior asked in English.

"When we're within a rifle shot of the knoll."

"You say. I teach these Earth Eaters."

"You'll need help."

Two Humps smiled hugely. "With them?" he said in utter contempt. "Nez Percé women better fighters."

An unforeseen delay arose. Chavez happened to glance at the woman again and saw her sagging off the far side of the horse. He yelled, caught hold of her arm, and everyone halted. The rope had to be retied and lightly looped around her arms so she wouldn't slip again.

The Shoshokos became noticeably nervous the closer they drew to their destination. Some fingered their sinew bow strings, unaware they did so. Coyote's Brother moved to one side so his back wouldn't be to the whites.

Nate slowed to ride beside the riverman and the tracker. "When I give a yell, cut to the west and head for those mountains yonder. Protect the woman at all costs. Two Humps and I will take care of these Diggers."

"I will fight also, *señor*," Chavez said. "The honor of the *señorita* demands it."

"First LeBeau, now you," Nate joked. "What is it about blonde women that they turn a man's head inside out and make him act half his age?"

"It is not what you think," Chavez replied. "This woman reminds me of another, a woman I care for very much, so much that I killed a man to keep him from abusing her."

"Did you fight a duel?" LeBeau asked. In St. Louis duels were a common occurrence. The local field of honor, Bloody Island in the Mississippi, had gained national notoriety after a number of prominent citizens lost their lives there.

"No," Chavez said. He pulled the brim of his sombrero lower. "Her name is Anita. We talked of marriage, she and I. But her father did not like my father and would not have given his consent. We tried to think of a way to change his mind. Then another man came along and wanted Anita for his own. She told him that she loved me but he would not listen. He imposed himself." Chavez stopped, touched his forehead. "One morning I waited at his stable and when he came, I called his name. He went for his *pistola*. I was faster."

"So that's why you're on the run," Nate said.

"The man's family is very powerful. They have much political influence. Had I stayed, my father, my mother, my whole family would have been ruined."

"I think you do not run for long, eh?" LeBeau said.

"No, *amigo,* not much longer," Chavez responded. "It was Anita's idea, hers and my father's. I did wrong listening to them. A man must stand on his own two legs or he is not a man."

"Do you ever hear from home?" Nate asked.

"Letters, *si.* Anita sends them with travelers when she can. She misses me but worries. Our enemies still hunt me." Chavez tilted his face to the sun. "Soon they will not have to run very far. After *Señor* Porter pays me, I am off to Tucson. It will end, one way or the other."

A low whoop from Two Humps drew their attention to the northeast, where a solitary knob rose from the plain.

"The knoll," Nate said.

"Soon, then?" LeBeau asked.

"Real soon."

The Shoshokos closed in tighter around the horsemen, either because they sensed trouble brewing or they were simply taking an added precaution now that their destination was in sight. Coyote's Brother unslung his bow and pretended to be examining it.

Nate pulled up next to the venerable Nez Percé. Two Humps held his lance loosely in his right hand, the pointed tip angled downward.

The distance lessened, the knoll growing larger and larger. Now that the moment of truth had arrived, Nate was tense, filled with doubt. Once he shouted, they would be committed. Their lives, and all those on the knoll, were forfeit if his ruse failed.

Glancing at Coyote's Brother, Nate smiled, then threw back his head and howled like a wolf.

All hell broke loose.

Chapter Fifteen

Despite Shakespeare McNair's vigilance, it was Zachary King who spotted the tendril of dust that marked the progress of Nate's party. At the boy's shout, the mountain man swiveled. He estimated the distance at four miles.

The shout also alerted the Shoshokos, who rose and congregated on the south side of the knoll. Arrows were notched to bows and knives loosened in their crudely made sheaths.

Shakespeare had already gone from person to person, alerting the greenhorns to the ruse and telling them what to do when he gave the signal. Now, one by one they drifted steadily closer to their mounts, doing their best not to be obvious, pretending they were interested in the dust.

Shakespeare watched the Shoshokos to see if they would catch on. Thankfully, the warriors were too preoccupied. He walked over to the expedition's leaders and said, "Are the two of you ready?"

"I hope this insane scheme works," Cyrus Porter said.

"Just remember to keep your heads low and ride like hell," Shakespeare said. "Once you're out of bow range, you'll be safe."

"How far can they shoot?" Adam Clark asked.

"A hundred yards or better. More when they angle their bows into the air."

Clark stared westward. The nearest cover of any sort was over a mile away. "Some of us won't make it," he predicted.

"That depends on how many Diggers take the bait," Shakespeare said. Leaving the leaders to fret, he went to where the women stood beside Winona's horse. She still had the cradleboard strapped to her back, but she had taken Evelyn out and tenderly held the girl in her arms. "It won't be long," he said.

"We know," Blue Water Woman said.

"Remember what I told you," Shakespeare reminded them. "Keep the pack horses between you and the Shoshokos. I'd rather lose an animal or two than either of you."

"You are so considerate," Blue Water Woman teased. She had a knack for staying cheerful in the midst of adversity that Shakespeare had always admired.

"Where's the sprout?" Shakespeare wondered. His question was answered when he spied Zach over by the rim, observing the Diggers. "Darn that boy. I told him to stay near his horse."

"He listens about as well as his father," Winona said. "I can only hope our daughter takes more after me."

Zach started when Shakespeare's hand fell on his shoulder. "Goodness, Uncle. You caught me by surprise."

"If you don't get over to your horse, I'm liable to catch you by the scruff of your neck and plant my foot on your backside," Shakespeare said.

"Shucks, you'd never lay a finger on me," Zach said, unruffled. "Told me so yourself. Said you liked the Indian notion of never beating their young ones."

"You're not so young any more." Shakespeare refused to be bested at his own game. "And there are those who say that if we spare the rod, we spoil the child."

"I was just curious," Zach said.

"There's a time and a place for everything," Shakespeare said. "For being born and for dying, for weeping and laughing, for talking and listening, and for being curious and knowing when not to be." He gave the boy a light push toward the horses. "Now do as I told you and don't give me any more nonsense."

By this time the returning party was approximately three miles off. Many of the Shoshokos stared at the top of the knoll as might a pack of starving wolves at a herd of elk. Shakespeare smiled and waved at them to make them think he was a bigger idiot than they suspected. Then, since there was nothing else he could do, he simply waited.

A few of the younger Shoshokos were too impatient for their own good. Several started toward the slope but were intercepted by older warriors and herded back.

Shakespeare tried to pick out the leader in Coyote's Brother's absence. A stocky warrior appeared to be the one; the man gave orders to a number of warriors who promptly did his bidding. "Chop off the head and the tail won't be of much use," Shakespeare said softly to himself.

As the dust came nearer, the Shoshokos worked themselves into a killing mood. More and more of them stomped the ground and quietly chanted, their arms stabbing the air as if they struck foes.

Rotating slowly on a heel, Shakespeare was pleased to note that every expedition member except him stood beside or close to a horse. Everyone, women and Zach included, had rifles in hand, pistols under their belts.

Out on the plain, the five riders were now visible. Shakespeare was upset at seeing the warriors who encircled them, and he could only hope Nate was able to break through. Walking a few yards to his left, he kept one eye on the stocky warrior and another on the plain.

Soon, Shakespeare told himself. It had to be soon. The seconds crawled by like snails. Nate and company rode closer, too close, in Shakespeare's opinion. Thumb on the hammer of his Hawken, Shakespeare wondered if something had gone wrong, if maybe Nate had changed his mind.

Ordeal

Suddenly, the air was rent by the wavering howl of a wolf. Gunshots rang out as a battle erupted on the plain. Swirling dust arose, enveloping the fighters like a veil.

The Shoshokos at the base of the knoll were riveted to the sight. At a bellow from the stocky warrior, they charged to the aid of their chief, momentarily forgetting about the whites they had trapped.

That was exactly what Shakespeare had counted on. Whirling, he bawled out, "Now!" and dashed to his white horse as the expedition members hurriedly mounted. He swung up, gripped the reins and lead rope in his left hand, and poked his heels to bring his horse to a gallop. Down the slope he raced. At the bottom he veered to the left and reined up, motioning urgently for the rest to bear to the west and keep on going.

All would have gone well if not for the New Englanders.

Shakespeare had placed Winona and Blue Water Woman right behind him, since those at the front stood the best chance of getting safely away. Behind the women rode Porter and Clark. The trouble started when Porter decided to get in front of the Shoshone and Flathead, and with Clark and a short string of pack animals in tow, he tried to swing around the women. There was barely room for four horses riding abreast, certainly not more, yet Porter paid no mind and crowded Blue Water Woman and Winona aside.

Shakespeare saw, and wanted to shoot the man then and there. The women wisely gave way, slowing so the New Englanders could get past them. But Clark, in passing Blue Water Woman, crowded her pack string too close, and one of his pack animals collided with one of hers. Both stumbled and almost fell. His pack animal squealed in pain, and it was this squeal which fell on the ears of a few slow Shoshokos.

Five or six warriors turned, realized a mass escape was under way, and yipped to warn the rest of the war party. More of them spun. By twos and threes they bounded back, raising their bows to shoulder height.

Cyrus Porter and Adam Clark swept out onto the plain and thundered westward. Winona was next, then Blue Water Woman. Winona bent low over Evelyn, protecting the girl with her own body. They had not gone ten yards when the arrows began to fly.

Shakespeare twisted, aimed at the foremost warrior, and fired. The Shoshoko pitched forward, arms akimbo, bow flying. Other warriors leaped over his twitching body or skirted him, loosing arrows right and left.

One of the pack horses being pulled by Blue Water Woman whinnied as a shaft penetrated its flank.

Another nickered when hit in the neck.

Zach and Brett Hughes were the next riders down from the knoll. Hughes snapped off a shot. Zach hugged his saddle and rode for dear life. Behind them came the rivermen.

Fully half of the Shoshokos had awakened to the deception played on them and were hastening back. They howled, whooped, yelled in their tongue.

Shakespeare had to discourage them. Whipping out a pistol, he took a bead on one of the fastest runners and put a ball through the warrior's head. The Shoshoko toppled without making a sound. A half-dozen others halted, sighted down their shafts, and gave their arrows wing.

Slapping his legs against his horse, Shakespeare sped westward beside one of the rivermen. Arrows rained down, some imbedding in the soil at the very spot he had just occupied. Other shafts fell wide. He jammed the spent flintlock under his belt.

Other Shoshokos fired. Shafts cleaved the air in swarms.

Shakespeare heard a horse screech, heard the buzz of an arrow that missed his ear by inches. Then a human scream added to the din. He shifted, saw the riverman transfixed through the neck.

The man let go of his reins to futilely tear at the shaft, but couldn't get a grip because of spurting blood. He coughed, spit more blood. His eyelids fluttered. Desperately, he tried holding on to his mount's mane but lost his grip and fell. He bounced once.

Scores of arrows cleaved the sky, seeking targets. Shakespeare weaved, making himself hard to hit. The rivermen shot wildly, using rifles and pistols both. Grouped together, they were easier to bring down, so more of the Shoshokos tried to do just that.

Shakespeare was unpleasantly surprised by the endurance of their pursuers. He had expected the warriors to tire quickly, but they didn't. Exhibiting the stamina of antelope, the nimble-footed Shoshokos held their own even though they were on foot.

Bit by bit the horses pulled head. A final flight of arrows, more than ever before, flashed down out of the blue. Men and horses cried out. An arrow clipped Shakespeare's elbow, shearing off a pair of whangs but leaving his flesh unhurt.

Shakespeare pulled his second pistol and swung it around. Some of the warriors had stopped. Others were slowing. A few went faster, expending their last iota of energy. Few of the random arrows scored.

Saving his shot, Shakespeare galloped westward at the tail end of the expedition. He could see dust where Nate had last been. It was impossible to determine whether the others had escaped. He offered a short prayer that Nate still lived, then devoted his attention to overtaking the women to see how they had fared.

As the first note of Nate King's wolf howl rang out over the plain, Coyote's Brother turned and brought up his bow. His reflexes were swift, but not swift enough. For as the bow leveled, Two Humps cut loose with a war whoop and hurled his lance.

The Nez Percé, though old, was as wiry as a man of 20 and stronger than most men half his age. His lance glittered as it cleaved the air, the point striking Coyote's Brother in the sternum. Shattering bone, ripping through flesh, it impaled the Shoshoko chief. Coyote's Brother looked in disbelief at the smooth new appendage jutting from his torso, whined, and toppled.

While the clash between chiefs occurred, others were also fighting for their lives. Simultaneous with Nate's howl, LeBeau wheeled his mount to the west and sought to break free of the warriors before one put an arrow into the woman.

LeBeau wasn't afraid for himself. He had a philosophical bent despite his youth, and he had long ago realized that when a man's time on this earth was up, there was nothing anyone could do to postpone the inevitable. So why bother worrying about it?

A pair of Shoshokos blocked LeBeau's path. In unison they swept bows into play. LeBeau already had his rifle pointed at one. He fired on the fly and the man crumpled. The second Shoshoko tried to leap aside and was bowled over when LeBeau ran him down.

Another warrior, unseen by the riverman, raised a bow to plant an arrow in LeBeau's back. A rifle cracked, and the warrior melted to the soil, having no idea which one of his enemies had struck him down.

It was Nate. On firing, he charged the line, swinging his Hawken like a club. An arrow zipped past his face. Another nicked his shoulder.

A Shoshoko leaped and caught hold of the stallion's reins. Clinging on, yelling for help, he tried to keep Nate from getting away. Nate swung the rifle but missed. He saw another warrior bearing down on him from the right, yet another from the left. Barbed arrow points were trained on him. They had him dead to rights.

Then two pistol shots boomed, so close together they sounded as one. The warriors spun and fell. Nate landed a heavy blow on the man holding his stallion, and the Shoshoko thudded to the earth.

Chavez appeared at Nate's side, smoke curling from both fancy dueling pistols. "Ride, *señor!*"

Nate needed no encouragement. Side by side they burst through the scattering Shoshokos. Ahead of them sped LeBeau. "Two Humps!" Nate remembered, slowing and glancing over a shoulder. He would not desert the Nez Percé.

On foot, wielding a tomahawk right and left, the aged warrior was holding his own against four Shoshokos, the rest having fled. He would already have been dead, but the quartet wanted him alive and were using knives instead of their bows.

Nate drew a pistol, turned the stallion, and voiced a lusty roar as he swooped to the rescue. A stringy Shoshoko spun to face him, and Nate sent a lead ball into the man's right eye. He rode into a second foe, trampling the man. The third fled. The fourth lay on the ground, his brow split wide. Over him stood Two Humps, beaming. "Come on!" Nate urged. "We've got to get out of here!"

"You go," Two Humps responded, and drew his knife. Leaning low, he inserted the blade under the Shoshoko's hair and sliced deftly, expertly.

Ordeal

Nate looked around, dreading another assault. But the Shoshokos still alive were sprinting toward the main war party, which was rushing to help in an enraged body. "We have to go!" he persisted.

Two Humps casually lifted the dripping scalp. He waved it high and shouted in his own tongue, "I thank you for this coup, Great Mystery! You gave this Earth Eater to me, and now my people will see my medicine is as strong as ever!"

The war party was almost within bow range. Nate bent to nudge the chief's shoulder. "Do you want to die?"

The Nez Percé shrugged off the hand. "Must have chief's," he said in English, and walked to Coyote's Brother.

Torn between self-preservation and loyalty, Nate took a gamble. He had no time to reload the Hawken, and the distance was too great for the pistol, but he fired the pistol anyway at the front ranks of Shoshokos. He relied on the Diggers having had little experience with guns. They wouldn't know how far the pistol could shoot.

Sure enough, the foremost Shoshokos slowed or dived for cover. It bought ten seconds, at most, before they were all up and charging once more.

Nate was about set to grab the Nez Percé and haul him off against his will when Two Humps raised a second trophy, pivoted, and bounded to his Appaloosa. Arrows started falling as they galloped westward. They soon caught up with

Chavez, who had stopped to wait for them. Half a mile off sat LeBeau.

"We did it!" Nate marveled.

"*Si,*" Chavez said. "I hope *Señor* McNair and the others were just as lucky."

Nate thought of his wife and son and picked up the pace.

Cyrus Porter and Adam Clark had both been bred in the lap of luxury. They were used to a comfortable, relaxed life where their most taxing task of the day was to take a carriage from their palatial homes to their favorite men's club.

Oddly enough, both men believed they were adventurous spirits, as brave as the next man, stronger than their peers. Lulled by the warmth of soft armchairs, they had waxed eloquent about how they would teach the heathens respect for the white race when they went west.

Experience had taught them a vast gulf existed between brave words and brave deeds. It was one thing to boast of facing down hordes of blood-thirsty savages, another to have a shrieking horde actually thirsting for their blood.

Neither man would admit it, but both had been badly scared several times during the long journey. The worst had been the awful moment when it appeared they would be overrun by Blackfeet. Neither thought anything worse could ever happen. Then along came the Shoshokos.

Surrounded, with no hope of escape, never knowing when the savages might see fit to storm the knoll and finish them off, Porter and Clark had barely held their fear in check. When the time came to flee, they had tried to behave calmly, rationally. But their fear, so long contained, overwhelmed them as they rode past the two Indian women, and when the arrows began falling thick and heavy, they beat their fists and kicked mercilessly to goad their mounts on.

Miles flew behind them, and still the greenhorns raced westward. The mountains beckoned them, havens, they thought, where they would be safe. They sent herds of antelope into panicked flight, sent birds into taking startled wing, and once, passing a gully, they both saw the head of a small grizzly rear above the rim. It added fuel to their flight.

Their horses flagged long before they came to the mountains. Both men slapped and kicked, but their mounts were played out. Having no choice, they reined up and looked behind them. A cloud of dust revealed the rest of the expedition was a full mile back.

"What a bunch of turtles," Clark jested.

"Remember this moment, Adam," Porter said. "We outrode mountain men and squaws. No one will ever doubt our horsemanship."

"Say," Clark said, holding his hands up and staring at his palms, "what happened to our pack horses?"

Cyrus Porter blinked. Each of them had been responsible for three animals. He remembered his three trailing him as he descended the knoll, and seemed to recall they had been with him for the initial hundred yards or so. After that, he couldn't account for them. "Why, they must have been so terrified, they tore loose."

"That's it!" Clark said. "For a second there I was worried we had been negligent."

"Not us."

"No, not us."

Climbing down, they sat on nearby boulders and fanned their hot faces with their dusty hats. After a while Clark laughed, then commented, "That wasn't so terrible, after all. McNair and King knew what they were doing."

"We escaped by the seat of our pants," Porter said. "Competent guides wouldn't have put us in such an untenable position in the first place."

"I suppose not."

"I only hope the next leg of our journey goes smoother," Porter said. "I'd hate to think we have to put up with various bands of simpleminded heathens the entire way."

"Say, that reminds me," Clark said. "What if this woman they found *is* Hetty? Then we don't need to go on. We can head back for Hartford right away."

"No, we can't."

"What?"

"We can't."

Adam Clark stared in amazement at the older man. "I don't understand, Cy. We've gone to all this trouble to find your daughter and take her back to the States. What do you mean, we *can't*?"

"If I could explain, I would. Just take my word for it and let the matter drop. You'll see Hartford again—eventually." Porter stretched his legs and smiled. "Maybe we'll sail instead of retracing our route and going through this ordeal again. Take a boat from San Francisco around the Cape. Wouldn't that be nice?"

"But what of Hetty? After the horrors she's been through, wouldn't it be wiser to return as rapidly as we can? A trip to San Francisco would take four or five more months than it would take us to return to St. Louis from here. And there's the added time needed for the ocean voyage."

Porter inspected his fingernails, then said coldly, "Do you want me to put in a good word for you with my daughter, or not?"

"Of course, but—"

"No buts, Adam. I will not tolerate opposition. For reasons unknown to you, I must continue westward. And I would be grateful if you never bring the subject up again."

Clark fell silent, but he was profoundly unhappy at the prospect of extending their trek any more than necessary. He fell into a sulk and sat with his chin in his hands watching the rest of their party approach.

Cyrus Porter rose and went to his horse. From a saddlebag he took a small silver flask which he tipped to his lips. When he lowered it, Clark was watching intently.

"I didn't know you had that."

"Knowing your weakness, do you really think I would tell you?"

The beat of hooves prefaced the arrival of Shakespeare McNair, who had pulled ahead of everyone else. The mountain man sprang from the saddle, stalked up to Porter, and seized him by the shirt before Porter quite knew what was what.

"Here's where I separate you from your teeth."

Chapter Sixteen

Shakespeare McNair wasn't a violent man by nature. When forced to defend his life he became fierce, but most of the time his level-headed disposition governed his actions. There were exceptions.

When Shakespeare had caught up with the women and seen that all three of the pack animals his wife led were wounded, when he saw that two of those Winona handled had arrows sticking from them, when he saw two shafts imbedded in Winona's cradleboard, he'd been seized by a rare fit of rage. He thought of how close the wives had come to losing their lives because of the New Englanders, and his fury mounted.

Blue Water Woman had sensed his mood and commented, "We cannot blame them, husband.

They are not used to life in the mountains."

"Mountains, hell!" Shakespeare spat. "It's basic decency we're talking about. They were thinking of their own hides first. That's cowardly in any book."

"What will you do?" Blue Water Woman asked.

Shakespeare himself hadn't known until he saw the pair up ahead. His legs pumped of their own accord. He seemed to see Porter and Clark through a red haze, as it were, and he was off his horse and had his fist drawn back to smash Porter in the mouth when a shout stopped him cold.

"Please, husband! No!"

Blue Water Woman had followed him. She sat her tired horse wearily, eloquent appeal in her eyes.

Shakespeare hesitated. "Give me one good reason why I shouldn't?"

"Because I am asking you not to."

Cyrus Porter, speechless with shock until this moment, found his voice and barked, "Here now, McNair! What is the meaning of this outrage!"

Conflicting emotions tore at Shakespeare. He had never wanted to punch anyone as much as he wanted to punch Porter, yet by the same token he had never refused his wife before. She wasn't a demanding woman and seldom asked a favor for herself. Which made the one she asked now all the more special. "Damn you!" Shakespeare roared, flinging Porter to the dirt. "Thank your lucky stars that my wife is more of a human being than you can ever hope to be!"

Ordeal

"What the hell has gotten into you?" Porter responded. "What are you babbling about?"

Shakespeare bent so their noses nearly touched. "You should have let the women go first!"

"I—" Porter said, then paused, about to lie that he had merely wanted to ride at the head of the column where the head of the expedition should ride. Instead, he said the one thing that would deflate the mountain man's rage, blurting it out by accident, not design. "I was scared," he said softly, so softly the only one who heard was McNair.

Shakespeare slowly straightened. Having the New Englander admit the truth was a jolt; he didn't think Porter had that much honesty in his soul. "It takes backbone to confess to a mistake," he said. "Just don't let it happen again."

"I won't," Porter said. "I assure you."

Soon the bulk of the expedition arrived. At Shakespeare's bidding, Zach rustled up enough scrub brush and tinder to make a fire. The wounded rivermen were examined, arrows removed. None of the wounds were life-threatening in themselves, but there was another danger Shakespeare attended to by taking the ramrod from his Hawken and heating an end in the fire.

Gaston, who had taken an arrow in the fleshy part of his thigh, looked up as the mountaineer walked toward him, the end of the ramrod glowing cherry red. "What do you think you are doing, *monsieur?*" he asked.

"I need to poke this into you," Shakespeare said, wagging the ramrod.

"Over my dead body."

"By then it will be too late and a terrible waste of time," Shakespeare said, squatting. He held out his other hand, which held a thick stick. "You might want to bite on this to keep from screaming."

Gaston couldn't take his eyes off that cherry-red metal. "I really would rather not," he said. "The hole is a small one. It will heal on its own."

"It's not the hole I'm thinking of. It's the poison."

"Poison?" Gaston said, unconsciously biting his lower lip.

"It's not common knowledge in the States, but Indians sometimes dip their arrow points in rattlesnake venom or the livers of dead animals. About half of those who get shot by arrows die from infection instead of the wounds."

"Poison," Gaston said again, staring at the exposed hole. He had cut his pants open with his knife when the shaft was removed.

"Come to think of it," Shakespeare went on, "we're lucky the Shoshokos aren't as devious as the Comanches and some other tribes. Those wicked devils attach the barbs to the shafts loosely, so the points will come off whenever someone tries to pull an arrow out. That way, if the arrows don't get you, infection will."

Gaston picked up the bloody shaft lying beside him, his stomach feeling queasy. "Were these poisoned, do you think?"

"I can't say," Shakespeare said, offering the stick again. "Do you want to take the chance they weren't?"

Ordeal

"No," Gaston said.

Others were gathering to observe. Young Zach didn't understand why the riverman was so anxious. Shoshone warriors treated arrow wounds all the time much as Shakespeare was about to do, and they neither hesitated nor squawked.

Adam Clark watched until the tip of the ramrod touched Gaston's flesh and there was a loud hiss. Eyes bulging, he clasped a hand to his mouth and hurried away.

One by one the rivermen were operated on. To their credit, not one cried out, although a man named Jonquiere nearly fainted as the burning metal seared into his body.

The wounded horses were not so easily treated. Twelve had taken arrows, but only a sorrel had been hit in a vital organ. Lungs filled with blood, it would die a horrible, lingering death. That thought provoked Shakespeare into drawing a pistol and stepping to the animal's head. It was on its side, wheezing like a bellows. He aimed, then checked his intent. Out of the corner of his eye he had noticed young Zach watching.

"Zach, why don't you put this animal out of its misery," he suggested.

The boy glanced up, swallowed, and said, "Me, Uncle Shakespeare?"

"You're the only member of this expedition called Zach as I recall."

"But why me?"

"Ever done it before?"

"Shot a stricken horse? No, sir."

"Then it's about time you learned." Shakespeare handed over the pistol. "Always try to make the first shot count. Miss, and the horse will suffer worse. You have to put the ball right in its brain."

"I don't know. Maybe I should wait for Pa—"

"Art thou a man? Thy form cries out thou art," Shakespeare quoted. "Your pa ain't here, and you're old enough to be doing man's work when it needs to be done."

"Yes, sir." Zach cocked the pistol and extended the barrel. He would show that he was capable of doing a man's job, and do it well. Then the sorrel looked at him, and his resolve faltered. Those big, watery eyes fixed on him seemed to plead with him not to pull the trigger. Which was a ridiculous notion, when he thought about it. His imagination was to blame, giving horses credit for emotions they didn't have.

"Take your time if you need to," Shakespeare said when the boy hesitated. He didn't want to rush it and have the experience turn sour. It was a big step for a boy Zach's age, one of many the boy must climb on the stairway to manhood. It had to be done just right.

Zach became aware of his mother staring at him. She wore a hopeful look, as she had that time he went off with his pa on his first elk hunt. It was important to her that he shoot. He stroked the trigger gently, as his pa had taught him.

At the retort, the sorrel stiffened, whinnied pitiably, blubbered blood, and died gasping.

"You did fine," Shakespeare said, taking the flintlock. "Right in the brain, like I told you."

Ordeal

The rest of the wounded horses had to be held down while the arrows were removed. Since there wasn't a horse alive that would hold still for having a hot ramrod pushed into its body, Shakespeare improvised. He fed grains of black powder into each hole, then applied a lit stick to the grains. The horses bucked and squealed and near went crazy with pain, but they lived.

It was late afternoon when riders appeared to the south. Winona saw them and moved to the edge of their camp. She had been watching since they stopped, her heart yearning for sight of the man she loved. She feared he had been slain by the Shoshokos, and she imagined him riddled with arrows, lying stiff in the dust of the plain.

The four riders materializing out of the haze brought a smile to Winona's lips. They were letting their mounts walk, the smart thing to do in such heat. Chavez's horse limped. LeBeau sat awkwardly in the saddle, bending slightly forward as if there was pressure on his back. She guessed why before they were within earshot. Rather than wait, she bounded to meet them. Nate rode on ahead and left his saddle on the run. She gave a throaty purr of joy when he leaped into her arms.

"I would have been here sooner," Nate said in her ear, "but one of the horses sprained a leg running from the Diggers, and LeBeau is riding double."

"I am just glad you lived," Winona said. She squeezed him as hard as she could.

"I couldn't let myself be rubbed out by Diggers," Nate said lightheartedly. "The embarrassment would be more than I could stand."

Shakespeare McNair had seen Nate arrive. He was rubbing dirt on his hands to get off some of the blood, so he delayed going over to offer a welcome. It was well he did, or he might have said something that would have deprived him of seeing a bastard get his due.

It started when Zach ran over and talked urgently, gesturing at Porter now and again. Nate's features turned flinty. They turned even harder when Zach showed him the cradleboard with the two arrows still embedded in it.

Then came the interesting part. Shakespeare saw Nate face Winona as they exchanged words. He knew what was coming next, knew Winona had to know, but she gave no indication of wanting to prevent Nate from doing it, the way Blue Water Woman had stopped him. To the contrary, she stroked his cheek and whispered something that made Nate's anger deepen.

As yet, Cyrus Porter and Adam Clark were unaware Nate King had returned. They were by the fire, their backs to the plain as they sat sipping coffee, so they hadn't seen the four riders. And since Nate had dismounted far from camp, they hadn't heard him, either.

Cyrus Porter was lifting a tin cup to his mouth when Nate's hand fell on his shoulder. He looked up, tried to say something, and was yanked to his feet as if he were weightless instead of a grown man. Porter dropped the cup, gripped Nate's wrist, and tried to push Nate's arm aside. He might as well have been trying to budge a tree.

Nate punched Porter on the chin. The blow sent Porter stumbling into Clark, and they toppled together, limbs locked. Dazed though Porter was, he scrambled to his knees, then stupidly tried to draw a pistol.

The fight was no contest. Nate clubbed Porter on the temple, and when the New Englander slumped, Nate grasped his wrist and bent it backward, eliciting a yelp and causing Porter to drop the gun. Porter swung wildly, but Nate blocked and slammed a fist into Porter's face.

By then Shakespeare was there. He was about to grab Nate to keep him from doing lasting damage when Adam Clark chose to rise to Porter's aid. Clark pulled a pistol and rose directly into the path of Shakespeare's fist. The younger man hit the ground flat on his back and didn't move.

Shakespeare turned to see Porter in a similar position. "Well, I reckon that will teach these two some manners," he said. "It's a shame no one ever taught them that ladies should always go first."

"I'm surprised you didn't get in a racket with them after what they did," Nate said, looking from Porter to Clark in the hope one or both still had some fight left in them.

"I wanted to," Shakespeare said. "Blue Water Woman wouldn't let me." He rubbed the knuckles of his right hand. "It's a sad state of affairs when a man can't thrash someone who needs a licking because his wife is getting soft in her old age." Shakespeare grinned. "Maybe you'd like to trade? An even swap, my wife for yours?"

The fight had drawn all those able to walk. Brett Hughes took it on himself to revive Porter and Clark by splashing water on their faces. Porter sputtered, shook his bullish head, and rose primed to explode. He would have, too, if he hadn't seen the three riders rein up. At sight of them all else was forgotten.

"*Hestia!*" Porter shouted, and ran to LeBeau's horse. He tried to lift the blonde woman down, then realized she was tied on, and snarled, "Hurry, man! Undo this rope so I can see how she is!"

"She is not good, *señor*," Chavez warned, coming around with a knife in hand. "The Indians . . ." He let the statement trail off.

The rope was cut, and Hestia Davin slid off into her father's arms. Porter's features underwent a remarkable transformation, from outrage to grief. His knees wobbled, but he carried her to the fire and laid her down gently. Tears rimmed his eyes as he cupped her dainty hand in his and said, "Dear, dear Hetty! What have those heathens done to you?"

The lovely young woman stared blankly at the empty sky, showing no recognition of her father at all.

"Talk to me, Hetty," Porter pleaded. "Please. You can talk to me."

Nate stood to one side with his family. In one respect, that of a father, he felt sympathy for Porter. No parent should live to see their children suffer so. To Winona, he said quietly, "Is there anything you can do?"

As was typical of Shoshone women, Winona had skill as a healer. As a girl, she had sat at her grandmother's knee and learned about the curative properties of many plants and various herbs. "I have *toza* chips in my parfleche. I can make her a tea, but I do not know if it will help. Her hurt is more of the spirit than of the body."

"Do what you can," Nate said.

Porter was fussing over his daughter, smoothing her hair and moistening his fingertips to wipe off the grime caking her cheeks. "You haven't washed in ages. And look at these clothes! Didn't those savages have any sense of decency?" He moved a palm in front of her eyes, sparking no reaction. "God. Your mind is gone. They've made a vegetable of you."

Someone groaned, but it wasn't Hestia. Adam Clark sat up, working his jaw back and forth, and declared in ignorance of those around him, "That old man is as strong as an ox." He went to reach for the pistol lying next to him and woke up to the fact that he wasn't alone. "What the—?" he said, then spied Hestia.

"Noooo!" Clark wailed, scuttling on hands and knees to her side. His shoulder bumped Porter and almost spilled the older man in the dirt. "Oh, no, no, no!" he cried shrilly. Placing a hand on either cheek, he shook her vigorously.

So swiftly had it happened that for a few seconds the spectators were too astounded to move. Nate and Shakespeare reached him at the same time and pulled him away from the woman.

"Let go of me!" Clark rasped. "Can't you see she needs me? Why won't she speak? What is wrong?"

"She can't talk," Shakespeare said.

"Can't?" Clark repeated, and looked at the woman in dawning horror. "But this isn't the way it's supposed to happen! She and I are going to be husband and wife. Her father promised me."

The disgust the mountain men felt was evident to all but the distraught greenhorn. Clark tried to break loose and was shoved onto his backside.

"You stay put until we've tended her," Shakespeare directed. "If you get up before I say so, this ox will smash you on the head again."

Zach King, like everyone else, had been watching Clark, amazed a grown man would blubber so. He looked back at the woman's father, who had tears streaking his cheeks. Zach remembered his doubts about Porter's affection and felt a twinge of guilt. The man did love her, after all.

No one noticed LeBeau. The handsome riverman had moved around to where he could see the blonde woman's face clearly, and he stood staring forlornly at her, his sadness, strangely enough, rivaling the father's.

Blue Water Woman appeared, holding a spare buckskin dress. "I will wash and dress her," she told Shakespeare, "but not with all these men around. Can you ask them to turn around?"

"I'll do better than that," her husband said, drawing a flintlock. Without ceremony he fired into the air, and when all eyes were on him, he bellowed, "All right, gentlemen. The ladies need privacy. So we'll count our supplies to learn how much we're missing and stake out the horses so they aren't stolen in the middle of the night."

"We staying here until morning?" a riverman asked. "There's no water."

"We have a few water skins," Shakespeare reminded him. "Or would you rather we toss Hestia Davin over a horse and put her through more hell while we ride all over creation looking for a spring or a stream?"

"You must know where one is," the man said.

"The nearest river is three day's ride."

That shut up the protester, and the men drifted to the packs to do as they had been told. Shakespeare went with them, but Nate walked over to Porter and said, "You too."

"I'm her father. I'll stay."

"No," Nate said.

Porter stood, his cheeks moist, lightning flashing from his eyes. "What do you mean, no? First you beat me senseless, now you presume to butt in where you aren't wanted. I'll settle with you later. Go help McNair and leave me alone."

"No."

Porter drew back a fist but stopped when he saw the dress in Blue Water Woman's arms. "Oh," he said simply. "I didn't know." He coughed sheepishly and shuffled off.

Winona passed him, a parfleche over her left shoulder. "I will make a tea," she told her husband. "We must feed her a cup four times before morning." Her mouth formed a small 'o,' a habit of hers when she was upset. "Once I had a friend who was taken by the Piegans. She had lived but sixteen winters and was the prettiest in our tribe. Our warriors went after the war party and tracked them for a whole moon. There was a battle and all the Piegans were killed."

"The girl?" Nate knew she wanted him to ask.

"She was brought back, but she did not live long. She would not speak, would not eat. She had crawled inside herself and would not come out. Nothing we did helped."

"Let's hope we have better luck with this one." Nate walked to the packs, pondering the frailty of all life. Angry voices put an end to his morbid musing. Shakespeare and Cyrus Porter were glowering at one another. "What's the matter now?" Nate asked.

"You won't believe this!" Shakespeare declared. "I just told him that we can head on back just as soon as his daughter is up to a long ride. I figured he'd be happy to be quits of this country after all his complaining and everything that's happened."

Nate looked at Porter. "We can't head back sooner. Your daughter needs rest."

Shakespeare shook his head. "That's not it. He doesn't want to go back at all. He wants to go *on*, clear to the Pacific."

There were some back in the States who believed all mountaineers were illiterate, unkempt brutes little better than the savages they lived among. In many a sitting room the intelligence of the average trapper had been compared, unfavorably, to that of a brick. While this was true in a minority of cases, such a comparison was largely unfair. Many trappers were well-read, many came from well-to-do families, many, like Nate King, were astute students of human nature. They had to be in order to survive.

But Nate was as surprised as his mentor by this latest revelation. He thought he had the Hartforder pegged. The very last thing he would ever expect Porter to want to do, Porter wanted to do. It rattled him, made him wary. "Why do you want to keep going west?"

"My reason is none of your business," Porter replied. "All that need concern you is keeping out of my hair from here on out." He paused. "I don't mind telling you that I don't want you along, King. Unfortunately, Mr. McNair has made it clear that if you go, he goes, and I can't do without him." Pivoting, Porter left them.

It was Shakespeare who expressed their shared sentiments. "I fear, Horatio, that something is rotten in the State of Denmark." He stared after Porter. "Very, very rotten indeed."

Chapter Seventeen

Two days later the Porter/Clark expedition resumed its trek westward. Shakespeare McNair spent nearly every waking minute trying to reason with Porter, but the man refused to change his mind. Unexpected allies, in the form of Clark and Brett Hughes, also pointed out the pitfalls of exposing themselves to further danger without good cause. Porter turned a deaf ear to all entreaties, nor would he give in and explain his reason for wanting to go on.

Finally, McNair agreed to continue as guide. Not out of any affection for Porter. He did so because it was clear that one way or the other Porter was going on, and he didn't want the deaths of the expedition members on his conscience. He would do what he could to see them safely through.

Ordeal

There was another reason, one Shakespeare never mentioned but which weighed as heavily in his thoughts. The reason's name was Hestia Davin. Like practically every other man there, his sympathy was mightily stirred by her pathetic plight. He wanted to do all in his power to restore her to a normal state of mind. To do that, he had to be handy in case she regained her mental faculties.

Everyone was deeply disappointed that Hestia showed no sign of recovering. Blue Water Woman and Winona used all their considerable skills as healers, without result. The young woman stared blankly at empty air hour after hour after hour. She never blinked, never twitched a muscle. Every ten hours or so she would drift asleep, but she would only slumber for a couple of hours before awakening to repeat the cycle all over again.

The two Indian women were saddened by their failure but never gave up. They hovered over Hestia like mothers who shared the same daughter, taking turns sitting up with her when one or the other needed to sleep.

Adam Clark sulked the whole time, and when not sulking he would take one of the rivermen and go for long walks to take his mind off the agony of uncertainty.

Cyrus Porter, strangely, spent little time in Hestia's presence. He checked on her condition every few hours but seldom lingered and never showed any fatherly affection. He was more interested in preparing for the next leg of their trek.

The rough and tumble rivermen kept a respectful distance so as not to disturb the women. All, that is, except one, who made it a point to never be far away. LeBeau contrived to spread out his blanket much closer to the fire than he had in the past, but not so close that Cyrus Porter was liable to take notice.

Nate King was least affected but not through any fault of his own. With everyone else preoccupied, someone had to see that the dozen and one daily chores were done, that wood was gathered, the horses fed, sentries posted. Zach helped when he could, but much to the boy's annoyance he had to spend a lot of time sitting watch over his little sister.

"Just my luck," he groused at one point within his father's hearing. "I come along to see something of this world and maybe have a few adventures, and what do I end up doing? Protecting Evelyn from killer flies and such."

"We protected you when you were a sprout," Nate shot back. "It's only fair you do the same for your sister." He chuckled. "As for those killer flies, if they're not mean enough for you, I'll see about scaring up a Blackfoot war party or maybe some Bloods. They ought to keep you from being bored to death."

"You're a caution, Pa," Zach said glumly.

On the night before the expedition departed, Nate was able to get Shakespeare alone. "Any ideas yet why Porter is so all-fired determined to go to the Pacific?"

"Not a clue," McNair said. "I've tried approaching the subject from every angle I could think of, but he was too canny and wouldn't take the bait."

Ordeal

"Does he have a route picked out?" Nate asked sarcastically, since they both knew Porter's sense of direction was about as keen as a rock's.

"Believe it or not, he does," Shakespeare said. "He wants us to follow the Columbia once we leave the Snake."

"That's the usual way, isn't it?"

"Yes. But you should have heard him."

"Why?"

"He got to asking me about distances, and how far it was between tributaries and landmarks. He knows the country awful well." Shakespeare became thoughtful. "I tell you, if I didn't know better, I'd swear he'd been there before."

"Is that possible?"

"Not according to him it isn't, but I wouldn't take every word the man says as gospel. Not unless you're fond of false prophets."

Nate stroked his beard. "So what do we do?"

"Keep our eyes skinned, for one thing. He might be the booshway, but that don't mean we let him take advantage of our sweet natures to hoodwink us," Shakespeare said with a straight face.

"If you ask me, Porter and Clark are no account any ways you lay your sight." Nate tapped his tomahawk. "I don't know which is worse. The way they lord it over us, or the fact they think they're so much better. Especially Porter."

"Why, man, he doth bestride the narrow world like a Colossus," Shakespeare quoted, "and we petty men walk under his huge legs and peep about to find ourselves dishonourable graves. Men at some time are masters of their fates.

The fault, dear Brutus, is not in our stars, but in ourselves, that we are underlings."

"I'm nobody's underling," Nate said.

"Spoken like a true mountaineer," Shakespeare complimented him. "But we'll have to go on acting the part until we reach Astoria. Then he's on his own, and I'm off to walk on the beach and let salt water tickle my toes."

Nate looked at him. "Sometimes you're worse than Zach."

"If you mean I can be as childish as the next person, then this coon is flattered. There's an art to staying young at heart that most people never learn. You could do with learning it yourself."

"What is this secret art?" Nate asked.

"I never said it was a secret. Half the answers to the so-called secrets of life are right there in front of our noses if we'll just open our eyes to see them." Shakespeare leaned closer and spoke confidentially. "It's the little things, Horatio. The little things."

"Flies and such?" Nate said, thinking of his son's comment.

"Did you get walloped by a rock when I wasn't looking? No, not insects, you dunderhead. I mean little things like a rosy sunrise on a cool morning or the taste of buffler steak when a man's half starved, or the scent of a woman when making love. Those kinds of little things."

"Who would have figured? You missed your calling. Instead of being a mountaineer, you should have been a philosopher."

Ordeal

"And waste my words of wisdom on uneducated minds? No thank you."

The next morning the expedition got under way. There was a short delay while Hestia was laid on the sturdy travois rigged for the purpose, then covered with a soft buffalo robe. Blue Water Woman rode the horse that pulled the travois. Close behind at any given minute of the day rode LeBeau.

Their course was along the Snake to its confluence with the mighty Columbia. Getting there took exhausting effort, as the country bordering the river had turned steeply mountainous. The river itself often contained rapids so treacherous a person dared not wade more than a few feet from shore for fear of being swept away.

Occasionally they passed tributaries of the Snake. At one with wide cotton willow bottoms, they accidentally flushed a grizzly and its cub. The she-bear roared at them but elected not to charge, instead making off noisily through the brush, much to everyone's relief.

They also passed several islands, from the largest of which rose a column of smoke. Since they were still in Nez Percé country, Two Humps stood on the bank and hailed the island for over five minutes, but no one appeared or answered.

Later they came upon the site where a village had recently stood. From the sign, Shakespeare deduced it had been a Nez Percé encampment and that the inhabitants had traveled northward, deeper into their domain.

Finally the expedition came to where the Columbia joined the Snake, from the northwest.

David Thompson

Shortly thereafter, as they were striking camp one morning, they heard chanting and the beating of drums. Presently a Nez Percé chief by the name of Wolf Running arrived along with over a hundred warriors. It turned out the expedition had been under surveillance for some time, and that the presence of Two Humps had assured Wolf Running that the whites were friendly, so he decided to make a formal visit.

There was a three-day delay while trade goods were swapped for pemmican and other items. Everyone had to smoke the peace pipe. Wolf Running showed Nate and Zach a large medal he wore which had been given to him by Lewis and Clark years before.

As a favor to Two Humps, Wolf Running drew a map of the Columbia on a piece of elk hide. This was rolled up and consulted as the need arose.

After a formal parting, the expedition moved on. They passed four islands the next day, and a severe rapid. On one of the islands stood five lodges made of poles and brush, unlike any they had ever seen. Two Humps became incensed, claiming that another tribe had encroached on Nez Percé territory. He wanted to ride back and inform Wolf Running, but Shakespeare convinced him not to since it would mean another delay. They went on.

The next day they stopped at noon at the base of a 200-foot-high cliff. A game trail to the top enabled Nate and his family to make the climb in short order.

Ordeal

"Gracious, Pa! Look!" Zach declared as he enjoyed the panoramic scene.

To the northwest reared a solitary majestic mountain of immense height, its crown layered in a pristine mantle of gleaming snow.

"It is beautiful," Winona said, holding Evelyn so the child could see.

Nate gazed down at their camp. From that height the men resembled bugs. He could see Shakespeare and Blue Water Woman, near the travois bearing Hestia Davin. The young woman had yet to show any sign of life. It was distressing in the extreme.

Nate was reminded of an incident the week before, when he had awakened in the middle of the night feeling a need to heed Nature's call. Being half asleep, he had shuffled toward the fire instead of away from it. He realized his error at the same instant he saw a shadowy shape on bent knee next to the travois.

The women had long since stopped staying up all night with Hestia. Nate assumed it must be her father. Startled into wakefulness, he crept closer, and was shocked to recognize LeBeau. The riverman had her hand in his and was whispering in her ear.

Nate's anger flared. It was improper of LeBeau to take such liberties with a woman who was helpless. Nate was about to storm forward and give LeBeau a piece of his mind when he overheard the words being spoken.

"—every night, and I will keep on every night, *petite*, until you are whole, *non?* I know you hear me. I know it. You be safe now. You are among friends."

There was more, in the same vein. Nate listened, and knew he need not worry. LeBeau would never disgrace himself or mistreat the woman. Treading silently, he melted into the night and left LeBeau to his tender ministrations.

Now, looking down at the unfortunate woman, Nate wondered what the riverman would do if she never came around. To be smitten by a woman who could neither think nor talk seemed the height of folly, but there was no explaining the designs of Cupid.

Not long after the expedition moved on, Shakespeare found three pieces of driftwood, the first they had seen. Two days later they came to a great falls. In the pools below swam a large number of sea otters, and one of the rivermen shot two for their supper. As they had done on previous evenings, they supplemented their diet with fish they caught. Porter, to the surprise of some, proved a competent angler.

That night only a single guard was posted. No one expected trouble. They were at the border of Nez Percé country, and the Nez Percé were friendly. In addition, there had been no problems with nocturnal prowlers in so long that recollections of the previous times had faded.

Shakespeare McNair slept under a buffalo robe, his body molded to his warm wife. He couldn't say what awakened him, but suddenly his eyes were open, his senses primed. For a few seconds he heard nothing, then a whinny split the night and four guns went off, one after the other.

Leaping erect, a pistol in each hand, Shakespeare beheld ten horses or more racing toward them in panicked flight. "Get up!" he bawled to Blue Water Woman and, stooping, slid his hands under her arms. She promptly woke up, but confusion froze her in place.

"What—?"

Shakespeare tried to run. The horses were almost upon them, manes and tails flying in the wind. He hurtled to the right, clasping his wife close. They fell, and the horses pounded past and on into the darkness.

Elsewhere, men shouted and milled in confusion. Shakespeare grabbed Blue Water Woman's hand and ran to where the string had been tied. The pale glow of the fire showed a riverman on the ground, blood trickling from a gashed temple. LeBeau was examining him.

"Is he dead?" Shakespeare asked.

"*Non*. Hurt bad."

Nate appeared, leading three pack horses. Other men had caught other animals and were bringing them back. "Did anyone get a good look at whoever scared our stock off?"

"All I got a good look at was the hind ends of horses headed west," Shakespeare said. "Hell of a sight to wake up to."

"Was anyone else hurt?" Nate asked.

"Not that I know of."

"What about Hestia?"

LeBeau went as rigid as a bean pole, leaped erect, and dashed toward the fire.

"What got into him?" Shakespeare said. "As if I can't guess." He let go of Blue Water Woman. "Why don't you see how badly our fixings were damaged while I help these pilgrims round up the horses?"

Fifteen minutes later two-thirds of the horses had been recovered. Cyrus Porter stomped back and forth, furious. "We should track down the savages who did this and make them pay in blood! We can't afford to lose that many horses. We'll need every one we have in order to reach Oregon."

"We maybe can trade for some between here and Astoria," Shakespeare said. "The Flatheads sometimes come to this region. And if we don't run into them, there may be some at the dalles."

"Is that a fort?" Clark asked. "I've never heard of it."

"The Chinooks, who happen to be the best damn traders this side of the Rockies, have one of their main villages there," Shakespeare disclosed. "Indians come from hundreds of miles around to barter. Think of it as the Indian answer to St. Louis, and you'll have a fair idea of what goes on."

"They won't put arrows into us when we show up?" Clark inquired, thinking of the attacks by the Blackfeet and the Diggers.

"They wouldn't dare." Shakespeare snickered. "Didn't you hear me? The Chinooks are traders. They'll give their eyeteeth for any supplies we'd care to part with, because they know they can turn around and get three to four times as much from other tribes for the same goods."

Ordeal

"Just so they have horses," Porter said with his typical single-minded persistence.

The sentry brought their conversation to an end by groaning. Winona had cleaned his wound with a wet cloth and bandaged it. His eyelids fluttered, then snapped open as he sat bolt upright in fear. Winona's smile and calm demeanor had a soothing effect on him. Shaking, he laid back down.

Shakespeare and Nate went over. "Up to talking a little?" the older man asked.

"*Oui*," the man said. "English mine but much poor."

That struck McNair's funny bone. "Lordy, son. You speak it worse than LeBeau, and that takes some doing."

"I heard that, *monsieur*," LeBeau said, joining them. He had stayed near Hestia Davin until assured she was unhurt by Blue Water Woman. Now he knelt beside his fellow riverman and questioned him in French. When he was done, he faced the free trappers. "Pierre says he did not see man who hit him."

"Wonderful," Shakespeare said dryly. "The way these coons keep getting the best of us, you'd think we were dealing with ghosts."

The jingle of spurs attended the arrival of Chavez, who appeared out of sorts. "My friends, one of us is missing," he announced.

"Who?" Nate asked, and the moment he did, he knew. "Two Humps!" he exclaimed, realizing there had been no sign of the old chief since the raid.

"*Si,*" Chavez said. "I wanted him to help me look for tracks. He is a fine tracker. Better than I am."

"Tarnation. Don't be so humble," Shakespeare said. "We still remember that night you tracked us from one end of the Rockies to the other, and you without a torch."

"You exaggerate, *amigo,*" Chavez said. "It was not more than twenty miles." He grinned slyly. "And it was not as hard as you believe. Two of your pack animals had horseshoes, did they not?"

"I seem to recollect they did. I never bother shoeing my animals, myself, but that pair had been traded to me by Bill Williams, and he's finicky about his stock. So?"

"So one of them was losing a front shoe. It dug big clods of earth from the ground, which were easy to see even in the dark. That is how I followed you."

"I'll be dogged," Shakespeare said.

Nate couldn't believe they were standing there idly discussing something that happened months ago when Two Humps might be lying in the woods somewhere, scalped and mutilated. He mentioned as much.

"The reason I'm not flustered," Shakespeare said, "is because I have eyes and know how to use them." He pointed.

Trotting toward them from the rear was the warrior, his lance in his right hand. He wore only leggings; he had been sleeping when the attack came and had not bothered to put on his shirt or robe. For a man of advanced years, his chest and arms rippled with muscle. "I followed them," he signed without preliminaries. "They have stopped and made camp. If we hurry, we can bring back the horses they stole."

"Question. How many?" Nate signed.

"Six."

"What tribe are they?" Shakespeare was curious. "Columbias? Spokans? Wenatchis?"

"They are white."

Something in the expressions of the mountain men prompted LeBeau to ask, "What is wrong, *mes amis?*"

Shakespeare told him, adding, "The only other whites I know of who might be in this area are British trappers. You saw for yourselves back at Fort Hall that the Britishers don't like Americans much, but I never figured them for this." He rubbed his belly and sighed. "Goes to show you the deplorable state this old world of ours has come to when a man can't go halfway across the country without being robbed."

They informed Porter. He was all for setting off after the culprits with Clark and half the men, but Shakespeare prevailed on him to only send four. So, dressed and armed to the teeth, McNair, Nate, Chavez and Two Humps entered the gloomy, foreboding forest in the dead of night and headed to the northwest. Chavez let Two Humps handle the tracking.

Progress was slow. The undergrowth was dastardly thick, denser than any in the central Rockies. The slopes were steeper, too. A man had to be half bighorn just to get around.

The night was vibrant with sounds; the guttural coughs of bears, the high-pitched shrieks of painters, the hooting of owls, the howling of wolves. Especially the latter. It seemed to Nate that he had never heard so many wolves in full throat at the same time.

Shakespeare was having a grand time. Having always been an adventurous soul, in his younger days he had craved excitement as children craved sweets. The rush of blood in his veins was like a tonic, reminding him of many glorious times he'd had. His sole complaint was that his Nez Percé friend was taking the hardest shortcut any man ever took in order to reach the camp of the horse thieves quickly. Shakespeare knew it was a shortcut even though he didn't ask, because no horse alive could have negotiated the terrain they were covering.

Five miles fell behind them. Suddenly, a flaring point of light stood out in stark contrast to the wilderness, serving as a beacon that drew them to the edge of the British camp.

The stolen horses were all there, strung out in a line, tethered securely. None of the thieves were asleep yet. Seated around their small fire, they passed a jug back and forth and bragged of their part in the enterprise.

Nate King was shocked. Not by the pleasure the English felt in having crippled the expedition, nor by the talk he heard, but because he recognized the man who had led the raid.

It was none other than Andrew Smythe-Barnes.

Chapter Eighteen

A dozen questions popped into Nate King's mind: What was Smythe-Barnes doing there on the Columbia? Had the man followed them all the way from Fort Hall, awaiting an opportunity to steal their stock? Was there any link between this theft and the previous two attempts made before they reached Fort Hall?

Nate studied the faces and recognized the man named Dinkus and those other ruffians who had given Winona such a hard time. He glanced at Shakespeare, who was looking at him. McNair motioned for him to go to the left. Nate complied, placing each foot carefully, his moccasins making no noise on the layer of pine needles. When he had circled partway around the camp, he halted and snaked forward on his belly until he was a mere 20 feet from the fire. The HBC men were gabbing so much, they never even noticed.

Nate wasn't particularly worried. He doubted Smythe-Barnes would make a fight of it over a bunch of horses. Rather, the weasely company man would concoct a bald-faced lie to explain the horses being there and try to snivel his way out of the fix he was in.

But events proved Nate wrong.

Shakespeare had crawled across the open space between the Britishers and the woods, freezing whenever one happened to glance in his direction. He held his face low to the ground so the firelight would not reflect off his skin. The Hawken he held in front of him, flush with the earth. When he was close enough, he laid still another few minutes to give everyone else time to get into position. The conversation of the HBC men interested him greatly.

"—raid them again before they reach Fort Astoria," Smythe-Barnes was saying in his clipped, impeccable English. "If we can make off with another fifteen or twenty head, the bloody Americans will have no choice but to turn around and go home."

"That's right, guv," Dinkus cackled. "We can't have them blighters comin' here and overrunnin' the country. Worse than a plague of locusts, they are. Makin' us go to all this trouble."

Smythe-Barnes lowered the jug and smacked his lips. "Might I remind you that we wouldn't be here if you had done your job back at the fort?"

Ordeal

"I tried, guv," Dinkus said. "As the Lord is my witness, I tried. But that King character was on us before we knew he was there. We had no time to shoot."

"The failure is your fault, not his," Smythe-Barnes said in disgust. "All you had to do was get him to go for a gun and shoot him dead. That's all. Then I could have blamed him and ordered their so-called expedition out of Oregon Country for violating the terms of the agreement between our two countries. But no. You and your mates couldn't beat one American trapper."

"He's tough, I tell you," Dinkus persisted. "And his punch is like the kick of a mule. I never been hit harder in all my days."

Another ruffian chimed in, "Seems to me we could have saved ourselves all this skulkin' about if we'd sent a rider on to Astoria and let them deal with the Americans."

"There would have been no guarantee the rider made it safely," Smythe-Barnes said. "The job was ours to do, and since we failed at Fort Hall, we've got to keep trying until it's done."

"I don't see why this bunch has those higher up so worried," commented another man. "What's one more party of Americans?"

"This one is special," Smythe-Barnes said, then took a healthy swallow.

"Special how?"

"One of them is a spy, sent by Washington, D.C.," Smythe-Barnes said.

"Why?" the man pressed.

"When I'm told I can pass on the information,

I will." Smythe-Barnes passed on the jug instead. "As it is, I've babbled too much already. It's this damn beer."

"Begging your pardon, sir," said yet another, grinning. "But this drink wouldn't addle a child. It's all arms and legs. Give me whiskey any day."

"You're worse than the Americans, Peeves," Smythe-Barnes groused. He noticed a spot of dirt on his coat and brushed at it with the back of his hand. "God, this miserable land. I can't wait to see London again."

Shakespeare had waited long enough. Rising slowly so as not to startle any of the HBC men into doing anything rash, he leveled his Hawken and advanced several strides. "You'll be lucky if you see Fort Hall again, let alone London," he said matter-of-factly.

Those Britishers with their backs to the mountain man spun, one spilling the jug in his haste. Those on the other side of the fire, including Smythe-Barnes, half rose, some reaching for their weapons.

From out of the night rushed Nate, Chavez, and Two Humps. The sight so shocked the HBC outfit that those who were rising sat back down and the ones who had whirled turned to stone.

"Glad to see you gents have some common sense," Shakespeare said, going nearer. "Not enough to keep you from stealing horses, but enough to keep you from being shot."

"McNair," Smythe-Barnes said in an awed tone that inferred he couldn't believe Shakespeare was there.

Ordeal

"Is that the best you can come up with after you've just been accused of being a horse thief? Tarnation, and here you British are supposed to be such wits."

Dinkus hissed like the serpent he was, then snapped, "Don't be insultin' us, Yank. We won't stand for it."

"Any more than we'll stand for having our stock taken," Shakespeare said. He made a show of studying them as if trying to make up his mind what to do. "The question is, do we shoot you outright or make you suffer a spell?"

Actually, McNair had no intention of doing them real harm. He'd shoot anyone in cold blood who affronted his wife, but not a pack of dim-witted horse thieves. Maybe he'd crack a skull or two to repay them for the sentry, but that was all.

The British trappers didn't know that. They exchanged anxious glances, Smythe-Barnes's the most anxious of all. The administrator coughed and said, "What's this about us appropriating your animals? We found this lot wandering in the forest and tethered them so they wouldn't wander."

Nate laughed. It was exactly as he had expected. "Sure you did," he said, "and you just happen to be along the same stretch of the Columbia we are. Did you go out for an evening stroll and lose your way?"

"What we're about is our business."

Shakespeare clucked like an irate hen. "Oh, please. I just heard you brag about taking them, so don't be so dumb as to try and deny it." He wagged his rifle. "On your feet. We'll let Porter vent his spleen on you so we don't have to listen to him bellyache for the next two weeks."

"We're not going anywhere with you, Yank," Smythe-Barnes said, producing a small pistol.

It was all so unexpected. Shakespeare had no intention of harming them, yet there was that pocket pistol swinging toward him, leaving him no choice but to whip the Hawken higher and fire from the hip. The recoil jerked his arms.

Smythe-Barnes was flung backward by the impact of the heavy ball, his arms flung out, a red stain spreading over his chest. His men were glued in place, but only for a few seconds. Venting snarls and curses, they swept to their feet and brought their weapons into play.

Nate King was mere yards from the one named Peeves. The man turned toward him, drawing a pistol. Nate shot him through the throat. He meant to shoot higher but in his haste didn't quite raise the Hawken high enough. Peeves collapsed, spurting like a geyser, blubbering like a baby.

At the same time, a pair of HBC men spun on Chavez. Both had rifles in hand. Both were fast. But neither was faster than the Mexican. Chavez drew his dueling pistols ambidextrously, and his two shots cracked simultaneously. He sent a slug tearing through each man's forehead.

Even as the tracker fired, Two Humps charged, his lance arm flinging far back. He was a single stride from a burly trapper armed with a large pistol when he hurled the lance, which tore clean through the trapper's body. The man tottered, squeezing a shot into the ground out of pure reflex. Then he collapsed.

Five of the six had been dispatched in as many seconds. Ironically, only Dinkus remained, and he showed his true colors by fleeing into the woods instead of fighting.

The Nez Percé saw him go and drew his tomahawk. He started to give chase but stopped when Shakespeare called his name.

"There's been enough killing. Let the coward go."

"Cowards make vengeful enemies. It is a mistake. I should scalp him now so he will not cause us trouble later."

"That worm?" Shakespeare walked to Smythe-Barnes and stared at the dead man's features. "Why art thou than exasperate," he recited the bard, "thou idle immaterial skein of sleave silk, thou green sarcenet flap for a sore eye, thou tassel of a prodigal's purse, thou? Ah, how the poor world is pestered with such waterflies, diminutives of nature."

Nate hardly heard his friend's recital. He stood over the man he'd shot in the throat, who thrashed and whined and kicked empty air but wouldn't die although he bled enough to fill two washtubs. "Someone should put you out of your misery," he said without thinking.

Two Humps's lance streaked out of the dark and caught the man in the center of the chest. He heaved off the ground once, gurgled, and expired, his tongue sticking over his lower lip.

The warrior walked up. In a smooth motion he yanked the lance free and wiped it on the dead man's shirt. "Kill clean, kill quick," he said in his broken English. "Best way, Grizzly Killer."

"I tried," Nate said lamely. In the heat of battle it was easy to misjudge and make a mistake, but he still felt a twinge of guilt for having missed the head.

The Nez Percé took it upon himself to go from body to body, verifying that each man was dead. Only one other stirred, but not for long. With a swift slash, Two Humps slit the man's throat.

Shakespeare was reloading his rifle. "I don't make it a habit to bury those who try to kill me," he commented, "but in this case I'll make an exception. I don't want the scavengers to get them."

The Britishers were buried in shallow graves. It took most of the night, since the ground was as hard as iron and they had to improvise digging implements. Nate used an axe, McNair a jagged limb. Chavez merely watched, while the Nez Percé occupied himself cleaning the scalps he had lifted.

Because the hour was late and they couldn't very well try to lead the horses back over the mountains in the dark, they made camp right there. The mountain men stayed up after their friends had dozed off, sipping coffee. Nate fed fuel to the flickering fire while listening to a painter screech high off in the mountains. "What do you make of all this?"

"As near as I can figure, we went and got caught

in the middle of a squabble between our government and England," Shakespeare answered. "The two have been feuding for years over who gets to keep the Oregon Country, as you well know." He opened his possibles bag, removed some kinnikinnick, and filled the bowl of his pipe before going on. "You heard Smythe-Barnes. There's more to this expedition than we've been told. Someone is working for the people in Washington. Why, I have no idea."

"It shouldn't be hard to figure out who it is," Nate said. He began ticking off the suspects. "The rivermen are just who they claim to be, and so is Chavez. That leaves Porter, Clark, and Hughes. Hughes was hired on in St. Louis, which leaves him out. Since Clark is a flash in the pan, my guess would be Porter."

"I don't know as I agree."

"Think about it a moment. The expedition was his idea, supposedly because he was fired up to find his daughter. But he never acted very upset about her welfare, not like I would do if Hestia were mine. Even Zach noticed, remember?"

"I do."

"So Porter is our man."

Shakespeare finished tamping the tobacco and took a tiny burning brand from the fire to light it. He puffed until smoke wafted from the bowl, then leaned back and remarked, "I think it's Clark."

"You must have been knocked on the head during the fight and not noticed. Clark is as worthless as a man can be and still go on breathing. Why pick him?"

"For that very reason. No man can be that incompetent. Maybe it's all an act."

"Could be," Nate said. "A man can't judge a book by its cover, but it seems to me you're giving that worthless coon credit for more intelligence than is his due. Besides, if he was the man sent by Washington, would he let Porter treat him the way Porter does? I think not."

Shakespeare took a slow drag on his pipe, savoring the sensation. He happened to glance skyward and beheld a marvelous spectacle: a fiery shooting star streaking across the sky in a blaze of glory. "I reckon we'll have to be on our guard more than ever from here on out. The British won't give up easy, and we still have a long trek ahead of us."

"Should we make Porter or Clark fess up?"

"To what purpose? Haven't you learned by now that you can't go sticking your nose into someone else's affairs? It's none of our business whether they are who they claim to be or not."

"Like hell. Our wives and my sprouts are in danger because of this nonsense. I should throttle the two greenhorns until they tell us the truth."

"You go right ahead if you want. Just don't expect me to hold him down while you do."

Nate made small talk until they turned in. He slept fitfully, deeply bothered by what they had learned. No matter who it was, the man should have been honest with them and told them at the very start of the journey that they were letting themselves in for a lot of unnecessary aggravation. It was unconscionable to him that the man had kept it a secret.

Ordeal

Nate was still thinking about the situation the next morning as they rode toward the Columbia River. Only a mile lay before them when a shocking idea hit him. Was it possible the government didn't want the man to let anyone know? Was it possible the *government* was keeping the secret from its own citizens?

Such an idea was shattering. Nate had always been one of those who believed that if the cream of political candidates were elected to government posts, the wheels of government would turn smoothly and honestly. Only after he'd met McNair, who held a deeply cynical view of politicians he never explained, did Nate realize that sometimes the government worked in its own best interests and not those of the people it was supposed to serve. George Washington and his ilk would roll over in their graves if they knew.

There was rejoicing in the camp when the stolen horses were brought back. Porter was one of the happiest, going to each of those who had taken part and clapping them on the back. Nate flinched when the man touched him, as he would if he were brushed by a snake.

"So who took them?" the New Englander asked. "More thieving savages, I presume?"

"It was Smythe-Barnes and some of his men," Shakespeare said. "We had to kill them."

A pall fell over the group. Winona and Blue Water Woman appeared confused. Brett Hughes looked shocked. Adam Clark turned crimson, whether from anger or another emotion it was hard to say. And Cyrus Porter made a wave of dismissal and remarked, "Good riddance! I haven't forgiven that man for his treatment of us at Fort Hall. If anyone ever deserved to die, it was him."

The expedition got under way within the hour. The river turned turbulent, posing one series of rapids after another. Both shorelines were harshly rugged, at times starkly steep. Slow progress was the order of the day, and the next several days.

Everyone was overjoyed when the Columbia finally widened and a large basin covered with lush grass opened up before them. At the end of the basin nearest the river stood a unique village.

"The Chinooks," Shakespeare said.

The dwellings were of two types. One was a simple lodge made from woven mats. These were shown to be temporary shelters used by visitors. The second type were underground homes covered by low plank roofs, the permanent dwellings of the Chinooks.

In addition, huge wooden racks made from cedar poles had been erected, from which hung enough drying salmon meat to feed half the population of the United States.

The basin buzzed with activity. Hundreds of Chinooks called the village home, while lined up along the shore were scores of dugout canoes hollowed from the trunks of trees, canoes belonging to Indians from other tribes who had traveled from far and wide for the privilege of trading.

"Do you speak their language?" Clark nervously asked McNair as the column moved into the open.

"Not all that well," Shakespeare said. "They've been trading with the Nootkas and Salish tribe for so long that they speak jargon made up of all three. It's hard on the tongue and I'm out of practice."

The expedition's arrival did not go unnoticed. A stream of Indians flowed from the dwellings to meet them, and four Chinooks stepped forward with arms raised to show their peaceful intentions. They were stocky, muscular men garbed in various fine animal skins, their hair cropped at the shoulders, their skin bronzed from the sun.

Shakespeare took Nate, Porter, and Clark with him to conduct the formal greeting. The Chinooks did not use sign as fluently as tribes to the east, but between the few signs they knew and the few Chinook words Shakespeare recollected, they were able to communicate.

The chief escorted them into the village and put a dozen mat dwellings at their disposal. Porter was all for pushing on, but Shakespeare made mention of the fact that their horses needed a few days to rest and graze, so he assented.

Nate took his family on a stroll. Everywhere they went they were surrounded by fascinated, smiling, friendly Chinooks. Children flocked to them in droves, many young girls pointing at Zach and giggling. Few weapons were in evidence. The men of the tribe were as open and frank as the women and children. No hint of hostility was ever seen.

The Chinook way of life was so distinctly different from the tribes with which Nate was familiar that it gave him much food for thought. Devoted as they were to trade and fishing, the Chinooks were as peaceable a people as Nate could imagine.

In contrast, the Shoshones, Crows, Sioux, Cheyennes, and many others were devoted to warfare. A man who had never been in battle, never gone on a raid, never counted a single coup, was accorded the status of a woman. War was exalted, peace looked down on as a state to be avoided at all costs.

It set Nate to wondering which was better, the Chinook mode of living or the warrior ways of the plains and Rocky Mountain tribes. Perhaps, he reasoned, it had more to do with the natures of the respective peoples. He couldn't see the Blackfeet giving up their passion for warfare any more than he could see the Chinooks adopting the customs of the warrior societies.

Three events of note took place during the expedition's stay. The first involved Two Humps. He created a sensation among the Chinooks, who acted timid around him. None would approach him too closely, and when he strolled through the village, the inhabitants made it a point to avoid him. Nate had no idea why until the afternoon of the next day, when he asked the warrior in sign language.

"They fear the Nez Percé," the chief responded. "We are brave fighters." Glancing around at the wary Chinooks, he added, "And many, many winters ago my people liked to slit Chinook throats. They still hold that against us."

The second incident happened during the evening meal hours later when Nate mentioned the warrior's comment to his mentor, saying, "The Chinooks must have been easy pickings for the Nez Percé."

"There's such a thing as being too friendly for your own good," Shakespeare said between puffs on his pipe.

"You really think so?"

The mountain man gestured at the village. "Look around you. What do you see?"

"One of the most peaceful villages I've ever been in. Why?"

"Remember it, Horatio. You might never see its like again."

Nate surveyed the picturesque setting. "I've lost your trail."

"The Chinooks you see here are about all that's left of their tribe. Chillarlawil, their chief, might well be their last." Shakespeare stared at several boys playing a game with a stick and several hoops. "Once there were thousands, all as friendly as those you see here. They welcomed everyone with open arms, including Lewis and Clark and white traders who sailed up the Columbia from the Pacific."

"What's wrong with that?"

"A few years ago smallpox wiped out nearly the entire tribe."

The third event did not transpire until the morning of the third day, only a few hours before the expedition was to resume its journey. The pack animals had been loaded with extra provisions obtained in trade. A formal delegation, headed by Chillarlawil, came to bid them farewell. Porter was fidgeting, impatient to be off, while Shakespeare said a fond good-bye to the chief on everyone's behalf. Just as McNair turned to give the signal that would start the column on its way, the most unforeseen event of all happened: Hestia Davin sat up.

Chapter Nineteen

Winona stood nearest the travois when it happened. She had just slung the cradleboard onto her back and was about to find Blue Water Woman to ask her to slide Evelyn into it when she heard a low groan and looked down to see the young white woman sitting up. She was so startled that she recoiled a step, clutching Evelyn to her bosom. After so many weeks, Winona had about resigned herself to the woman never recovering.

Hestia Davin blinked a few times, squinting at the blazing sun in the azure sky. Then she gazed calmly all around her at the Chinook village and the various expedition members, none of whom had yet noticed the miracle. She said two words, softly as if to herself, but not so softly that Winona didn't hear: "At last."

Winona felt foolish for having acted as she did. Stepping to the travois, she said in her best English, "I am Winona King, Miss Davin. Do not be afraid. You are in good hands."

"I know," the blonde said, smiling. "I know who you are. I know who all of you are."

"How is that possible?" Winona asked, wondering if the woman's mind had gone. It wasn't uncommon for captives to suffer so severely they lost their power to reason or else lived in imaginary worlds of their own devising.

"It's hard to explain," Hestia said, pressing a hand to her brow. "All this time I could hear every word being spoken and see all of you going about your daily work, as if through a heavy fog. But I couldn't bring myself to talk, couldn't make my vocal chords move to let you know I was conscious. I couldn't move a muscle. It was as if I were frozen solid."

"And now?" Winona queried, putting a hand on the woman's face. She found no trace of fever.

"There was this strange feeling in my head just a minute ago, as if something inside of me had snapped, and I realized I was whole again." Hestia looked at Winona, tears of relief rimming her eyes. "I'm whole," she repeated in amazement. "It's almost too good to be true. I fear I might be dreaming."

"You are not," Winona assured her. She had witnessed astounding recoveries before, most notably a Shoshone chief who had been attacked by a grizzly and lost the use of all his limbs. For several years the man had been cared for by his wife and sons, who refused to leave him behind. Then one day, for no apparent reason, the chief had risen from his pallet, fully recovered.

"Thank you, Lord," Hestia said, her lids hooded. She sniffed, dabbed at her eyes with her sleeve, and said, "I know all that you have done for me, Mrs. King. You and Blue Water Woman. I know you gave me medicines. I could feel you washing me and changing me and hear you talking, but I couldn't respond. I'm so sorry to have put you through such an ordeal."

Winona decided on the spot that she liked the young woman. Anyone who was so considerate of others after having suffered so terribly had to be a good person. She squeezed Hestia's shoulder, saying, "I wish our medicine had worked sooner. Your father will be very happy to have you healthy again."

At the mention of Porter, Hestia's features clouded darkly. "Yes, my dear, doting father," she said, lacing the last word with scorn.

Winona turned and saw Shakespeare about to give the signal to move on out. "No!" she cried, drawing the gaze of all those within earshot. "Look!"

Shock was the widespread reaction. In moments they came from all directions, not only the New Englanders and Brett Hughes, but the rivermen too and many of the Chinooks who had stood and stared at the poor white woman, feeling sorry for her. Winona noticed fear creep into Hestia's eyes and gripped her elbow. "It will be all right," she said quietly. "No one will hurt you."

David Thompson

Cyrus Porter barreled through the throng heedless of those he knocked aside. He halted in front of his daughter, mouth working soundlessly, aglow with his happiness. "You're well again!" he finally exclaimed, astounded. "You're well again!" Impulsively he swooped Hestia into his arms and whirled her around, laughing merrily until he observed the look she gave him.

"Put me down, father."

Porter slowly complied, his elation giving way to apprehension. "What's the matter, sweetheart? Did I make you dizzy?"

"No, father," Hestia said icily.

Winona didn't understand her behavior, nor why her father grit his teeth as if in pain.

"Still?" Porter said. "After all I went through on your behalf?" He seemed about to give his daughter a verbal lashing. Then he glanced at the milling faces and changed his mind. "Later, Hetty. I expect you to look me up once you have a free moment so we won't have to air our dirty linen in front of these riffraff." As mad as a wet badger, he stormed off.

Adam Clark was next to step close to her. "Sweet Hetty," he said, in awe of her beauty. "It's so wonderful to have you back among the living again."

"No, Adam," Hestia said.

"But it is," he stated. "You have no idea how much I've worried about you ever since your father told me that you had gone off with that worthless Davin. You have no idea how much I've missed you."

"As usual, you're thinking of yourself first," Hestia said. "And when I said no, I wasn't talking about my recovery. I was referring to the reason you came with my father." She paused. "I heard, you know. Every time the two of you stood close to me and discussed your plans, I heard every word."

"You did?" Clark said, losing some of his confidence. "Well, that was merely idle talk."

"All those times you told my father that you loved me? That you couldn't wait to make me your wife?"

Clark blanched and licked his lips. "I meant every word of that, my dear. I've never stopped dreaming that we would be reunited."

"We were never united in the first place," Hestia said. "We dated a few times, is all. You don't have a claim on my heart. Frankly, you never will."

Crestfallen, Clark walked off, head bowed.

Winona was going to leave, herself. She felt as if she were prying into the blonde woman's personal affairs. But as she began to turn, Hestia clutched the travois for support and sagged. Winona had her arm around the woman's shoulder in an instant. "Are you all right?"

"Too much, too soon," Hestia said sadly. "I feel so weak, so tired. But how can that be, when I did nothing except lie on my back for days on end?"

"Your head has healed but your body has not," Winona said. "You are very thin, and you have not used your muscles in many moons. You must go slowly."

Hestia nodded, her gaze roving the crowd. "Where is he?" she asked urgently.

"Who?"

"I don't know his name, but I will know his face when I see it."

At a loss to guess whom she meant, Winona helped Hestia sit down. Blue Water Woman appeared and lent a hand.

A few yards away, Shakespeare McNair and Nate King had witnessed the exchanges with interest. "I reckon we should stay over another night," the older man said.

"I'll pass the word," Nate volunteered.

It was shortly before sunset when Winona walked to the Columbia and took a seat on a flat boulder partially ringed by tall weeds to nurse Evelyn. The child had grown so much since leaving the Rockies that soon Winona must wean her, a thought that saddened Winona very much. She liked having a baby to brighten her days, liked the soft warmth and cheerful smiles and the playful antics. Once they had returned to their cabin, she would convince Nate to have another. If he refused, she felt strongly enough about it to have him get her pregnant anyway. Which would be easy to do. In the heat of passion men were easily swayed and could rarely control themselves.

For an hour Winona sat, savoring the rare privacy and peace. During the arduous trek she had seldom enjoyed such a luxury. Either she had been tending the stricken woman or the baby or spending time with her husband and son.

292

Ordeal

Winona admired the setting of the sun, the sky resplendent with a rainbow of vivid colors. A refreshing breeze blowing in from the ocean stirred her long hair and cooled her brow. She was in no great hurry to return to the village.

Now and then Winona heard voices as Chinooks came to the river to fish or stroll. None noticed her, hidden by the weeds as she was. A new set of voices carried to her ears as she sat stroking Evelyn's brow, and these drew her interest because the speakers used English.

"—thank you for going for this walk with me."

Winona identified Cyrus Porter and hoped he wouldn't see her. She always felt uncomfortable around him, as she would around anyone who secretly despised her because she didn't have the same color skin that they did.

"You didn't leave me much choice, dragging me away from the fire the way you did."

That was Hestia Davin. Winona debated whether to get up and go before she heard things rightfully not meant for her ears, or simply to stay put in the hope they would wander elsewhere and she could relish a few more minutes of tranquility. The next she knew, they were within ten feet of her, to the left, only the tops of their heads visible above the weeds.

"We had to talk whether you cared to or not," Porter said. "We have to clear the air now so there are no misunderstandings."

"I understand you perfectly, father," Hestia said.

"Don't start in on me already. We haven't been out here two minutes."

"We've been here long enough."

Winona was about to stand when she heard the sound of a slap. Since to rise now would only subject Hestia to embarrassment, she stayed where she was.

"How dare you!" Cyrus Porter declared.

"I'll thank you not to put your hands on me, father. If I want to go, I'll go. You have no right to pull me back."

"But all I want to do is *talk*," Porter pleaded. "Is that a cardinal sin? For a man to want to have a few words with his only daughter?" He paused, and apparently Hestia didn't leave. "I know that you haven't thought much of me since your mother died, but I've tried my utmost to be the best parent I could be. I think I've proved my devotion by arranging this expedition to find you."

When Hestia spoke, her voice reminded Winona of the icicles that sometimes hung from the roof of the cabin in the winter.

"I haven't thought much of you since mother's passing, father, because I blame you for her death. She would have lived a lot longer had you not neglected her so."

"Neglected her?" Porter snorted. "Why, I gave her every luxury a woman could want. I bought her anything her heart desired whenever she wanted it. Tell me I didn't. I defy you."

"Money can't love. She wanted you by her side, needed your companionship more than the rings and furs and lavish gifts. She died of a broken heart because you were never home. You cared more for your social clubs and business associates than you did for your own wife."

"I did not," Porter said, but his tone lacked conviction.

"As for the expedition," Hestia went on, showing no mercy, "you came out here with the express purpose of taking me back to the States whether I wanted to go or not. You even had the audacity to bring that fool Adam in the hope I would take up with him and leave my poor Oliver."

Porter tried to talk but was cut off.

"Don't interrupt. You wanted to talk, well, I'm talking. And if you don't like what you're hearing, you have only yourself to blame." Hestia took a breath. "You can't seem to get it through your head that I am my own woman and always will be. I'm not like mother, willing to be bossed around and told how to live my life by someone who thinks he has the God-given right to lord it over everyone. I married Oliver because I loved him with all my heart. Now he's dead and I have to take up the strands and go on. It's not easy, but I'll do it, father, because in one respect I am a lot like you. I can be just as hardheaded." Again she paused. "I don't know what my plans are yet, but I do know that once we're back in the States—if I go back—we will part company for good. I like to think of you in your old age, sitting on a rocking chair in the parlor with no one around to comfort you, just sitting and staring at the walls as mother used to do."

"You can be cruel when you want to, Hetty."

"No crueler than you."

Winona listened to footsteps drag into the night. She put a hand under her to stand, then froze on hearing a new sound, the soft, choking sobs of a young woman crying. Her keen ears picked up more footsteps, Porter coming back, she assumed, until a new voice proved her wrong.

"You be okay, *petite?*"

A sharp intake of breath greeted the question, followed by a breathless exclamation.

"You! At last! Where have you been? Didn't you know I had recovered?"

"I knew," LeBeau said.

"Then why haven't you shown yourself until now?"

"The truth. I was afraid."

"Of what, for land's sake?"

"You, *petite.*"

"Me?"

"That maybe you throw a stone, eh, and tell me to jump off one of these here cliffs. They say you remember everything. They say you were awake but not awake." LeBeau's voice dropped so low Winona could barely hear it. "I think maybe you think me an idiot. I think maybe you laugh."

"Never," Hestia said, somehow contriving to make the single word a declaration of abiding affection.

There were footsteps, the rustling of a dress.

"Why did you do that, *petite?*" LeBeau asked.

"I wanted to."

"Your father, he'll shoot me if he sees."

"He tries, and I'll shoot him."

Ordeal

They laughed softly, and then Hestia turned serious.

"Yes, I know what you did. I laid there listening, night after night after night, as you held my hand and talked of anything and everything that came into your head. You poured your heart and soul out to me, Armand. And you kept saying that you knew I could hear you, knew I would understand. How did you know?"

"I—" LeBeau began, but stopped.

"I know this is crazy. I know you know little about me. But I would like you to learn more." Hestia coughed. "You have to understand. Lying so helpless, with no way of communicating, ignored by everyone, many times I wanted to die. Then you came into my life, and you were kind and gentle and never once took advantage. Day after day I couldn't wait for you to come to me, to hear you soothing me." She paused. "You told me that you thought I was the most beautiful woman in all the world, and you prayed I would get better so you could court me. Were those lies, or did you mean it?"

"Every word." LeBeau was having difficulty talking.

The next sounds Winona heard puzzled her a few moments, until the blonde woman moaned. Aware she must not let them discover her at any cost, she held Evelen close to her breast and gently rocked back and forth to lull her daughter to sleep and keep her from crying or making some other noise.

Later that night, after Winona told her husband, Nate draped an arm over her shoulder and commented, "We'd better keep our eyes on Porter. He won't take kindly to Hetty taking a fancy to LeBeau."

"What can he do?" Winona asked. "Hetty is a grown woman. She can do as she pleases, can she not?"

"I wish it were that simple," Nate said. "Her father is the kind of man who doesn't take failure well. He'll find some way to break them apart. Mark my words."

Cyrus Porter's mood the next day bore Nate out. Porter was as foul-tempered as the storm clouds that had appeared to the northwest. He stalked around barking orders to the rivermen and Hughes as if they were his personal servants. Adam Clark also felt his wrath several times, but Clark's only crime appeared to be that he was breathing.

Toward the middle of the morning the expedition got under way. Shakespeare wanted to stay longer to give Hestia Davin more time to recuperate, but she would not hear of it. Assuring him she was well enough to ride and badly needed the exercise, she convinced him to strike out for the Pacific.

The Chinooks gave them a fine send-off. Nate was almost sorry to go, he liked the peaceable tribe so much. He noticed Zach bidding farewell to a Chinook girl with tears in her eyes and reminded himself that before he knew it, his son would be a man.

Ordeal

Nate also noticed Hestia and LeBeau riding side by side; occasionally, hand in hand. They were in the full flush of first love, in their own little world, oblivious to all else. And being so, they were particularly vulnerable. Nate made it a point to keep a watch on her father as much as he could, but often his duties took him off scouting or hunting.

It proved fortunate the expedition wasn't relying on boats or canoes. Shortly after leaving the village, they found that the Columbia narrowed, the rushing flow compressed into a 45-yard gap that extended for over a quarter of a mile. Beyond, the river widened to 200 yards for a couple of miles, but then the current encountered a massive blockade of enormous rocks.

Farther on, the river was divided by two islands of sheer rock, the lower one situated in the very middle and creating rapids of the most hazardous order.

The fourth day out from the village, as the column passed high bluffs on their left, Nate spied numbers of Indians observing them from on high. He galloped ahead to where McNair rode with Chavez and pointed the watchers out.

"We spotted them 20 minutes ago, Horatio," Shakespeare said. "Your brain has been dulled from too much easy living."

"Are they Chinooks?"

"No. I can't say as I've seen them before. Let's hope they're friendly, though. If they take to shoving some of those big boulders down on us, we'd lose a lot of horses and supplies. Not to mention a lot of lives."

The threat so unsettled Nate that for the next two hours he could hardly stand to tear his gaze from the craggy bluffs. The Indians seemed content to shadow the expedition, but it prickled the short hairs at the nape of his neck to have them up there, peering down on him. It also gave him a crick in the neck before they finally vanished as mysteriously as they had appeared.

Not a day later they saw more Indians, this time across the river, fishing for salmon. The Indians panicked on seeing the whites and took to the forest as fast as their feet would fly. A few were brave enough to peek from behind trees, but none would answer no matter how loudly Shakespeare hailed them.

That evening the party camped on a level bench beside the roaring river. After supper Nate strolled with his son down to the water's edge. Zach acted restless, fidgeting and gnawing on his lower lip as if he were practicing to be a beaver. As they stood thrilled by the gorgeous spectacle of the setting sun, he turned to his father and cleared his throat.

"Mind if I ask you a question, Pa?"

"When have I ever minded?"

Zach toyed with a pebble with his toe. "This is sort of a different kind of question. It's hard for me to ask because you'll think I'm being silly."

"Your mother claims men are born silly," Nate joked, "so you have no need to feel awkward." He put a hand on the boy's head. "Ask away."

Ordeal

"What can you tell me about girls?" Zach blurted out. For days he had wrestled with whether to broach the subject or not, and now that he had he felt extremely ill at ease. His father had always been open to him in every regard, but there were some things that were hard to bring up.

Girls were one of them. They had never interested Zach much until the time he was a captive among the Blackfeet and met a certain young maiden who had taken a shine to him. But their friendship, as he preferred to think of it, hadn't troubled him as much as a recent incident.

"Can you be a little more specific, son?" Nate requested. Several years ago he had sat the boy down and explained about men and women in embarrassing detail, so he was at a loss to understand his son's quandary.

"Ever had one stick her tongue in your mouth?"

Nate pinched himself to keep from chuckling. Boys took such matters far too seriously, and he didn't want to upset Zach. "Once or twice, I guess. Why? Has it happened to you?"

"Yes, sir. Back at the Chinook village. I made friends with a girl and we went walking the last night we were there." Zach could hardly bring himself to go on, but he did. "We stopped to admire the stars, and she leaned over and kissed me plumb on the mouth. I was so shocked I kept it open, and the next thing I knew her tongue was wrestling with mine."

"Did you like it?"

"At the time, I was shocked. No girl ever did that to me before. Now that I've had time to think about it, yes, I liked it a lot more than I've ever liked anything."

Nate smiled and clapped the boy on the back. "It's normal to like to kiss. People have been doing it since the Garden of Eden, and—"

At that juncture, shattering the quiet night, a shot rang out from the direction of the camp.

Chapter Twenty

"Stay close!" Nate King instructed his son, and sped off to investigate as a second shot punctured the crisp air. At that time of the day there was no reason for anyone to be firing a gun. Several possibilities occurred to him, none of them pleasant. Either a wild animal had invaded the camp, hostile Indians had shown, or one of the expedition members had fired at another.

A commotion was taking place. Nate saw everyone streaming toward the east side of the encampment and joined the flow, his son at his side. Winona and Blue Water Woman were 20 feet to the right, hurrying along.

In a shadowy nook where a large log lay, Armand LeBeau and Hestia Davin stood facing the murky forest. He had a smoking pistol in his right hand. She, distraught, was doing something to his left sleeve.

Shakespeare McNair and Two Humps were at the forefront of the company. The mountain man stopped and looked around, his Hawken leveled. "What was all the fuss about?" he asked them. "What did you shoot at?"

"Someone who shot at me," LeBeau answered, turning. High on his left arm was a bullet hole from which blood trickled.

"Was it an Indian?" Nate queried, stopping beside his mentor.

Hestia answered. "We didn't get a good look at him, but I don't think so. He ran off," she pointed, "that way."

Shakespeare nudged Nate and Two Humps, and the three of them dashed into the darkening woods. They went 20 yards before pausing to scour the dense vegetation. Behind them brush crackled, and they were joined by Chavez.

"You left without me, *amigos*. My feelings are hurt."

"It's your fault," Shakespeare said. "You'd be able to run a lot faster if you weren't wearing spurs big enough to plow a field." He motioned. "Spread out. It's almost too dark to find tracks, but we might get lucky."

They didn't. Although they hunted for the better part of an hour, the four of them converged on the camp later without having found a trace of the person. LeBeau had been bandaged and was near the fire, surrounded by the women and Zach.

Ordeal

"Anything, Pa?"

"No," Nate informed them. "Whoever was responsible planned it well." He addressed the riverman. "How bad were you hit?"

"A flesh wound, *mon ami*," LeBeau said. He was staring toward the spot a dozen yards away where the rest of the rivermen were seated in a cluster.

Hestia had her arm looped through his good one. "He was lucky. If he hadn't moved just when he did, the ball would have gone through his chest instead."

LeBeau shrugged. "It probably be an Indian, *non?*"

Nate said nothing, but he doubted it. Ammunition was hard for Indians to come by. A warrior wouldn't waste a precious bullet unless there was plunder to be gained, or a scalp to be taken. And according to McNair, none of the tribes in the region took scalps.

"We'll post extra men tonight," Shakespeare said. "Just in case."

The aroma of bubbling coffee drew Nate to the pot resting on red-hot coals. As he knelt to pour himself a cup, he glanced across the fire and saw Cyrus Porter over by the horses, staring in their direction. He couldn't see Porter's eyes, but the man's grim countenance left no doubt as to his thoughts.

Nate wondered if Porter had been to blame. He tried to recall if he had seen their intrepid leader among those racing to the scene after the gunshot. Lacking proof, he shouldn't say anything, but he resolved to watch Porter more diligently from then on.

The rest of the night passed uneventfully. At daylight a hasty breakfast was eaten, the packs were loaded, and the horses saddled.

Shakespeare was lifting his foot to a stirrup when a splashing noise caught his ear. Turning, he beheld three canoes bearing toward the thin strip of shore bordering the Columbia. They were filled with warriors. It took him a moment to identify them, and when he did, he shifted and called out, "On your guard, everyone! Trouble has come calling!"

The Indians were Kelawatsets. Of all the tribes in the plateau and coast region, they were the most outspoken in their dislike of whites. Shakespeare knew why.

About a decade ago a famed American trapper named Jedediah Smith had brought a large party into Kelawatset territory to trap. One day an axe turned up missing. The trappers blamed the Kelawatsets and demanded its return. When the Indians refused, the trappers tied up a chief and held him at the point of their flintlocks until the axe was produced.

Immediately upon returning to their village, the Kelawatsets held a council, and the offended chief pushed to make war. He was overruled by a higher chief who liked the Americans and felt his fellows had brought the harsh treatment on themselves by stealing the axe. The high chief then went to visit the camp and while there took it into his head to mount a horse and ride around.

Ordeal

The Kelawatsets had never seen horses before Smith's party appeared. They had been so astounded that many had run off in stark fear. Later the trappers had been amused to see some of the warriors walk up to their horses and speak to the animals in sign, fully expecting the horses to answer.

The chief who climbed on the horse that day had no intention of stealing it. He had seen the whites ride the magnificent animals and merely wanted to do the same. Yet no sooner had he climbed up than one of the trappers brandished a rifle and ordered him to get down or be shot.

Insulted, the high chief added his voice to that of the other one, and before long a band of over 100 warriors showed up at the trappers' camp.

It was fortunate for Jed Smith that he was gone that day, scouting, or he would have been slaughtered with those who had stayed behind. The Kelawatsets butchered every one, in their rage hacking some to bits with tomahawks.

There had been bad blood between the tribe and white men ever since—Americans in particular.

As the 15 warriors stepped from their canoes, Shakespeare, with Nate, Zach and Chavez, advanced to meet them. He used sign, saying, "We greet our red brothers in peace."

The warriors were a colorful bunch. Some wore red or blue blankets draped over their shoulders, others had on sailor jackets and pants, a few wore sailor caps. Eight of them carried rifles or pistols, the rest had war clubs, lances, and bows.

"What do you make of their garb?" Nate asked.

"Spoils taken from a ship they attacked at anchor," Shakespeare guessed. "Coast tribes do it from time to time. They wipe out the sailors, loot the hold, and burn the ship so no one will be the wiser. Spread the word. These men are killers, and if we let down our guard for a minute, they'll pounce."

"Do it," Nate directed Zach, and the boy spun and ran off.

Shakespeare raised his hands in sign language. "We greet you in peace, red brothers."

An imposing warrior wearing a greatcoat that must have belonged to the ship's captain, grunted and answered, "White men far from home. White men in our country."

Shakespeare knew that for a lie. The Kelawatsets lived well to the north. He deduced they were on their way to the Chinook village to trade and signed as much.

"Maybe we trade with them," the warrior signed in return. The sign language he used employed slightly different gestures than that of the Plains tribes but was close enough for Shakespeare to understand. "Maybe we trade with you."

"We do not want to trade," Shakespeare said. He was alarmed by the furtive manner in which the warriors were fanning out, some moving toward the horses, others toward the expedition members, most of whom were clustered on the river side of the stock.

Ordeal

The tall warrior frowned. "You are whites. Whites always have many goods. You make us glad. You trade with us."

Shakespeare glanced at Nate and said out of the corner of his mouth. "We're in for it. I'll take this son of a bitch. You protect the women."

As Nate melted away, Shakespeare shifted the Hawken from the crook of his left elbow to his right, then signed, "You do not have anything we want. Let us smoke a pipe in peace and we will be on our way."

"We smoke after we trade," the warrior insisted.

One of the Kelawatsets was nervously fingering the trigger of his rifle. Shakespeare made a mental note to shoot that one second and turned so the leader and the eager brave were both in front of him. He paid particular attention to the man doing all the signing, since he was the one who would give the signal to attack. A glance showed the majority of the warriors had mingled with the rivermen and the rest, some pretending to admire clothing or guns, others standing aloof. This was bad, he reflected. Very, very bad.

It suddenly got worse.

Cyrus Porter, with his shadow Adam Clark dogging his heels like a whipped cur, walked up and stood between Shakespeare and the pair of warriors. "What the hell is the delay, McNair? What do these heathens want?"

"Move out of the way," Shakespeare said as calmly as he could.

"What? Why?" Porter said angrily. "We don't have time to waste coddling every miserable group of Indians that comes along. Tell this band to get in their canoes and shove off."

Shakespeare saw the leader of the Kelawatsets glance at the warrior with the itchy finger. "For God's sake, Porter, get out of my way before they shoot."

"Shoot?" Porter responded, puzzled. "Why would they do that? We've done them no harm."

Unbidden to Shakespeare's mind came gory memories of all the trapping parties and travelers wiped out by Indians over the years. It had always amazed him that so many of the whites had been massacred because they foolishly let down their guard at the wrong moment. Now he saw how easily it could happen. All it took was one idiot like Porter, and dozens of people would pay the price with their lives. "Damn it, move!" he commanded.

Porter's nose tilted into the air and his jaw muscles quivered with indignation. "Who do you think you are, using that tone on me? Must I remind you which one of us is in charge and which one is the hired help?"

Shakespeare gripped his Hawken with both hands. The two Kelawatsets had moved closer to one another. To Shakespeare's right, Chavez was slowly edging around Porter to get a clear shot at the pair. Before the tracker could, all hell broke loose.

The leader of the war party suddenly threw back his head and howled like a wolf. At the first note the Kelawatsets exploded into furious action, foremost among them the warrior who had been fingering the trigger of his rifle. He raised the barrel and shot Adam Clark in the back.

War whoops, shrieks, and the blasts of guns filled the air as Shakespeare darted to the left so he could kill the leader, who was taking aim on a stunned Cyrus Porter. Before Shakespeare could squeeze off a shot, though, two pistols cracked and the leader and the warrior who had downed Clark both pitched to the ground with holes in their foreheads.

Shakespeare pivoted, saw smoke curling from Chavez's dueling pistols. Behind the tracker a warrior was lifting a war club to bash him on the head. Quickly Shakespeare sighted and fired. The ball bored the Kelawatset's chest and toppled the man backward.

Pandemonium reined. The expedition members were fighting for their lives, some locked in mortal combat, others firing, others reloading. Clouds of gunsmoke shrouded the battleground.

Nate had reached the women just as the wolf howl rang out. A stocky Kelawatset charged Winona. Nate whipped his Hawken to his shoulder but she fired first, shooting from the hip, hitting the Kelawatset high in the chest. The warrior twisted, clutched himself, and fell.

Zach and Blue Water Woman cut loose at the same instant. Unwittingly they had both aimed at the same warrior, and the man went down with two balls in his head.

Nate moved closer to cover them while they reloaded. Without warning steely arms encircled him from behind, and he was wrenched off his feet and flung to the earth. He tried to land on his knees so he could turn and shoot, but his shoulder smacked the ground instead and he lost his grip on the Hawken. As he put both palms flat to push up, his assailant leaped onto his back. A knee gouged his flesh, lancing pain seared his spine. A hand seized his hair and his head was snapped back. He saw a knife blade materialize in front of his face, then swoop toward his throat.

In desperation Nate lifted his right hand, catching hold of the warrior's wrist. In doing so, he fell forward, accidentally flipping the Kelawatset over his shoulders. He rolled to the right to gain room to maneuver and felt a stinging sensation in his left shoulder. Leaping to his feet, he discovered he had been cut, but not deeply.

The warrior with the knife was also erect. Slashing savagely, he closed, trying to rip Nate open.

Retreating, Nate palmed his tomahawk but held it close to his leg so the Kelawatset wouldn't notice. Then, as the warrior lunged at his chest and missed, he arced the tomahawk up and around and buried the sharp edge in the Kelawatset's skull. Skin and bone were cleaved like so much butter. Screeching, spouting blood, the warrior collapsed.

Elsewhere the fight raged on. By now the clash was being waged largely hand to hand. Bodies littered the ground. The women and Zach were untouched, huddled back to back, Evelyn perched in her cradleboard on Winona.

Ordeal

Nate wedged the bloody tomahawk under his belt and drew both of his pistols. A muscular Kelawatset was astride one of the rivermen, about to sink a war axe into the man. Nate shot the warrior in the side. He jumped like a stricken jackrabbit, then sagged.

A scream pierced the din. Nate whirled, spotted LeBeau in trouble. The young riverman fought two warriors, all three using knives, all three dotted with crimson splotches. A seeping wound on LeBeau's right thigh slowed his reactions, making him easy prey for the confident Kelawatsets.

Nate ran up close and shot one in the back of the head at point-blank range. The warrior's forehead blew out, spraying LeBeau, and the other Kelawatset turned toward Nate. In a flash, LeBeau rammed his knife into the warrior's throat.

Nate heard hooves drum heavily. Two Kelawatsets, on horseback, were leading nine pack animals eastward along the river bank just as rapidly as they could flee. In the river the three canoes were streaking eastward as well, each manned by a single warrior.

Of a sudden Nate realized the battle was over. He straightened, his eyes stinging from the thick gunsmoke, his wound throbbing. The wives and his son were fine. Nearby, Hestia Davin hugged LeBeau in relief at his deliverance. To the left, Brett Hughes was on one knee next to a dead warrior. Of the other rivermen, only three were alive, one of them Gaston. Over by the water's edge stood Cyrus Porter, mouth agape, miraculously unscathed. Two Humps was scalping a slain foe.

Shakespeare came over, his buckskins peppered with scarlet dots. "I'm not one to hold a grudge, but for two cents I'd rub out the whole damn tribe."

"It was so sudden," Nate said. He'd thought that he was used to the random violence of frontier life, but the stark butchery had effected him as deeply as it always did.

"Death usually is," Shakespeare noted, and moved to help the wounded. He stepped over a riverman he assumed was dead, but the man groaned and opened his eyes.

"Help me, s'il vous plait!"

It was hopeless. The man had a nasty bullet wound above the heart. In addition, his stomach had been torn open from side to side and his intestines were visible. "There's nothing I can do, son," Shakespeare said gently. "Unless you'd like a blanket or a drink."

"Kill me."

The fervent appeal in the riverman's eyes touched Shakespeare's soul. "Are you sure?" he asked in a whisper.

"Please," the man repeated, coughing up blood. "The pain . . ."

Without further comment Shakespeare pulled one of his pistols, touched the muzzle to the man's forehead, and fired. The riverman arched his back, eyelids quivering, then sighed as his body went as limp as melted wax. Shakespeare closed the man's eyes and slowly stood. "I wish I could have done more."

"Shakespeare! Behind you!"

Ordeal

Nate's shout came a hair too late. Shakespeare was struck between the shoulder blades and knocked to his knees. He looked around, thinking a Kelawatset had been playing possum, but it was Cyrus Porter who had attacked him, hitting him with a rifle stock. "What—?" he said in a daze, his limbs refusing to move him out of harm's way.

"Are you insane? He was one of ours! You didn't have to kill him!" Porter elevated the rifle for another blow. "This is all your fault! I should have done this long ago."

A buckskin clad avenger hurtled out of the air, barreling into Porter and plowing him over. The New Englander attempted to scramble to his feet, but Nate grasped him by the front of his coat and bodily threw him down again.

"Enough, Horatio!" Shakespeare shouted when Nate made a grab for a pistol. "You can't!"

Nate paused, the pistol half drawn. "Watch me," he said.

Porter cringed, not even trying to hide his fear. "Wait!" he exclaimed. "I wasn't really going to hurt him. I just never expected him to kill one of our own."

Shakespeare managed to stand. "I had to," he said. "The man didn't have a prayer." He was ready to spring, to stop Nate from killing in cold blood and having to bear the stain on his conscience for the rest of his life, but there was no need. Nate shoved the pistol down, glared in disgust a few moments, then walked back to his family.

Shakespeare was of half a mind to punch Porter in the mouth, just for the hell of it. He might have, too, had Porter not done the one thing that would save him; the man who had brought so much misery on others buried his face in his hands and cried like a baby.

To the men and women looking on, it was the final straw. Whatever lingering vestige of sympathy for Porter any of them had felt, died. These were mature men and women who had learned to wrestle life on its own terms, not pampered aristocrats who had life's riches doled to them on silver platters. They knew how to stand on their own two feet and take the good life had to offer with the bad. They saw Porter's tears for what they were, the selfish act of a man too timid to face reality.

LeBeau and Hetty looked on in disgust, their hands entwined. Winona and Blue Water Woman turned away, as was Indian custom when a person behaved badly. Brett Hughes scowled. And the surviving rivermen wore black expressions of bitter resentment. This was the man who had hired them, who had bossed them around for so long, who had lorded it over them as if they were his personal servants. They felt more than disgust. The rivermen felt revulsion.

Then the moment passed, broken by another cry for help, this time from near the river.

Nate reached Clark before any of the others. The young man lay on his back, his knees slightly bent, blood oozing from both corners of his mouth and his nostrils. His eyes were wide in fright, his breaths short and fast. The ball had ripped clean through him, shattering the sternum as it exited.

"Help me," Clark begged again, tears rolling down his cheeks. "Please, King. I don't want to die. Not like this. Not here."

"There's nothing we can do," Nate said.

"There must be something," Clark said weakly. "Get your squaw to mix a poultice."

The corners of Nate's mouth crinkled as he held his temper in check.

"It was her herbs that brought Hetty around," Clark continued. "I'm sure of it." Feebly, he put a hand on Nate's arm. "Call her. Have her mend me."

"She can't do the impossible," Nate said. "You must accept what has happened. It will be easier for you if you do."

"Accept dying?" Clark's fear rivaled Porter's. "No one can do that. I'm afraid, King. Afraid of what lies on the other side. Afraid because I've wasted my life and have nothing to show for it. Please—" He had a coughing fit, his whole body convulsing. When it was over he could barely speak. "Oh, God! Save me! I'm rich, King. I'll give you half my fortune if you'll only save me!"

"I don't want your money," Nate said.

"What kind of man are you? Everyone wants money. Lots and lots of money. With it a man can do as he pleases. Fine women, a mansion, the best food and clothes." Clark's features had a dreamy quality. "Money has meant everything to me, King. It made me the man I am, made me a respectable citizen. It gave me all any man could want."

"Did it give you the woman you love?"

Adam Clark blinked. "No," he croaked, choking on more than blood. His eyes slowly widened until they seemed as big as saucers. "Oh God!" he whispered. Then, once more, at the top of his lungs, *"Oh God!"* And with that, he died.

Nate stared at Clark's face until a warm hand brushed his brow. It was Winona.

"Are you all right, my husband?"

"Never better," Nate said, standing. He slipped an arm around her. "Never, ever better."

Chapter Twenty-one

It was a disheartened company of weary travelers who set out shortly after dawn the next day. They left behind them a long line of shallow graves topped by makeshift crosses, a concession to Hestia Davin. Zachary King looked back before the trees closed around them and saw the crosses silhouetted against the glare of the rising sun, an image that burned itself into his brain and would not let go. It served as a reminder that no one could let down their guard in the wilderness, not for a minute, not if they cared to go on breathing.

Shakespeare, Nate, and their wives rode at the head of the shortened column. Next came LeBeau and Hetty. Then Hughes. A dozen yards behind them the three rivermen led the pack animals. Gaston wore a mask of pure hatred, which everyone assumed was meant for the man who brought up the rear.

No one wanted anything to do with Cyrus Porter. He plodded along, hardly aware he was in a saddle, his eyes as vacant as the air, his features pale as if he were sick when in fact he was as healthy as the horse he rode.

Nate glanced at the expedition's leader just once, and remarked to no one in particular, "He brought it on himself. The fool should never have left Hartford."

"True enough," Shakespeare said. "You never see a duck pretending it's a cougar."

Nate wondered what that had to do with Porter, but he held his tongue. Once McNair got started on a subject, he might talk for hours. And Nate relished the cool quiet of the new day. It let him see how grateful he should be for his family's deliverance. Any one of them could have been slain. It had been a stroke of warped luck that the Kelawatsets were mainly interested in plunder and not rubbing the expedition out to the last man, woman and child.

Up ahead hiked Chavez and Two Humps. Nate glimpsed them every so often through the vegetation. Shakespeare had advised them to keep their eyes skinned for more Kelawatsets. For that matter, once word of the fight spread, any tribe in the region might decide to teach the white interlopers a lesson and attack them when they were least prepared.

Nate was almost sorry he had agreed to come, that he'd brought his family along. Almost, but not quite. Though there had been a few harrowing experiences along the way, there had been more pleasant ones, plus plenty of marvelous sights they would remember for the rest of their lives. And the journey was only half over. Who knew what wonders lay in store for them?

There was, however, a cloud hanging over their future. They had to figure out how to go about returning to their neck of the Rockies. Making the trip with the few men they had left invited disaster. They wouldn't be able to defend themselves against the smallest of war parties.

The night before, during a heated talk around the camp fire, Gaston had pushed to bend their steps immediately for the Mississippi. He had been seconded in his opinion by the other two rivermen and, surprisingly, Brett Hughes. None of them had been very happy when Shakespeare bluntly refused, citing the safety of them all. It was his opinion that their sole hope lay in reaching Fort Astoria. Or, in case they found themselves cut off from the trapping post there, they should cross the Columbia and try to reach Fort Vancouver, an HBC post run by a Scotsman named McLoughlin.

At one point, Nate had felt sure Gaston was going to wade into Shakespeare with fists flying. He had even put a hand on a pistol to stop the riverman if need be, but Gaston had reluctantly backed down.

Beset as they were with so many problems, Nate was more than mildly bewildered when he happened to glance at his wife and saw her smiling broadly. "Care to let me in on your secret?" he asked.

"My secret?"

"How you can be so happy at a time like this?"

Winona partially turned and nodded toward the young lovers strolling behind them. "They remind me of us, my dearest, when we were their age. They bring back memories long forgotten."

Nate recalled the first time he had stood under a buffalo robe with Winona, recalled the exquisitely sweet sensation as their lips touched for the first time, and smiled himself. "Those were fine days," he sighed.

"You speak as if you were an old man," Winona said, "and you have not seen much more than thirty winters."

"Sometimes I feel older than I am," Nate admitted. "It's this life we lead."

Shakespeare had been listening and picked that moment to interject. "Wrong. It's not life but the way we live it that makes us feel old or young. Attack life like you would a haunch of venison when you're starved, and you'll always feel young."

"As usual you lead us on a word goose-chase," Nate commented. "We don't eat life. We live it."

"Nay, if thy wits run the wild-goose chase, I have done," Shakespeare quoted, "for thou hast more of the wild-goose in one of thy wits than, I am sure, I have in my whole five."

Nate was trying to figure out if he had been insulted or not when Two Humps came flying back along the trail and pointed out across the broad river.

"Canoes."

Sure enough, a pair of canoes were making their way inland, hugging the opposite shore. Each was filled with warriors, but since the far bank now lay hundreds of feet away, it was impossible to tell whether they were Kelawatsets.

"If they are," Shakespeare voiced the thought uppermost on all their minds, "they'll be back once they overtake their friends and learn what happened. We'd better travel faster."

Except for a brief halt to rest and water the horses, the expedition pushed on through the remainder of the day, covering at least five more miles than they ordinarily would. Since they didn't care to have the Kelawatsets spot their camp, Shakespeare directed a cold camp to be made. They ate jerky and pemmican and sat huddled under their blankets.

All the men took turns keeping watch. All, that is, except for Cyrus Porter. He would neither eat nor drink and simply laid down on his side once they had called a halt, refusing to talk to anyone.

Zach was elated when his father asked him to take a turn at standing guard. He had never been asked before, and he considered the request a token of his father's faith in his ability, yet another step on his long road to manhood. He was so excited, he couldn't sleep a wink between nightfall and his shift at midnight. When he heard LeBeau coming for him, he jumped up so suddenly that LeBeau was startled.

"You have a snake in your pants, young one?"

"No, sir," Zach answered, grinning. "I'm raring to go, is all."

"So I see. Be careful you not shoot yourself, eh?"

It wasn't until close to two in the morning that Zach heard or saw anything unusual. He was making his fiftieth circuit of the remaining horses, his Hawken cocked in case he should be jumped, when a twig snapped in the forest to the south. It was just one twig, and it might have been broken by an animal or even the strong wind that blew down the Columbia gorge at night, but Zach suspected differently. He crouched and listened, straining his ears until he thought they would burst, yet he heard nothing else. He pondered whether to wake his father and decided against it. His father needed rest, and he would feel like an idiot if he sounded an alarm and there was no cause for concern.

Zach felt differently the next morning when he did mention the incident. He thought he'd done the right thing, but it was apparent by the look his father gave him that he had made a mistake.

"I thank you for thinking of how tired I was," Nate said sternly, "but the safety of all of us is more important. It might have been a hostile Indian. Or a grizzly. We should have gone to see."

"I'm sorry," Zach said. "I won't ever let it happen again."

The very next night Zach had an opportunity to test his vow. He had been on watch for only an hour when he heard rustling in the high grass bordering the river. They were camped on a wide strip of flat land abutting a barren bluff, which made approach from any direction difficult. Uncle Shakespeare had been quite pleased with the site, and his father too, so Zach hadn't expected anyone would try to sneak up on them. That is, until the grass rustled.

Zach was between the grass and the horses. He promptly crouched low as his father had taught him. Moving figures at night were easier to spot from ground level than when erect, and he was able to see the tops of the grass bending ever so slightly as if to the pressure of a body snaking along close to the water. Was it a prowling beast? Zach wondered. He aimed the Hawken, and when the rustling stopped, he crept nearer. But he only went two steps when he thought of his promise. If he was right, and if there was something lurking out there that might threaten all their lives, his first duty was to tell his father.

Nate came instantly awake when Zach's hand fell on his shoulder. He glanced at Winona, who slept soundly with Evelyn nestled in her arms, then whispered, "What is it?"

"Something, Pa. Over by the river."

Grabbing his rifle, Nate padded on his son's heels to a spot halfway between the string and the shore. Zach pointed. Nate nodded, motioned for the boy to stay there, and advanced alone. He hadn't said anything to the others, but he was extremely worried about the Kelawatsets. Shakespeare had told him enough about the tribe for him to know they would never leave the deaths of those warriors unavenged. Even if the warriors had brought their fate on themselves.

Nate stopped every few feet to look and listen. His ears registered the various sounds, identifying them; the fluttering gusts of wind, the gurgling rush of the water, the swaying of the grass. He suspected that Zach had seen the grass bend under the wind and assumed a living creature had been responsible. A moment later he saw the bump.

Nate couldn't quite make it out, at first. But poised above the stems, off to the right perhaps 20 feet, was the dark outline of something that didn't quite fit. It resembled nothing so much as an oversized bump on a log.

Although Nate couldn't distinguish any features, he had a gut feeling that unseen eyes were on him. His skin crawled of its own accord. Were they the eyes of men or a roving predator? He hefted the Hawken, then stalked forward slowly, body in a crouch. Ten feet from the strange shape he began to think his mind was playing tricks on him and there must be a perfectly natural explanation.

Suddenly the bump dipped from sight. The grass moved, bending swiftly as whatever it was moved with lightning speed toward the Columbia.

Nate rose and ran, the rifle tucked to his shoulder. He was still yards off when he spied a long, slender form slip into the water and disappear under the surface. In the dim light he couldn't be sure what he had seen. He stopped a yard shy of the edge in case it tried to spring out and seize him. The water bubbled briefly, then rippled as something made off underwater, moving parallel with the bank.

Nate gave chase, treading carefully since a misstep might plunge him in the icy river. The grass ended, replaced by a gravel strip. His moccasins crunched as he sprinted. He came to the end of the gravel and drew up short. Belatedly, he realized the ripples had vanished.

Whirling, Nate scanned the glassy surface. He thought he saw a few bubbles farther out, but they were swept away before he could be certain. Then a stick poked out—at least, it appeared to be a stick—and was carried off by the flow, soon blending into the darkness to the east.

Puzzled by the occurrence, Nate walked back. Zach met him at the grass.

"What was that thing, Pa? I didn't get a good look."

"You're not the only one."

"Want me to stand guard by the river for the rest of the night in case it comes back?" Zach asked eagerly.

The question gave Nate pause. He was going to say yes, confident his son could handle the chore, but a vague premonition made him change his mind. "I was the one who let the thing get away, so I figure I should be the one to keep watch for it. You go get some rest."

Zach turned, then glanced back. "Pa, you're not shooing me off because you think I can't handle myself, are you?"

"Never," Nate said sincerely. "If I've learned nothing else on this journey, it's that I have to start thinking of you as a man and not as a little boy." He could tell his son was downcast, so he elaborated. "You have to understand, son. Fathers love their children just as much as mothers do. We might not say it as much. And we might not show it like women do. But the fact is, we do. I care for you so much that sometimes I hurt inside." Nate gestured at the Columbia. "This has nothing to do with whether you can handle the job or not. It has to do with me not wanting any harm to come to you. Do you understand?"

"I'm not sure, but I'll take your word for it."

Nate watched his son hasten off and smiled in the heartfelt satisfaction only the proud fathers of sons can ever know. He went in search of the other guard and found a riverman standing close to the barren hill. It was Gaston. "Quiet over here?" he asked casually.

"Quiet enough," the riverman answered sullenly.

Since the battle, Nate had not shared three words with Gaston. They seldom talked as it was, due in part to Gaston's resentment of the beating he had suffered that day he attacked McNair. Nate thought to mend fences and said, "You'll probably be glad as can be when you see the Mississippi again."

"More glad than you can imagine," Gaston said in his heavily accented English. There was no hint of friendliness in his voice.

Nate gazed at the camp and saw LeBeau and Hestia Davin sleeping close to one another. They had become inseparable, and Nate fully expected them to marry at the earliest opportunity. "I know someone else who will be happy to reach civilization," he remarked. "LeBeau probably can't wait to set up house."

Gaston's tone, surprisingly, hardened. "*Oui*. He is the only one who has come out of this nightmare with a prize worth the hardships. Or he thinks he is the only one."

"What does that mean?" Nate asked.

"Nothing."

Gaston strolled off, leaving Nate perplexed. He suspected there had been more to the comment than the riverman let on, but he had no idea what it might be. The sinister growl in Gaston's tone troubled him. He chalked it up to jealousy; Hetty was a beautiful woman and Gaston was envious that she had taken a fancy to LeBeau and not to him.

The rest of the night passed quietly. Shortly before noon of the next day, as they came to the crest of a high hill opposite a gigantic rock, they saw in the dim distance a great shimmering haze and a wide expanse of water.

"The Pacific Ocean," Shakespeare announced with reverence.

"Really?" Zach was elated. "How much longer before we reach it, Uncle?"

"Three or four days at the most," Shakespeare said, "if we don't have any more trouble."

No one needed to ask what kind of trouble. The reminder bothered Nate, for it brought to mind the strange occurrence of the night before. He moved closer to the Columbia as they continued on, studying the opposite shore and the forest behind them. He became so engrossed, he fell a little ways behind the column but didn't realize he had done so until one of the pack horses whinnied.

Lifting the reins, Nate prepared to catch up. He looked to the left and held still. Over in the trees stood two figures. At first he suspected they were Indians spying on the expedition, but then a stray shaft of sunlight streaming through the branches bathed both, revealing Cyrus Porter and Gaston. It shocked Nate to see them together, since they cared little for one another.

As Nate watched, unseen, they talked in low tones. Or *argued*, would be more to the point, because Gaston was gesturing sharply and Porter was shaking his head. They had a heated exchange, Porter as red as a beet. For a moment Nate thought Porter would strike the riverman. But no such thing happened. Instead, Hetty's father nodded, and the two men shook hands. With furtive glances, they hastened after the column, moving their mounts apart.

Nate was confused and greatly alarmed. Porter and Gaston acted as if they were up to no good, but what could it be? And why then, of all times? Weren't they all in enough danger without those two adding to their woes? He had half a mind to ride up to each of them and demand to know what was going on, but he knew he'd be wasting his time. They'd deny his accusation, and short of beating the truth out of them, there was nothing he could do.

Ordeal

For the rest of the day, though, Nate kept them both in sight. They didn't speak to one another again. Indeed, it seemed to him as if they went out of their way to avoid each other, which strengthened his suspicions.

That evening, as everyone sat around eating a buck Two Humps had brought down with his bow, Nate strolled over to where Shakespeare and Blue Water Woman sat. McNair had charge of assigning guard shifts to the men, so to McNair Nate said, "What time does Gaston pull his shift tonight?"

"Two in the morning," Shakespeare disclosed, his brow knitting. "Why?"

"I'd like to share it with him," Nate said. He didn't care to elaborate until he had proof.

Shakespeare scratched his beard a moment. "How now. Mighty strange that you should ask such a thing. Last I heard, Gaston rated you on a par with rancid polecat meat." The mountain man leaned forward to whisper. "What's this all about, young prince?"

"I can't say as yet."

"Why not? Don't you trust me?"

"With my life. But this is something I'd rather take care of myself. If I'm wrong, then no one is offended. If I'm right—" Nate didn't complete the statement because he had no idea what would happen if he was right.

"In the reproof of chance lies the true proof of men," Shakespeare quoted. "As for Gaston," he said, and quoted again, "a false-hearted rogue, a most unjust knave. I will no more trust him when he leers than I will a serpent when he hisses."

"That makes two of us," Nate assured him. He saw Porter off by himself, eating a steak. Gaston was with the other two rivermen, acting perfectly ordinary.

"I hate it when someone keeps a secret from me," Shakespeare said. "Makes it downright hard for me to sleep."

"Do your best," Nate said, and walked off before McNair quizzed him to death. He plunked down beside Winona, who promptly handed Evelyn to him.

"Here, husband. It has been so long since last you held your daughter, she has forgotten what you look like."

Evelyn squealed in delight and grabbed Nate's chin, tugging on his facial hair. He smiled, pecked her on the forehead, and held her high over his head. She giggled, her little legs waving.

"Do you ever wish we had another child?" Winona asked out of the blue.

Nate glanced at her. "Are you—?"

"No. Sometimes I want to be. I would be happy to bear you another one."

"I'll keep it in mind," Nate said, marveling that she could think of such a thing at such a time. "We'll see if you still feel the same when we're home." He didn't add that for all they knew, none of them would see their cabin ever again.

They went on talking until dark claimed the land. Nate lay with Winona cuddled in his arms but was too high strung to sleep. He stared at the sparkling stars, so many they filled the heavens, and listened to the men making their rounds of the camp. Against his will he drifted off.

Approaching footsteps awakened him. Nate sat up slowly so as not to disturb his wife and children and looked at Chavez.

"Your turn, *amigo*."

"See anything unusual tonight?" Nate asked as he rose.

"I thought I saw a light across the river, to the northwest. It might have been a camp fire."

"This coon will keep his eyes skinned," Nate promised. Some of the sleepers were snoring loudly as he made his way to the string and verified that the horses were tethered. He looked around for Gaston but saw no trace of him. Disturbed, he headed back toward the knot of prone forms to see if the riverman was among them. He spotted LeBeau and Hetty, closest to the trees, then Shakespeare and Blue Water Woman.

A slight noise behind Nate made him spin and raise the Hawken. Gaston stood a few yards away, grinning.

"You have bad nerves tonight, King. That is not good. You might shoot me by mistake."

"I'd never put a ball into you by mistake," Nate said.

The riverman walked off toward the horses, so Nate went to the bank of the Columbia and sought sign of the light Chavez had seen. Every 15 to 20 minutes over the next two hours he checked again. He had about given up on ever seeing it when, sometime around four in the morning, he spotted a flickering glow miles off. Halting with his back to the encampment, he stared intently at the distant fire, so intently he didn't sense that someone was behind him until a fraction of a second before a heavy object slammed into the back of his head. He fell forward, pain lancing his skull, dropping the rifle as he sagged. A second blow to the small of his back sent him flying—right into the river.

Chapter Twenty-two

Nate King owed the Columbia River his life. For no sooner did he sink under the surface than the cold water revived him with a jolt. He gasped, and nearly drowned. Water poured into his mouth, into his throat. Although he closed his mouth promptly, he had precious little air in his lungs.

Above Nate the surface glistened dully. He pumped his arms and legs, kicking furiously as he was swept along by the strong current. His face broke free and he sucked in air. Twisting, he was astounded to find he had been swept 15 yards from the camp in just the few seconds he had been under.

Weighted down by his buckskins and moccasins, Nate struck out for the shore, a mere ten feet away. It might as well have been ten miles. The current fought him every inch of the way.

For every foot he gained, he was carried another three eastward. Suddenly fate smiled on him. Nate's feet made contact and he was able to stand and resist the pull of the mighty river.

Slowly feeling his way with his toes, Nate reached the shore and collapsed on the bank. He had only been in the water a minute or two, yet it seemed like an eternity. He was soaked to the skin and so exhausted he could do no more than lie there panting. Then he thought of the blows that felled him.

Had it been Gaston? Or a hostile Indian? That question spurred Nate into pushing up off the ground. He swayed, feeling as chilled as ice, goose bumps breaking out all over. Marshaling his strength, he headed for the camp. His legs refused to work at first, and he had to compel them through sheer force of will.

Nate navigated by instinct. There was no moon, only starlight. The camp fire had burned so low that mere fingers of flames were all that remained. He sought movement, listened for sounds, seeking anything that would pinpoint his attacker's whereabouts.

All seemed quiet enough. The horses were undisturbed, some grazing, some dozing. And the expedition members still slept, still snored, their hump-shaped silhouettes a lighter shade against the inky backdrop of the night.

Nate stopped in confusion. If an Indian had been responsible, the warrior would have stolen a few horses or dallied to slit the throats of some of the sleepers. Yet neither had happened. And it made no sense for Gaston to have hit him, since what could the riverman hope to gain?

Abruptly, a shadow moved, detaching itself from the trees on the south side of the clearing and creeping toward the slumbering couple nearest the forest. In the shadow's hand something shone palely.

The truth shocked Nate into action. He had no time to retrieve the Hawken, no time to reload the wet pistols. Pulling his tomahawk, he bent low and stealthily hurried to intercept the shadow before it struck. He recognized the bulky form long before he saw the man's features.

Gaston stood over LeBeau, a knife clutched in his right hand. He glared at the younger man, then glanced at Hetty as if to assure himself she slept soundly. Raising the knife overhead, he tensed to plunge the blade into LeBeau's chest. One stroke was all it would take, and then Gaston could whirl and dart into the trees before Hetty opened her eyes.

Nate was six feet from the riverman when he made his move. "Gaston!" he roared, and charged, swinging the tomahawk in a tremendous downward arc that would have split Gaston's head like a rotten melon had Gaston not spun and parried the blow with the knife. Nate backed up, swung again. Gaston skipped to one side and slashed at his wrist, but Nate was too fast for him.

Pivoting, Nate drove the tomahawk at the riverman's chest. Again Gaston danced aside, his features contorted in hatred. Rumbling like a bear, Gaston flicked his long knife twice, trying to stab

Nate in the torso. Nate swerved, felt the razor tip nick him, and rammed the flat of the tomahawk into the riverman's head.

Gaston was staggered but didn't go down. He had the constitution of a bull and the temper to match. Mad now, he swung wildly.

All around them shouts erupted. People were rushing toward them. But neither paid any attention. To suffer a lapse in concentration was a death warrant.

Nate blocked a thrust at his throat, ducked under a swing aimed at his face, and lashed out at Gaston's midsection. The riverman screeched in agony as his stomach was ripped open from hip to hip.

Behind Nate there was a commotion, the sound of a scuffle, then the thud of a body hitting the ground. Nate dared not look. Gaston was still on his feet, still holding the knife. Uttering a feral cry, the riverman made a desperate leap, the gleam in his eyes the gleam of unbridled rage. Gaston was going to kill Nate with his dying breath if he could.

Nate was ready for him. He had the tomahawk up to ward off any blows and could easily have sidestepped the riverman's clumsy attack. But apparently someone didn't think so because an instant later a rifle cracked and Gaston was flung backward, a new hole in the center of his forehead. Gaston hit the ground hard and lay still.

Slowly straightening, Nate turned. He thought he would see one of his family or Shakespeare or even LeBeau holding the smoking gun that had laid Gaston low, but to his astonishment the only one with a smoking rifle was Cyrus Porter.

Winona and Zach hurried up, Winona with Evelyn in her arms. "Are you all right, husband?" she asked.

"Did he hurt you, Pa?" Zach threw in.

"Just a scratch," Nate said mechanically, unable to make sense of Porter's intervention.

Shakespeare also walked over, his own Hawken in hand. "I tried staying up to see what would happen, but damned if I didn't doze off. These old bones aren't what they used to be." He nodded at Porter. "Hard to believe he actually had the gumption to shoot someone."

"Yes, isn't it?" Nate said. He noticed another of the rivermen unconscious nearby.

"The rascal tried to help Gaston," Shakespeare said. "I guess no one ever told him that heads weren't made to be pounded on by rifle stocks."

LeBeau joined them, a pistol in one hand, a knife in the other. "What be happening here, *mon ami?*" he asked. "Why did you fight?"

"Gaston was set to kill you," Nate revealed. He turned to the body, then squatted. The knife Gaston had used lay in the damp grass at his feet and he picked it up.

"But why would he try to kill Armand?" This from Hestia Davin. "I'll admit they weren't very close, but they were both rivermen. They shared a bond of sorts."

Nate slowly rose, the answer in his left hand. "He tried to make wolf meat of your man because your father offered him a lot of money to do just that."

A stunned silence greeted the revelation. All eyes fixed on Cyrus Porter, who stood as calmly unruffled as if he were back in Hartford at one of the exclusive clubs he patronized. "That's perfectly absurd," he said. "King must have been hit on the head during the altercation."

"I know what I'm talking about," Nate said.

Hestia stepped forward, an odd look about her. "You've made a monstrous accusation. I know my father is capable of many things—but murder? Do you have proof?"

"I saw your father talking to Gaston earlier today, off in the woods where no one would see them," Nate said.

"So they talked?" Hetty challenged him. "That hardly constitutes proof."

Nate was surprised by her attitude. She was the last person he'd expect to defend her father. Evidently, as the old saw went, blood was thicker than water. Or maybe, in this case, it was simply a matter of her not *wanting* to believe her father guilty. "Gaston also talked about some sort of prize he was getting out of the expedition. I think he meant the large amount of money your father promised to pay him."

"Again, you've failed to show us definite proof," Hetty said. "Perhaps you were wrong about Gaston trying to kill Armand. Perhaps you only thought he was, and attacked him without cause."

"Gaston meant to kill LeBeau, all right," Nate insisted.

LeBeau appeared skeptical himself. "How can you be certain?" he demanded.

Nate held up the knife, a Kelawatset knife with the hilt carved from an elk horn and the crude blade fashioned from a sheet of metal no doubt obtained in trade from whites. Then he pointed at Gaston's own knife, the knife Gaston had carried with him ever since leaving the Mississippi, clearly visible on the dead riverman's hip. "Why do you think he bothered to take this knife from a dead Kelawatset? Why did he keep it hidden until just a few minutes ago? I'll tell you why. He planned to kill you with it so the Kelawatsets would get the blame."

"Sounds reasonable to me," Shakespeare said on Nate's behalf. He believed every word but could see that the daughter still doubted.

"I don't know what to think," Hetty said. Suddenly turning on her father, she said, "Tell me it isn't so. Look me in the eyes and give me your solemn oath that you didn't hire Gaston."

Porter shifted from one foot to the other. "I've already said the very idea is absurd. That ought to be enough."

"I need more," Hetty said, stepping close to him and gripping his arm. "Please, father. For both our sakes. Swear before God that everything Nate King claims is wrong."

"The Bible says not to swear by the Lord's name," Porter said, "so I'll do no such thing."

"Then swear by the memory of my mother," Hetty said, "the kindest, most beautiful woman who ever lived." She shook his arm. "Swear it,

father, or so help me, I'll never utter another
word to you for as long as the two of us shall
live."

Everyone there saw Cyrus Porter squirm, saw
him lick his lips and avert his gaze. He opened
and closed his mouth twice before he responded,
and when he did reply, he stared at the ground,
not at her face. "I swear by the memory of my
sainted wife that I never did any such thing."

Hestia Davin went pale right before their eyes.
Her arm dropped limply at her side and moisture
filled her eyes. "Oh, father. How could you?" she
said softly.

Porter's head snapped up. "What do you mean?"
he asked. "I swore, just as you wanted me to."

"You did it," Hetty said, each word laden with
sorrow. "You really did it."

"Are you as insane as the rest of these barbarians?" Porter huffed, grabbing her wrist. "You
asked me to swear and I did. What more do you
want?"

Hetty fixed her sad eyes on him and declared
with unexpected vehemence, "I want you to shoot
yourself. But kindly have the decency to go off by
yourself when you do it to spare us from having
to watch your crowning act of cowardice."

"You can't be serious!"

Porter wasn't the only one shocked by her
request. LeBeau gaped, Shakespeare whistled,
and Nate King looked in bewilderment at Winona,
who stared solemnly at the younger woman.

"I have never been more serious about anything in my life," Hetty said, turning her back on

Cyrus. "And those are the last words I will ever speak to you."

"Please, Hetty!" Porter said, trying to swing her around to face him. "Don't act this way in front of everyone else. It's childish and embarrassing."

Hetty jerked her wrist free and walked to LeBeau, who put his arm over her drooping shoulders. Together they walked toward the river, Hetty's shoulders shaking ever so slightly.

"Hestia Porter!" Porter snapped. "You come back here this instant! I won't be treated this way, not by you or any other person." He paused, his countenance showing a hint of panic as it began to sink in that she had meant every word. "I'm your father," he said, trying another angle. "I helped raise you, damn it. I went for medicine when you were sick, at least once that I can recall. And I let your mother hold those silly parties on your birthdays. I think I've earned some respect!"

Nate tossed the Kelawatset knife down and took Winona's arm. He had seldom felt such revulsion toward another human being as he did toward the leader of their expedition. Walking off, he fell into step next to McNair and Blue Water Woman. Shakespeare, for once, had no comment to make, no quote to share.

Porter wasn't done trying. "Please, Hestia!" he called out forlornly. "You're all I have left in this world. My sister died last year, and with your mother gone, the house feels so empty. Please come back with me, and I promise not to hold any of this against you." He took a few steps after her. "Say you'll come, and you can bring your riverman with you. He can stay in the servants' quarters until we sort this affair out and you regain your senses." There was a pregnant pause. *"Please!"*

A pall fell over the camp, and even young Zach was affected. No one spoke unless spoken to. And everyone, without exception, shunned Cyrus Porter. Gaston was buried near the Columbia by his two surviving companions, and one other. When the pair began digging, LeBeau went over and took a turn working the shovel. No one said any words over the grave.

The next day dawned gray and overcast. A drizzle fell as they ate breakfast and showed no sign of letting up as they loaded their packs and resumed their arduous trek. The tracker and the Nez Percé took the lead. But before they walked off, Two Humps stared at the sky, then at the river, then at them all and announced, "This day will be bad day."

Two hours of travel brought them to a hill from which they could see a long stretch of the river to the west. The Columbia widened, the current grew stronger. From the water marks left on the bordering rocks it was plain that there were pronounced high and low tides.

"It's a sign the ocean isn't far off," Shakespeare commented. He pointed at several sea gulls winging out over the water. "There's another."

Until noon they rode, and then McNair called a halt to rest the horses. They were on a narrow strip of land between the river and a formidable ridge, hemmed in by water and rock. There was grass, though, enough for their needs.

Nate and Shakespeare were about to dismount when LeBeau and a riverman named Pierre trotted up.

"We have trouble," LeBeau told them.

"What else is new?" Shakespeare said wearily. "What is it now?"

"Francois and five of the horses are gone."

Nate rose in the stirrups to scan their back trail. Francois was the third remaining riverman, the same one who had tried to interfere the night before. "Where could he have gotten to? Surely he wouldn't have gone off by himself, not out here in the middle of nowhere?"

"We'll go look for him," LeBeau offered.

Shakespeare shook his head. "No, you stay with your sweetheart. Pierre, you watch the rest of the horses. Nate and I will hunt for him. We shouldn't be gone long." He lifted his reins, then bent so only the two rivermen could hear. "If we're not back in an hour, head for the Pacific just as fast as you can. Two Humps can lead you to Astoria. You'll be safe there."

Nate verified that his Hawken was loaded, then followed McNair. He waved to his family, who appeared upset that he was going off. "I'll be back soon," he called out to reassure them, and then promptly wished he hadn't. Knowing McNair as he did, they weren't about to stop until Francois had been found, and there was no way of telling how long that would take.

David Thompson

At a trot the two mountain men covered a quarter of a mile. They rode with their rifles braced on their thighs for ready use.

Shakespeare half suspected the riverman of stealing the pack horses, a notion he dismissed because they were so far from civilization.

Nate worried about hostiles, and felt sure Francois had fallen to them. The last time he'd seen the man, Francois had been riding last in the column. It would have been child's play for enemy warriors to pounce on him and slit his throat before he could utter a sound.

Almost half a mile from where they had left the expedition, they came to a point in the trail where it hooked around the bend of a towering cliff. Shakespeare was in the lead, and he heard the heavy beating of large wings first. Slowing to a walk, he leveled his Hawken and eased forward until he could see around the bend. The sight he beheld chilled him to the marrow even though he had witnessed similar atrocities many, many times.

Nate pulled alongside his friend, then sharply drew rein and exclaimed bitterly, "Damn. I knew it. I just knew it."

Francois the riverman lay on his back in bare earth, his arms at right angles to his body, his legs bent at the knees. His chest bristled with arrows, so many it seemed as if he lay in a patch of river reeds. Both hands and both feet had been chopped off. His eyes had been cut out, his tongue chopped in half. And as if that had not been enough, his attackers had castrated him. Five ungainly black buzzards were feasting on his intestines, which they had pulled from his sliced abdomen.

"One arrow would have been enough," Nate commented bleakly.

"It's their way of saying they're out for our blood," Shakespeare said. "They won't stop until every last one of us is dead."

"The Kelawatsets, you reckon?"

"Or another tribe friendly to them." Shakespeare turned the white mare. "Let's get back to the others express."

"You don't want to bury him?" Nate asked, although he had no such desire, himself.

"What I want to do and what we need to do are two different things," Shakespeare said. "The band that did this must be shadowing the expedition. With us gone they might think they'd have a better chance of wiping out the rest."

Nate hadn't thought of that, and it left him cold inside. "Hurry, then. What are you sitting there jawing for?" He lashed his reins as McNair loped westward, hoping he wouldn't hear gunshots before they got there. If his loved ones were rubbed out he didn't know what he would do with himself. Probably avenge them as best he could before being killed himself.

Shakespeare was upset, but for a different reason. Since Cyrus Porter had crawled into a shell and wouldn't speak to a soul, Shakespeare had become the man everyone else relied on. When decisions needed to be made, he made them. When anyone had a problem, they came to him. He was responsible for all their lives, and as such he should have kept a better watch and noticed the second Francois disappeared. Had he done so, the riverman might still be alive.

The pair covered hundreds of yards. Nate glanced across the river, then to his left at a ridge. A tingle ran down his spine, for standing in plain sight, watching them, was a swarthy warrior. He blinked, and the man was gone. "Shakespeare!" he called out.

"I saw him," McNair replied. "Ride, son! Ride!"

They flew now, riding recklessly. At times their horses were so close to the water's edge that a single misstep would plunge them in. At other times the forest on their left closed in so close that a lurking foe could have stuck a knife into them as they flashed past.

Nate felt more and more uneasy the farther they went. He swore unseen eyes were on them every foot of the way. His imagination got the better of him. Every bush hid a bloodthirsty warrior waiting to pounce; every tree hid two or three. His skin crawled and he tried looking in all directions at once in anticipation of being set upon.

A large boulder with a deep cleft at the top appeared. It was a landmark Nate recollected seeing about a minute after he had waved to his family. Seeing it again cheered him, for it meant he would soon be reunited with them. Whatever danger awaited, they would face it together. He wouldn't die alone, as Francois had.

Then the arrows streaked out of the air, three of them having long shafts and barbed points. They thudded into the stallion, two above the front shoulder, the third into the ribs. Before Nate quite knew what had happened, his horse had died under him and pitched forward into a roll that could prove fatal to him if he were to be crushed underneath it. He threw himself clear a heartbeat before the stallion would have smashed down on him. Rolling on one shoulder, he pushed to his feet, the Hawken at his waist.

From out of the brush charged a pair of brawny Kelawatsets, one with a war club, the other holding an eyedagg. They yipped fiercely, their faces alight with burning hatred.

Nate shot the foremost warrior in the stomach at such close range the shot left powder burns on the man's skin. It also left a hole the size of a walnut. The warrior shrieked and toppled, his war club flying. Undaunted, the second Kelawatset kept coming while waving the eyedagg overhead. Nate back-pedaled and clawed at a pistol. He was in the act of drawing when a rifle cracked. Cored through the forehead, the second warrior toppled like a felled tree.

"Climb on, son! Hurry!" Shakespeare urged, riding up in a flurry of dust.

Nate needed no incentive. More arrows flew past, one clipping his beaver hat. He vaulted on behind McNair and they fled, Kelawatsets streaming out of the forest in their wake. Nate was elated. They had survived an ambush and could rally the others.

The elation was short-lived, however. Nate was reaching for his powder horn to try and reload, when the stiff breeze brought to his ears sounds that filled him with dismay and made his breath catch in his throat. Coming from over the next rise, where the expedition should be, were piercing war whoops, the thunderous boom of guns, and screams.

Awful, lingering screams.

Chapter Twenty-three

The Kelawatset war party, numbering 40 strong, ambushed the Porter Expedition as the column crossed a shallow basin bordering the surging Columbia River. Shrieking war whoops and yipping like coyotes, painted warriors poured from the wall of vegetation flanking the lowland, many unleashing arrows, others hurling lances, still others racing to get in close so they could use their war clubs or knives.

The Kelawatsets picked the site because the basin was wide enough for all of them to attack at once. They were relying on surprise and their greater force of numbers to carry the fight in their favor; they hoped to overwhelm the whites in minutes. But the reason they had for picking the spot actually worked against them.

The expedition members were close to the

water, not the trees. It was a precaution Shakespeare had insisted they take to thwart hostiles.
They were riding in a loose cluster, alert for danger since Francois had gone missing. With McNair
and Nate gone and Porter in another of his moody
sulks, LeBeau was considered the man in charge
and rode at the head of the column.

The young riverman had no delusions about his
ability, though. LeBeau knew that Winona and
Blue Water Woman had forgotten more about
wilderness life than he would ever learn, so he
intended to rely on their judgement should the
need arise. He counted on the two mountain men
returning long before he had to.

Winona kept looking back. She wished there
had been an opportunity for her to say a few
words to Nate before he left, to let him know
that her intuition was acting up, telling her that
all wasn't well and would shortly get worse. But
he'd gone off with a cheery wave, leaving her
with gnawing worry and no one to tell about it.
Except for Blue Water Woman, the others might
think she was being silly, and she didn't care to
have Cyrus Porter laugh at her. She might forget
herself and shoot him.

For the tenth time since her husband left,
Winona shifted to see if he was on his way
back. As her gaze roved over the trees to the
south, she saw a bush move. Yet, at that moment,
there was no breeze. She stared at the bush and
made out the outline of a figure crouched behind
it. Suddenly she saw another, to the right of the
first, and divining the reason and their intent, she

cried out, "Protect yourselves! We are going to be attacked!"

Everyone looked at her, then at the woods. A heartbeat later the air echoed to war whoops, and the Kelawatsets charged in a ragged line. Had they not been spotted, they would have been among the horses in seconds.

LeBeau whipped his rifle to his shoulder to fire, then thought better of the idea. There were too many Indians. If all the expedition members fired at random, the warriors would be among them in a twinkling. "Hold your fire!" he bawled. "Wait for me to say!"

Winona had been about to squeeze the trigger, but she did as the riverman wanted. It was one of the hardest things she ever had to do, sitting there calmly, waiting word to shoot, while dozens of bloodthirsty warriors bore down on them, and arrows and lances whizzed through the air in swarms. The natural impulse was to shoot, shoot, shoot. She glanced at Zach, saw him awaiting the signal too, his features as grim as death.

"Now!" LeBeau roared when the leading Kelawatsets were less than 30 feet away.

Six rifles blasted at once, and six warriors fell. The line of Kelawatsets wavered but didn't break. They surged forward again, more determined than ever to punish the whites.

The fate of the expedition hung in the balance. The women and men drew pistols and fired another volley almost in the faces of their attackers. And at just that juncture, a Nez Percé war whoop rent the air as Two Humps and Chavez galloped onto the scene, the old chief firing his bow with uncanny skill and speed, the Mexican adding his dueling pistols to the fray.

Five more Kelawatsets fell, but so did Pierre, pierced by a lance. LeBeau also toppled from the saddle as his horse was shot out from under him, one of nine animals that had gone down and were thrashing madly on the ground. LeBeau jumped clear and sprang to his feet, but as he did, an arrow transfixed his left thigh. He heard Hetty scream as he sank in agony to his knees.

Winona had fired both of her pistols and was trying to reload before the Kelawatsets reached her. On her back Evelyn squirmed, upset by the din and the gunsmoke. The child's frantic movements made it impossible for Winona to reload while mounted, so she slid off. Opening her powder horn, she set the stock of her Hawken on the ground and went to pour in the black powder.

"Ma! Look out!"

Zach's shout made Winona look up. A burly warrior holding an ax was almost upon her. No hint of mercy animated his dark eyes. No trace of compassion lined his features. He would split her skull with no more regret than he would feel splitting a log. In that respect he was no different from a Blackfoot, Crow, or Shoshone. When most tribes made war, they did so with a ferocity terrible to behold. Men, women, often even children were routinely wiped out.

Winona knew all this. So when she saw the burly warrior's uplifted arm, saw his ax glinting in the sunlight, and realized she could not stop his arm from descending, she thought her time had come. A fleeting pang of sorrow filled her heart for the husband she would never see again, and for their children. Then a miracle occurred.

A horse bearing two riders charged into the midst of the warriors, scattering them right and left. A muscular figure launched itself from the back of the horse, straight at the burly Kelawatset. The warrior tried to turn, but Nate King slammed into him and bore them both to the ground. Nate pushed up on one knee, then rammed the stock of his rifle into the warrior's brow as the warrior was rising. The burly Kelawatset fell. Before the man could rise, Nate drew a pistol, pressed the muzzle against the warrior's ribs, and fired.

Shakespeare McNair, still astride his mare, saw Blue Water Woman being pressed by a pair of Kelawatsets. They both had knives and were trying to get close enough to use them, but she had a cocked flintlock in her hand and kept them at bay by pointing it at first one, then the other. It was only a matter of moments before one slipped her guard, though, and stabbed her.

Howling like a banshee, Shakespeare rode the mare into the nearest warrior and sent the man sprawling. Shifting in the saddle, he put a ball into the left eye of the other Kelawatset.

The first one leaped up and went to throw his knife into the mountain man's unprotected back, but the crack of Blue Water Woman's flintlock ended his throw before it had hardly begun.

Moments later the war party retreated, taking their wounded. They didn't go far, only to the

355

edge of the trees where they regrouped under the leadership of a warrior sporting a short head-dress made from owl feathers.

Shakespeare immediately assumed command. He gave Blue Water Woman's arm a squeeze, then surveyed the carnage. Over half their horses were dead or dying, and many others had fled. The only riverman still alive was LeBeau, propped behind a dead horse, Hetty at his side. Nate had ushered his family behind another horse, and they were loading guns as fast as they could. Cyrus Porter, who had sustained a shoulder wound, squatted behind a boulder near the river. Chavez was the only one still on horseback. And Two Humps calmly walked from one slain Kelawatset to another, taking scalps. The Nez Percé noticed Shakespeare's look, and grinned.

"I will have enough to make a robe if they attack us again."

The Kelawatsets were preparing to do just that. Shakespeare saw there were more than enough left to overrun the expedition. He slid off the mare and took his wife's wrist. "Climb on up. You can escape if you hug the shore. Ride west to Astoria for help. We'll hold them off."

"I would never leave you," Blue Water Woman said. "And I am hurt you would even ask."

"I'm not asking. I'm telling you," Shakespeare insisted. "Hurry, before they come at us."

"No."

"But—"

Blue Water Woman jabbed him in the chest with her pistol. "Husband, you insult me. What kind of wife would I be if I ran off and left my husband when he was fighting for his life? And what about our friends? You know as well as I that I would not reach Astoria in time." She lowered her pistol and began reloading. "If anyone should go, it is Zach and Evelyn. They have their whole lives to live yet."

The rebuke stung Shakespeare. He would have argued, but it was too late. The Kelawatsets had fanned out and blocked escape to both the east and the west.

"Any second now," Nate said.

Shakespeare beckoned the Nez Percé and the tracker. "Get back here, behind a dead animal. And make every shot count."

Chavez complied, but Two Humps took up a position in front of the uneven row of dead animals and hefted his lance. "I am a chief. I will die as a chief."

"Please, old friend," Shakespeare said.

Whether Two Humps would or wouldn't became moot the very next second, as with a riotous chorus of yells and yips the Kelawatsets charged once more.

"Don't fire until they're closer," Shakespeare cautioned. Abruptly, he realized he had neglected to reload his guns in his concern for his wife. Quickly he started, knowing full well he wouldn't have time. Then a pistol was shoved into his hand.

"Take one of mine, husband," Blue Water Woman said. Her eyes conveyed the depth of her love. "We will die together, as we have lived."

David Thompson

Winona King shared those sentiments about her own mate. She crouched at his side, ready to sell her life if need be to protect his. Evelyn now lay next to the belly of the dead horse, grinning happily as only a child her age could, completely unaware of the tragedy about to happen.

"Ma, Pa," Zach said. "I know I never say it much, but I love both of you."

A lump formed in Winona's throat. And then the battle was joined as Nate became the first to fire, dropping the warrior with the headdress at 40 yards. The rest never slowed, never broke ranks. Screaming and waving their weapons, they bounded over the ground like a horde of panthers.

"I thought it might stop them," Nate remarked.

But nothing did. Not the expedition's rifle volley, which dropped a half-dozen, nor the pistol volley, which felled even more. The Kelawatsets reached the dead horses and closed in mortal combat.

Nate shot a skinny warrior with his second pistol and drew his tomahawk as the man keeled over. Another warrior was perched on the dead horse, about to fling a lance into Zach, who was so busy taking aim at a different foe that he hadn't noticed. Nate threw the tomahawk with all his might. The blade bit into the warrior's neck, severing veins and flesh alike, and the Kelawatset fell, blood spurting everywhere.

Guns thundered. Arrows buzzed. A thick cloud of gunsmoke hung in the air above the battleground.

Ordeal

Nate, Winona, and Zach formed a ring around Evelyn, wielding their knives and tomahawks to keep the Kelawatsets at bay.

Shakespeare and Blue Water Woman were back to back, Blue Water Woman with blood on her right side.

Not far off, LeBeau and Hestia Davin were also back to back, on their knees, LeBeau slashing right and left with a dagger, Hetty awkwardly swinging a lance she had picked up after it had been dropped by a warrior LeBeau shot.

Two Humps had gone down under a pack of enemies.

Chavez's dueling pistols were empty and he was swinging a Hall's rifle like a club, trying to hold back three Kelawatsets at once.

And over by the river, unnoticed by anyone, Cyrus Porter cowered behind the boulder, quaking with fear.

Lives hung in the balance. The war party was on the verge of victory, of overrunning the weakening defenders. No gunshots had sounded for over a minute, but suddenly there were several, followed by a half-dozen more, then a blistering volley that felled over half the remaining warriors.

Startled, some of the Kelawatsets looked around for the source of the shots and were shocked to behold buckskin clad frontiersmen rushing toward them from the west. Ten, 20, 30 in all, all armed to the teeth. The Kelawatsets shouted to warn their fellows, whirled, and made for the pines, the frontiersmen in swift pursuit.

Nate King saw the newcomers but couldn't

credit the testimony of his own eyes. He stood rigid with surprise, watching Kelawatset after Kelawatset be slain, marveling at the almost military precision of their rescuers. In mere moments the hostile warriors were all gone, either dead or vanished in the forest. Ten of the frontiersmen gave chase, but the rest drew up short at a command from their leader, a huge, powerfully built giant with flowing white hair.

"Well, I'll be damned," Shakespeare said.

Bewildered, Nate turned. Winona and Zach were both alive and untouched, their faces caked with sweat, smudged by black marks, and covered with red dots. Evelyn still grinned, her small fingers waving in the air. "Thank God," Nate said softly.

Lifting his head, Nate saw Two Humps and frowned. The old chief had three lances and two knives sticking from his chest. Over on the right, Chavez had taken an arrow in the fleshy part of the upper arm.

A mournful screech pricked the short hairs on Nate's neck. He spun, thinking a Kelawatset had played possum and just killed someone. But that wasn't the case.

Hestia Davin was bent over Armand LeBeau, who lay on his side with a shaft protruding from the center of his back. She wept uncontrollably, her body convulsing in great sobs, her sorrow soul-wrenching.

"No," Nate said softly. "Not him too." He looked toward the river and saw Cryus Porter erect, staring in the direction of Hetty. Porter was smiling.

Ordeal

The sight so enraged Nate that he would have shot Porter if he'd had a loaded gun. He glanced down to find one, but just then the man with the white hair and the company of frontiersmen came up.

"Hello, McNair," the giant said.

Shakespeare wearily nodded. "It's been a long time, John. You're quite a ways from Fort Vancouver."

"Twice a year I pay the Chinooks a visit," the white-haired man said. "You can thank your lucky stars that this happened to be one of them." Turning to Nate, he walked over and offered his brawny hand. "John McLoughlin. I'm chief factor of the Hudson's Bay Company in this region." He indicated the sturdy men with him. "These are all HBC men, the cream of the crop as far as I'm concerned. I'll only have the best working for me."

"Nate King. Pleased to meet you," Nate said. "More than I can ever say."

"Some of my boys are old hands at tending wounds," McLoughlin said, and snapped his fingers. Four HBC men moved to minister to the wounded. "We'll set up camp here and stay until you're ready to push on." He paused. "Oh. And before I forget. I think I've found someone you lost." The six-foot-four-inch administrator raised a hand and waved twice.

From the west approached three more men. Nate was amazed to see Brett Hughes in the middle. Only then did he realize that Hughes had been missing during the battle.

"That's Hughes, the clerk of this expedition,"

Shakespeare said. "I was wondering what happened to him. Thought maybe the Kelawatsets got him when no one was looking."

McLoughlin stared hard at the clerk, who seemed to be trying to wither into the ground. "Hughes, you say?" McLoughlin said. "Bloody hell. His name is Harkness and he works for the HBC. Something very strange is going on here, and I intend to get to the bottom of it after we've set up camp."

The chief factor proved as good as his word. Once all the wounded had been bandaged, the dead were buried and the supplies moved to the west end of the basin, away from the dead horses. There a fire was built, and the exhausted expedition members sat around it, sipping coffee. All except for Hetty, who was off by herself, crying without cease, refusing to be consoled by anyone. She had become hysterical when LeBeau was lowered into the ground, throwing herself on his blanket-shrouded form and tearing at it as if to crawl in beside him. Three men had been needed to pry her off and hold her still long enough for the burial to be finished.

Nate stared at the poor woman's bent back and wished there was something they could do to lessen her heartache. Inwardly he gave thanks that his family had been spared, for if they hadn't, he knew he'd be in worse shape than poor Hetty.

None of the wounds suffered by the rest were life-threatening. The arrow that caught Chavez in the arm had missed vital veins. Blue Water Woman's cut in her side was shallow. And Cyrus

Ordeal

Porter's shoulder wound was a clean one.

Nate found himself thinking that it was unfortunate Porter hadn't been subjected to the same fate as Two Humps. He avoided even looking at the man, so much did Porter disgust him. Instead, he stared at Brett Hughes, who sat a dozen yards away under the watchful eyes of a pair of beefy HBC men. John McLoughlin had been questioning Hughes for the better part of an hour, and it was clear that Hughes's answers had made McLoughlin steadily madder.

Presently McLoughlin nodded at the beefy pair, who hauled Hughes to his feet and brought him along as the chief factor came to the fire. McLoughlin squatted, thunder eminent on his brow. "I can't tell you how sorry I am for all that has happened," he said. "He greatly exceeded his authority."

"Who did?" Shakespeare asked. "Hughes or Harkness or whatever his real name is?"

"It's Harkness, all right. Gregory Harkness," McLoughlin revealed. "For the last several years he was stationed at Fort Hall, working under Andrew Smythe-Barnes." At their looks of astonishment, he smiled grimly. "Thought that would get your interest. It seems Smythe-Barnes took his orders far too literally."

"What orders?" Nate asked.

"It's no secret that Hudson's Bay wants to discourage American settlement and competition in this region. The Company had notified all administrators to that effect. I told them that I'd be damned if I was going to treat anyone unfairly

363

or unjustly, Americans or no. They don't like my
attitude, but I'm the best chief factor they've ever
had, and they're not about to take me to task for
sticking to my principles." McLoughlin sighed.
"Smythe-Barnes didn't have any principles. And
he went too far in his efforts to carry out HBC
policy. The Company didn't tell him to cheat
Americans outright, or to drive them from their
homes once they had settled." He glanced at
Hughes. "Or to send men to St. Louis for the
express purpose of hiring on with American parties bound for the Oregon Country, and then to
have these men do what they could to keep the
Americans from getting there."

Nate had a flash of insight. "You were the one
who kept trying to run off our horses at night,"
he addressed Harkness. "What else are you guilty
of?"

In a perfect English accent, Harkness replied,
"I've said all I'm going to. Mr. McLoughlin tells
me that he intends to file a formal complaint
against me with the HBC office in London, so
I'm not saying another word until I've talked to
my solicitor."

"Your what?" Nate asked.

"His lawyer," Shakespeare explained.

McLoughlin went on. "I suspect Smythe-Barnes
was out to line his own pockets and used HBC
policy as an excuse to commit his crimes. They will
be as outraged as I am by his actions. I wouldn't be
surprised if they offer you an official apology."

Shakespeare gazed at the row of earthen
mounds over by the river. He thought of all

those they had lost, of all the hardships they had faced, and of the fight with the HBC men that had resulted in Smythe-Barnes's death. "I reckon an apology is better than nothing. It's too bad, though, that when governments squabble, ordinary people like us have to suffer."

"There's one more thing," McLoughlin said, facing Cyrus Porter. "Harkness tells me that Smythe-Barnes, through contacts in your government, learned they were concerned about rumors of British forts being built along the frontier in preparation for war. Washington wanted someone to act as a spy, to come into the territory and either verify or refute the rumors." He stuck a finger at Porter. "You were the spy they picked."

"What nonsense!" Porter declared. "The only reason I came was to find my missing daughter."

"Smythe-Barnes was of the opinion you used her only as an excuse. He told Harkness that you had done similar work for Washington before."

"I flatly deny it," Porter said. "Obviously it was another story that man concocted to excuse his dastardly acts."

"Perhaps," McLoughlin said, unconvinced.

Nate said nothing. All the pieces to the puzzle fit, and they only added to his contempt of Porter. He wanted nothing whatsoever to do with the man ever again. And he could see that he wasn't the only one.

That evening a decision was made. John McLoughlin would return to Fort Vancouver instead of going to the Chinook village. Hughes would be taken back under arrest. As for the expedition members, McLoughlin offered to see them safely as far as Astoria.

Cyrus Porter announced to one and all that he intended to take the first ship that came along back to the States. He said he would pay the fare of anyone else who wanted to go, but no one took him up on it. When he made the statement, he looked pointedly at his daughter, who ignored him.

Later, Hetty stopped weeping long enough to tell everyone that she was going to stay in the Oregon Country and make a new life for herself. Her father objected, but she refused to even speak to him.

Five days later, Nate King, Winona, Zach and Evelyn were on a sandy dune, a stiff sea breeze fanning their faces and hair. Nate inhaled the tangy air and stared out over the awe-inspiring vastness of the Pacific Ocean. He had forgotten how immense an ocean could be, and he grinned at the childhood memories it stirred, of carefree summer days when his father took the family to the beach at Atlantic City.

Zach plucked at Nate's sleeve. "Pa, there's something I've been meaning to ask."

"Ask away."

"Was it worth it? All we went through to get here, I mean?"

Nate looked down at his son's earnest expression, then at the laughing pair who played in the rolling surf. Shakespeare had an arm around

Ordeal

Blue Water Woman, and they were kicking at the waves, their naked feet splashing water right and left. Nate had never seen his mentor look so young, so happy, so very alive. "Yes, son," he said. "I think it was."